SECOND SON

THE SULLIVAN GRAY SERIES

H.P. BAYNE

BAYNE
INDEPENDENT
PUBLISHING

SULLY HADN'T COUNTED on being back here.

The manor stood before him, expansive, bleak and foreboding. The windows were like the eyes of a spider, many and watching. Behind them, he could sense the building's inhabitants, former occupants who'd decided to stay after death and other spirits who had gravitated here. They were, almost to a one, bad-tempered and malicious, driving from these walls anyone whom they disliked. That meant most people.

Sullivan "Sully" Gray wasn't most people.

For some reason, they put up with him. Perhaps because of Pax. Sully wasn't sure, but he believed the dog had belonged to the last owner, an old man who had been crotchety enough to fit in with his home's miserable otherworldly inhabitants. He'd once heard Linton Blackmoor was the only buyer to live more than a year in the place. He'd lasted more than twenty.

Then came the flood.

Blackmoor refused to leave the house that had meant everything to him. Like most others who'd stayed behind, the decision became his last.

Sully had never seen him; his ability to see ghosts was limited to those who had died by someone else's hand. Blackmoor, like the rest of the ghosts of Ravenwood Hall, remained invisible to him.

Of course, unseen didn't mean unnoticeable. Ravenwood had its own poltergeist, a ghost Sully had nicknamed Noisy Ned. Naming the entity had seemed like a way to inject some humour, or at least some humanity, into a terrifying situation.

It hadn't worked.

Ned still threw things at odd hours of the night, startling Sully awake and putting him on high alert for intruders. Here in The Forks these days, intruders carried far more danger than violent ghosts.

Thankfully, the house's reputation preceded it. Few dared to visit. Those who did regretted it quickly.

It made Ravenwood Hall the safest place for Sully to be.

Given the situation in which he'd landed, The Forks was the safest place for him in all of Kimotan Rapids.

And the loneliest.

But, right now, his being alone was the safest thing for everyone else.

In a weird way, it might also be a relief. The house came with its own ghosts, and it didn't like outside spirits any more than living intruders. Sully had first noticed Prescott Montague's ghost shortly after leaving Emily's apartment, and the spirit had trailed him here, a constant angry presence at his shoulder. The possibility of being somewhere he couldn't easily follow was a welcome one.

As Sully approached the manor's threshold, he avoided seeking out the image of Montague. Instead, his gaze drifted to the happy sight of the dog next to him.

"You and me, Pax." He stretched out a hand and rubbed his dog's head. Pax turned brown eyes up to meet Sully, his tongue lolling out the side of his mouth as he regarded his human. Whether the dog made the expression on purpose or not didn't matter. Sully laughed anyway.

He needed it. He hadn't found much to laugh at in the past couple of days.

Giving Pax one more pat, he returned his attention to the house.

Then he led the way inside.

Dez hadn't counted on being back here.

Not permanently, anyway.

It felt like forever since Eva had kicked him out, told him his drinking and foul moods were hurting their daughter. He'd gone, not entirely willingly, but with the acceptance that what Eva had said was true. He'd been a screwup, caught in a depression he couldn't pull himself out of. But even then, the last thing he wanted was to drag anyone down with him.

Especially his little girl.

He'd left, found himself a dumpy apartment in the Riverview area. He'd stayed there until a couple of days ago, when his brother had revealed to him the details of a secret so dark, it risked throwing Dez right back into the pit he'd clawed his way out of.

He'd hoped being back here, back at his own home with Eva and their little girl Kayleigh, would be enough.

It wasn't.

"Dez, you need to deal with this."

He looked up at Eva from the downstairs sofa, redirecting his gaze from the TV show he hadn't really been watching. He hadn't even heard her approach.

"I'm trying."

"No. You're not. You're doing what you did before, what you always do when things are bad, and you feel like everything's out of your control. You're brooding. And you won't talk to me about it."

"I don't need to drag anyone else down."

Eva closed the remaining distance between them and settled onto the couch next to him. "Newsflash, Snowman. I'm already down there with you. So talk to me."

"I told you everything."

"About Lowell and about the fight you had with Sully. What you haven't told me is what's going on in your head because of it. That's a lot for anyone to deal with, and you aren't dealing. So talk."

Dez sighed, met her eye. "What do you want me to say? That I've never wanted to kill anyone so bad in all my life as my own uncle? That my regret alternates between punching Sully and not punching him again? I'm pissed off, Eva. Like, beyond pissed. It's taking everything I have not to get up and leave and find Lowell, to beat a damn confession out of him. Hell, even coming here instead of going to look for him took every bit of self-control I had."

"I know. And I'm sorry this is happening. But we need to get this sorted out, you and me, before it destroys you. I don't want to see you go down the same road you did after you lost your dad and Sully. Especially now, when we're just getting *us* back."

"I don't want to see that either."

"So let's talk about what we can do."

Dez raised his hands, palms up, a demonstration of helplessness. "Do? There's nothing I *can* do. The only person alive with any information isn't supposed to *be* alive. I can't just drag my brother into a police station and get him to sit down with an investigator, can I?"

"Not unless he's willing."

"He won't be. He's got too much to lose, and he's already been through the wringer because of this. Anyway, who'd believe him over Lowell?"

"You never know. If he's being honest, investigators will figure that out, especially once they start digging."

"Eva, my uncle is one of the richest men in town, maybe *the* richest. He's charming, well-respected and popular. Sully is a scruffy, shy homeless guy who was once the suspect in a murder investigation, spent a couple of months as a patient at a mental hospital, and faked his own death. There won't be any digging. No one will take him seriously enough to even go to the trouble of a sit-down interview. And I think that was Lowell's plan all along. If killing him didn't work, discrediting him was a solid second option."

"What about Forbes? He might listen."

Dez lowered his head into a hand and massaged his temples. "He's not exactly the most competent detective on the force. And I'm not sure I'd trust him with this."

"So how about Lachlan? He loves a challenge. And he's got some well-placed contacts."

"Lachlan would salivate over this."

"So tell him. See what he comes up with."

"I'll think about it."

"Good. In the meantime, you need to go talk to your brother. You can't leave things like this."

"Like what? I've got every right to be mad at him."

"I know. But you also need to remember where he's coming from. Given what he went through, I can understand why he wouldn't want to talk about it."

"But this is my *family*, Eva. He knew how badly I needed to know about Aiden, and he knew I'd want to know about Dad. Hell, about him too. And he shut me out. He lied to me."

"He thought it was for your own good. He wasn't sure you could handle the truth."

"Please, don't quote *A Few Good Men*."

Eva smiled. "Dez. I'm being serious here. The effect it's

having on you, the depression you're slipping back into, the way you're battling yourself not to confront Lowell, those are things he would have expected. He wouldn't have wanted that for you."

"So, what? His plan was for us to go to our graves with me not knowing?"

"I don't know what his plan was. You should ask him. Talk to him, Dez. Half the reason you're sitting here in the dark, stewing, is because of the fight you two had."

"I'm not in the dark."

Eva looked around the room as if to make a liar out of him. Sure, he'd only turned on the pop lights above the couch, but still....

"Honey, it's dark," Eva concluded. "And you're in a bad place. Finding a way to deal with Lowell is a big challenge. I get it. But this thing with Sully—that, you can fix."

"I don't know if I can."

"Why not?"

He hadn't told Eva this part, too ashamed of himself to say it out loud. Now, he had no option. "I said some things to him too.... One thing, really."

"What?"

Dez took a breath, held it, let it go before answering. "I told him about Gerhardt being his father."

"Oh, Jesus, Dez, you didn't. Not like that."

"I was angry. It just came out as I was leaving. It was that or beat the crap out of him, so I chose the non-violent method."

"I can't believe you."

Dez's temper rose at the criticism, but almost as quickly, he tamped it back down. She was right. Hell, at least part of his current anger was directed at himself for having thrown the comment out there, like it meant nothing. He couldn't believe *himself.*

"I know I was an ass. And I regret it, but it's done."

"You need to make this right."

"*I* need to make this right? Look, I know blurting it out was low, but he held out on me too."

Eva's glare suggested she wasn't sold. "Look. You can sit here, arguing with me about who's right, or you can *make* things right. Which one of you was more wrong doesn't matter in the end. What matters is the two of you love each other, and if you don't fix this, you might lose him. You can be angry, Dez. You have every right to be. But don't let this cost you more than you can afford to pay. It's not worth your relationship with your brother."

He knew she was right. There was no question, the stupidity of costing himself a still-living family member over two who were already gone.

"I'll go look for him."

"Good. Do you want me to go with you?"

"No, you work today."

"Not until two."

"This might take longer than that. Anyway, it's something I need to deal with myself."

He looked down as Eva's hand slid over his, and he turned his own hand to weave his fingers through hers.

"I know it's hard," she said. "And I know you're angry. But you'll get through this, Dez. You've got me and Kayleigh and your mom, and you've got Sully. No matter what happened back at your apartment, he'll be there for you."

———

"HE'S NOT HERE."

Emily peered up at him as she uttered the words, her head tilted back, far beyond comfort level so she could look Dez in the eye.

He'd arrived back at his apartment to find his spare set of keys on the floor, just the other side of the door, and all of Sully's things gone. On the counter lay a two-word note in his brother's handwriting saying only, "I'm sorry." Worst of all, though, there was no Sully.

"Where is he?" he asked now. "Did he say anything?"

She shook her head. "He said he had to go. And he said he couldn't tell me where. 'The fewer people who know, the better.' That's what he said. He told me he couldn't risk anyone else he cared about; he needed to handle things alone."

"Damn it."

"Why don't you come in for a minute? We can talk."

"I don't have time. The jerk always does this when the chips are down. He goes off on his own to deal with things, and he gets himself into serious trouble."

"I didn't get the impression he was about to take immediate action. I think he was going somewhere to lie low a while. That was the feeling I got, anyway. He wasn't angry, really. Just sad. Really, really sad."

This wasn't helping. "Thanks, Emily. I'm going to call a couple of people and see if they've heard from him. In the meantime, please call me if he contacts you, okay?"

"I will."

Dez nodded and offered a forced smile before leaving the building and returning to his vehicle. He didn't want to be inside the apartment right now.

He'd tried calling Sully before driving over here, but got nothing other than a single ring and voicemail. Another attempt now got him no further.

He tried their mom next.

"What happened?" she said as soon as he asked if Sully was there.

"Why do you think something happened?"

"I hear it in your voice. What's wrong?"

"I'll explain later."

"Is one of you in trouble again?"

"No, nothing like that. We had a fight and I'm trying to reach him, is all."

"What about?"

Crap. Amidst his own anger and depression, he'd forgotten one other person was likely to be even more shattered by this news. Mara Braddock didn't even know Aiden's death had been anything other than a tragic accidental drowning. She'd have to be told about him. And about Flynn.

But that was a conversation for another time, preferably when both her sons could be there with her. For now, he had some ducking to do.

"I'll tell you later. Right now, I need to focus on finding Sully."

"I haven't heard from him. I'm sorry. He's not in any danger, is he?"

Dez sought to erase his mother's worry with words he didn't fully believe himself. "There are risks, but he knows how to avoid them."

"Are you sure?"

Nope. "Yeah, I'm sure. Call me if you hear from him, okay?"

"I will."

"Thanks, Mom."

"You look after yourself, all right? You know how you get."

Dez rolled his eyes. "Yeah, yeah, okay."

He hung up, then tried Marc Echoles, but got a similar response. At his urging, he next tried Raiya Everton. Again, nothing.

Dez was about to try Bulldog when his phone rang. He'd hoped to see his brother's fake name, Oliver, show up on his call display.

What he got was Lachlan.

Dez pulled into traffic, hoping for at least a few minutes of scanning the streets for a scruffy guy with a large, black dog.

"This isn't a good time," Dez said by way of greeting.

"In my experience, good times are rare. Listen, I want to talk to you and your brother about my other ghost. Now that we've figured out what happened to Nora Silversmith and her son—"

"That's going to be a problem. You need Sully for that, and I can't find him. You haven't heard from him by chance, have you?"

"No, I haven't. What happened?"

"We had a fight."

"Big deal. Brothers fight all the time. Hell, I haven't talked to mine in twenty-two years."

"Sully and I aren't like that. We're tight, always have been. This was bad. Really bad."

"Come pick me up and you can fill me in."

"You really care?"

"No. But I do care about finding your brother. He's the only way I'm going to bring an end to this other case that's been nagging me. I'll expect you within the half-hour."

Lachlan hung up, preventing further argument.

Just as well, since a call to Bulldog left Dez with no additional answers as to Sully's whereabouts.

He'd driven less than five minutes when his phone rang. His hopes were dashed when he saw the number on his call display.

Then again, a member of the Major Crimes Unit might have information after all. Information Dez wouldn't want to hear.

He pressed the Bluetooth button, allowing the call to come through his vehicle's speaker system.

"Raynor?"

Sergeant Forbes Raynor didn't often bother with small talk. "Where's your brother?"

"I don't know. Why?"

"Don't bullshit me, Braddock. Where is he?"

"I'm not lying to you. I really don't know."

"You don't know, as in he's gone out and didn't tell you where he was going? Or he's gone?"

"The latter. I'm trying to find him. Still leads me back to my question though. Why are you looking for him?"

"It's not something I'm at liberty to discuss."

"Then I won't be at liberty to share his whereabouts when I find him."

"You're a real stubborn asshole, you know that?"

"Takes one to know one."

"All right," Forbes said after a pause. "Here's the thing. You heard on the news about a shooting the night before last?"

"There's a shooting every couple of days. What's special about this one?"

"We haven't released the victim's name publicly yet. Trying to keep things under our hats as long as we can, particularly given the shit storm that's going to blow in the moment it goes public. The dead guy is Prescott Montague."

The information had Dez pulling to the side of the road. "What happened?"

"We seized surveillance video from his house. He had a camera mounted over the front door and at the front gate. The front door camera recorded a man in a hoodie running out at the approximate time one of the neighbours reported hearing a gunshot. I've analyzed and reanalyzed the footage, and I keep drawing the same conclusion. I think the guy in the video is Sullivan."

"Bloody hell. You can't seriously think he'd be responsible for a shooting. He's no killer."

"Well, the fact is, he isn't the one who pulled the trigger. The shot was from a high-powered sniper rifle, and it came from outside the house. As near as we can tell, the shooter must have been set up on top of Montague's boathouse out back."

"So there you are. Even if it was Sully inside the house, he didn't do anything wrong."

"It doesn't let him off the hook, especially now he's done a runner. Until we're able to eliminate him, we're treating him as a potential suspect. It could be he and the shooter were working together."

"Hang on," Dez said. "You didn't expose Sully to any of the other cops, did you?"

"No, but I can't keep it quiet forever. Your brother is either a suspect or a key witness. I need to talk to him so I can decide how I'm going to handle everything."

"This is all supposing he actually is the guy in the video. You said he's wearing a hood. I know Sully does that, but so do lots of other people."

"His size, build, his movements, it all points to Sullivan. You're welcome to watch the footage, if that will convince you."

"I can't just—"

"I'll make a copy and meet you somewhere out of the way. I think you'll want to see this."

DEZ FOUND Forbes where he said he'd be, sitting on a bench on the edge of a small park five minutes' walk from the police station.

The cop had been bold enough to bring a laptop with him, taking a chance no one would mug him for his electronics. Dez grudgingly sat next to him, and Forbes unfolded the laptop without bothering with a greeting.

A couple of clicks later, Dez was looking at a video from the inside of Montague's house. The image was dark, but the camera switched to night vision after nightfall, enabling him to see a slim male figure rushing toward the front door and turning the lock with gloved hands before dashing outside.

Little about the video could tell anyone who the man was. He never turned toward the camera, and he wasn't wearing anything particularly distinguishing. But Dez—who'd known Sully most of his life—saw what Forbes had.

The man in the video was almost definitely his brother.

"Enough to convince you?" Forbes asked.

Dez realized his mouth was open, and he shut it before thinking through his answer. "It could be anyone in that video."

"But it isn't, is it? I don't know Sullivan as well as you do, obviously, but I've gotten to know him well enough. That's him. I'm sure of it."

"Look, if it is him, he wasn't there to do anything bad."

"You sure about that? Montague had, after all, nearly killed him. Plus he's implicated in the attempt on your life at the caves. And Sullivan told me about wanting to go back to try to talk to him about…." Forbes trailed off, as if he'd remembered something.

Dez knew what it was. "About Lowell. I know. Sully filled me in. I know he told you about his suspicions. And I know the judge threw Lowell's name out there when he was arrested, hoping his info might buy him a deal."

"Right. So there's another reason he might have gone down there with bad intentions. He knew Montague was mixed up in something seedy with Lowell, and he knew the judge said he had information that could take Lowell down. I think Sullivan went down there to confront him, to try to get some answers. Maybe he went with some backup, someone who would take the shot if things went sideways or if Montague refused to talk."

"That's weak," Dez said. "First off, what good would killing him do? Sully wanted to know what info he had. If he's dead, he can't share it, and nothing can be proved. Second, Sully doesn't know anyone who'd be capable and willing to pull off a hit like that. It's not even close to being his style. Sully's no killer. You know it as well as I do. If he did go down there to talk to Montague, it was on his own. This assassin or whatever, he had to have been working independently, or for someone else. If that is Sully on the video, he was in the wrong place at the wrong time. Not like he hasn't been in that situation before."

"All right. Let's say I believe you. That still puts him front and centre in this thing as a crucial witness. We're going to have to talk to him, and I need you to make that happen."

"You know I can't do that. Not now. The risks to him are too great."

Forbes shut the laptop and focused fully on Dez. "There's something I hadn't planned on telling you, but I don't think I can avoid it. There was more than one shot. From what we've been able to piece together, Montague was taken down by one of the first bullets. The others, we believe, were directed at the person in the video. What we don't know is whether the shooter was trying to take out a witness, or whether he was looking to tie up a loose end by eliminating his accomplice. Either way, the guy on the video was a target as well. These risks you're talking about—they exist, whether or not he's in hiding. It might be he's safer coming forward and allowing us to get him some proper protection until we can get the shooter safely behind bars."

"Hold on a sec. You're telling me you think this assassin was firing at Sully? You didn't find any evidence he was hit, did you?"

"We didn't find any other blood in the house or on the grounds, other than a couple of transfer stains we believe will come back as Montague's DNA. So, no, there's no obvious evidence of him being hit."

"Thank God."

"Look, I showed you this because I thought you'd need some convincing. I guess I've got no choice but to leave it up to you to decide how to handle it. But Braddock? You need to handle it. I can't sit on this forever. You need to get him to come forward. He's not on the hook for the Betty Schuster shooting, if that helps convince you any."

It didn't. The facts remained the same. If Sully was outed, particularly in the midst of a case bound to draw national media attention, he'd not only be a walking target for this shooter, whoever he or she was. Lowell would be next in line with the Dules not far behind. Add Gerhardt to the mix, looking for a way to get Sully recommitted, and you had a whole lot of bad with no real end in sight—at least, no end that wouldn't leave Sully destroyed.

No way in hell Dez was playing a role in that.

Forbes wasn't likely to take that as an answer. Not for long anyway. So Dez gave him what little he could.

"I'll think about it."

"Don't think too long." Forbes stood from the bench, casting one more meaningful look at Dez before walking off in the direction of the police station.

3

When Dez pulled up to Lachlan's home in the North Bank area, he was waiting on the front stoop. Dez unlocked the door and, staying true to form, by skipping the greetings, Lachlan dropped into the passenger seat and got right down to business.

"Did you already contact everyone he might have had reason to speak with?"

"Yeah," Dez said. "Given the whole pretending-to-be-dead thing, it's a pretty short list."

"And nothing from any of them?"

"Nope. Nothing. Doesn't surprise me, I guess. If he's gone to ground, he'll make sure he's doing it alone. Last person who saw him was Emily, my neighbour across the hall. She confirmed it, said he was basically taking himself off the radar for awhile."

Lachlan snorted, his expression mirroring the incredulity in the noise. "And this is just because the two of you had a fight?"

"Of course not. It's a lot more than that. More than I even realized."

"You going to fill me in, or are you hoping to turn this into a fun new guessing game?"

Dez broke it down for Lachlan, filling him in on what Sully had told him two days ago, leaving nothing out. He then added what he'd just learned from Forbes. By the time he'd finished, Lachlan's eyes were huge.

"Christ, Braddock, this is big."

"Yeah, I'd kind of realized that, thanks."

"No, I mean big. Like really big."

Dez allowed his annoyance to show in his expression and tone. "Yeah, I know, okay? So what do I do about it?"

"I don't know yet. But I'll give it some thought, that's for sure. Wow. Okay, well, since you've tried everyone else to no avail, I've got to ask: any chance your brother's gone to confront Lowell?"

It was a possibility Dez hadn't considered. His blood pressure spiked as he considered it was exactly what Sully had done when Lowell and Hackman had nearly killed him two years ago.

"Jesus. I hope not."

"I'm thinking taking you to pay your uncle a visit isn't a good idea, given your propensity to fly off the handle."

"I don't fly off the handle."

"Uh, yeah, you do."

"And could you not refer to him as my uncle? Far as I'm concerned, he's nothing to me now, so just call him by his name, all right?"

Lachlan looked like he was about to retort, but clamped his lips together instead. He gave it a moment, then replied. "Right. I get it. Lowell. Sorry, Braddock. I forget sometimes, when I get my teeth into the bit, these are real people and not just a great case. We're talking about your family here, so I'm sorry. Your dad was a great man, and I know you didn't exactly invite me to this party willingly, but I would be honoured if I could play a role in bringing his killer to justice. All right?"

It was the nicest thing Lachlan had ever said to him. It made Dez feel uncomfortable as hell, and he pulled back onto the road before answering. "Thanks."

"Don't mention it. So back to the uncle from hell. Is it worth a check to see if Sullivan went there?"

"I don't know. I can't think why he'd confront him now. The

last time we were anywhere near Lowell, Sully bailed out of the car and hid until Lowell left. He's done everything he can to avoid him."

"Everyone has a breaking point. But let's leave that possibility alone for a moment. You said you think Raynor's right, that Sullivan went to talk to Montague the night of the murder. I know you're not going to want to hear this, but is there a chance he was hit? Any idea how carefully the area was checked afterward? If he took a bullet, he could be lying under the bushes in someone's yard."

"Jesus Christ, Lachlan."

"Well? The question needs asked."

"Not to me. I can't think that way."

Lachlan pulled out his phone and started scrolling through something on his screen.

"What are you doing?"

"Calling the Humane Society," Lachlan said. "Checking to see if anyone reported a big, black dog on the loose."

With this new possibility to dread—not every bullet wound bled badly enough to leave a clear trail, especially if the victim was wearing several layers of clothes—Dez white-knuckled the steering wheel as Lachlan made the call. He received an answer in the negative.

"Doesn't necessarily eliminate the possibility, but it's probably good news," Lachlan said. "When did your neighbour see him? Before or after the shooting?"

"I don't know."

Lachlan made a rotating gesture with his hand. "Well, can we find out? It might help us figure out whether he had a hitman on his tail when he left Montague's."

Dez got on the phone in a hurry, hoping both Emily and Forbes could provide answers to soothe his new fear.

"Shooting happened around ten," Dez said. "Emily saw him between midnight and one in the morning."

"That's a good sign," Lachlan said to Dez's great relief. "If he made it there without being taken out, he probably slipped any tail he might have had. Of course, it also leaves us back at square one. Any idea where to start looking? You know him best. Where would he go?"

"If he's worried about putting people at risk, he's proven he can drop right off the radar. If he doesn't want to be found, he won't be."

"That's a cop-out. Everyone can be found if you've got the right people looking. If you and I aren't the right people, they don't exist. Let's break it down. He doesn't have a lot of options. I've been paying him under the table for his work, but it won't be enough for a long-term hotel or major transportation. Did he ever get set up with fake ID?"

"No, we never approached anyone about that sort of thing."

"So that limits where he can go and how far. We're sure he's got his dog with him?"

"He wouldn't go anywhere without Pax."

"So more limits. Plus, he'll be eager to keep his mug from being seen in public too much. How did he avoid it the two years he was away? Where did he go? What did he do?"

The answer hit Dez like a brick. He could have kicked himself for not thinking of it sooner.

"The Forks," he said. "He told me he stayed there during those couple of years."

"Did he say where, specifically?"

Dez's stomach rolled as he said the words out loud. "Ravenwood Hall."

"The mansion on the east side of the island? The one everyone talks about being haunted?"

"Yeah, that one."

"Well, if there's one place to find a guy who sees ghosts, why not try the most haunted place in town?"

Dez scrubbed a hand down his face. "Crap. Guess I'm going to have to go there."

"That gives us another problem. Driving through The Forks is not what I'd call an option. We'd only be setting ourselves up for carjacking and murder."

"You've got a better idea?"

Lachlan grinned. "Damn straight I do."

4

THERE WAS a chill in the air when Sully poked his head out from under three layers of blankets.

Winter was coming, and while the snow had yet to fall, the cold suggested it wasn't far off.

Sully had spent two miserable winters here, nearly dying during one particularly bad cold snap.

A champ at fires, he'd found a parlour toward the back of the house small enough to heat easily. Now, once again, he made the room his home. After lighting the fire last night, he'd curled up on the fainting couch, Pax curled on the floor next to him.

Previously, his routine had been to awaken every hour or two to stoke the fire. But he'd gotten comfortable during his return to his old life. His body clock had forgotten its preset survival alarms, and when he awoke inside the parlour, the fire was completely out.

He stayed where he was a moment, shivering beneath the blankets as he mentally prepared for the extra dose of cold he'd feel once he fully emerged from his cocoon.

Pax next to him exhaled noisily in his slumber. The cold rarely bothered him, thick coat of black fur protecting him from the worst of the elements. But every animal had its limits, and Sully felt guilty for the dog's sake at having neglected his duties with the fireplace.

He was still thinking about getting up when the distant creak of footsteps somewhere on the other side of the closed door made the decision for him.

Of course, the sound might not be human-caused. He'd heard footsteps before, usually overhead and often in the dead of night. But in a house like this, with its history and inhabitants, you learned quickly to tell the difference between physical and ghostly.

The footsteps he heard now were not made by invisible feet.

Someone was here.

Someone living.

Visitors to an abandoned building in The Forks took on a far different meaning from those anywhere else. Here, the person was likely to be an escaped convict or a messed-up meth user rather than a college kid with a video camera.

Sully jumped up, leaving the blankets where they fell as he lunged for the fireplace poker next to the fainting couch. Pax rose and stood to attention next to him, ears perked and a low growl sounding in his throat. Sully angled his body as he faced the door, heavy, wrought-iron poker drawn back in a batter's stance.

A crash sounded within the house, then a series of increasingly loud bangs. Noisy Ned had taken longer than usual to realize a newcomer was within his territory and to begin showing his displeasure. The poltergeist tolerated Sully, but he was as good as an alarm system for anyone else.

Noisy Ned was losing his touch, but he'd still prove a helpful ally.

Sully. Pax. Ned. If this intruder was up to no good, they were in for an unpleasant surprise.

A second crash sounded, vibrated the walls as Ned closed in.

This one was followed by a human exclamation. "Bloody hell! Sully! Sully!"

The wrought iron poker dropped to the ground with a dull

clatter the same moment as Pax's growls gave way to a gentle woof.

"Dez?" Sully said, voice not loud enough to carry beyond the room.

He left the parlour, Pax on his heels. A short hall led past a kitchen on one side and a large dining room on the other. From there, it emptied into what would have been a grand entry hall in the house's pre-flood days. Dez had backed himself up against one of the wood-panelled walls, palms flat against it as his head swivelled to allow saucer-like eyes to scan for hidden dangers in every shadowed corner.

A solid object cutting through the air whistled past Sully as Ned threw his latest improvised missile. Dez ducked just as a rusted brass serving tray clanged against the panel where his head had just been.

"Sully!"

Sully closed the distance to his brother. "I'm here." Then louder, for the poltergeist's benefit: "Cut it out! He's not a threat!" Waiting a moment, he listened for further movement from Ned, but all had fallen silent. The ghost had either decided to grant Sully the benefit of the doubt, or he'd exhausted himself with that last throw. It didn't really matter which, as long as Dez was able to go home with no cuts, bruises or broken bones.

Dez had gone from ducking heavy objects to wrestling with Pax's enthusiastic welcome. "What the hell was that, Sully?"

"I call him Noisy Ned for lack of an actual name. No idea who he really is, but he comes in pretty handy when someone shows up unexpectedly."

"Is there somewhere we can talk where Ned *isn't*?"

"I generally have no idea where he is, but we can try."

Dez fell into step beside Sully as he led them back down the hall and into the parlour he'd just left.

"So it's true," Dez said. "This place being haunted, I mean. It wasn't just some stupid story kids told each other in school."

"Nope, it's all true. Near as I can tell, there are at least six separate entities here, and most of them are in a bad mood daily. They all tolerate me, probably because they like Pax and they know I'm looking after him. I think he was Linton Blackmoor's dog."

"The most recent owner? The guy who died here in the flood?"

"Yeah. He's still here, too, I think. I don't know how to help him or anyone else since I can't see them or communicate with them, so we just put up with each other. Kind of like a really bad roommate situation."

Dez looked around the room, eyes settling on the rumpled pile of blankets on the fainting couch and what was left of last night's now-extinguished fire. "And you've been living here? I mean, you spent two years in this place by yourself?"

"I had Pax."

"I know. I just meant…. Bloody hell, Sully."

"It's not so bad. I've got a roof over my head, a way to more or less keep warm, and a stockroom with canned stuff and seeds for the garden out back. And I've got Pax and the best security setup a guy could ask for with Noisy Ned."

"Yeah, but…. Bloody hell."

It seemed like the right time to try again to fix things. "Dez, I'm really sorry. I didn't mean—"

"I know, okay? I get it."

"I didn't keep it from you because I—"

"I heard you the first time. I don't want to talk about it."

"You haven't… done anything about it, have you?"

"Killed Lowell, you mean? I thought about it. Hell, I think about it at least once every five minutes. But I haven't confronted him. Eva's been keeping an eye on me, making sure I'm not about to fly off in a murderous rage. Listen, I don't want to stay long, and I can't. Lachlan's waiting on the riverbank, guarding a boat we borrowed from some ex-cop buddy of his. Raynor called me, looking for you. He said Montague was shot to death, apparently by a sniper. And he thinks you were involved. Surveillance video shows a guy running out of the house. Someone who looks a lot like you. And… you don't look surprised by any of this."

Sully shrugged. "There's nothing to be surprised about. It was me. I was there."

Dez's mouth drew together in a tight line, the calm before the storm. Sully waited, watching as the blood filled the vessels in his brother's face, then decided he'd better step in to head off the worst of the explosion.

"He said he had answers, and I needed to get him to talk. If there's a way to take Lowell down for what he did to our family, I had to try."

"So you broke into his house and confronted him?" Dez was angry, no question, but Sully counted himself a win that the question was growled rather than shouted.

"Sort of. I snuck in while he wasn't looking and I talked to his back, pretending I was armed."

Sully filled Dez in on the conversation with Montague that had followed, right up to the point where the bullets started flying. When he'd finished, Dez's fury had reduced to a more comfortable level of angry.

"You're an idiot, you know that? Damn it, Sully. You could have been killed. Do you get that?"

"I know. I didn't count on a sniper in the backyard."

"The police aren't sure if you were in on it or if you're just a witness they need to talk to. Either way, they want you in there for a statement."

"I can't do that."

"I know. And Raynor knows, I think. But he's talking about outing you if you don't come forward soon on your own."

"So what am I supposed to do?"

"No clue. Maybe if you considered the consequences before going off and doing stupid crap, you wouldn't end up in these situations."

"I couldn't have predicted an assassination."

"But you had to have known the chances of things going bad were pretty damn good. You went anyway."

"If he could help us take down Lowell, I wasn't about to leave that stone unturned. I'd have thought you'd be onside with that."

"I would have been onside with a sit-down conversation that didn't involve a break and enter and threats."

"He wasn't going to say anything without serious incentive," Sully said. "You have to see that."

Dez's sigh and subsequent subject change suggested he did see that. "Still leaves us with what we're going to do about you."

"I'm already doing the only thing I can think of. I've removed myself from the situation, and I'm somewhere no one will look."

"I know this doesn't solve the Raynor problem, but no one ever looked for you at my apartment, did they? You could stay there."

"Dez—"

"Listen, Sully, I drove into The Forks just one time, when Raynor and I came to look for you at the Dules' old house. We almost didn't get out alive."

"I lived here for two years on my own. I'm not saying it was without problems, but I managed it. I can do it again."

There'd been a time, not so long ago, when this conversation might have gone very differently. Dez would have laid down an argument as to why Sully needed to be somewhere safe and, failing that, would have resorted to force to get his younger brother to such a place.

Things had changed. Sully could see it in the conflicting emotions passing across his brother's face. Sully had spent much of his life struggling to exert his independence with Dez, his ability to make his own decisions and mistakes. Now that he was here, it wasn't without some regret.

"I think you're making another stupid mistake, but I'm done arguing," Dez said. "You'll do what you want. You always do. But I came here for something else. I'm pissed at you with good reason, but I had no call to say what I did to you. I'm sorry I just blurted it out like that. The Gerhardt thing, I mean."

Sully dropped his head at the reminder, scanning the tops of his and Dez's boots. The name reopened the door, one Sully had spent the last two days trying to hold shut.

"Sully?"

"It's okay, Dez. After everything I told you—everything I hadn't told you—I get it."

"It didn't give me the right to nail you with that. Not the way I did. It was wrong. *I* was wrong. It was a dick thing to do, and I'm sorry."

Sully forced his head up, his gaze making it as far as Dez's chin. He couldn't quite meet his eyes. "It's okay. Like I said, I understand."

Dez nodded, muscles in his face relaxing a little. But not entirely. They'd each made their apologies, but words hadn't fixed what their secrets had broken. Sully wasn't angry at Dez for what he'd said—what he hadn't said until two days ago. He was too busy being angry with himself. He'd held out on Dez, had kept from him a truth he had every right to know. Intentions didn't matter, not to Dez. He was an action guy, and it was actions that counted. Sully's had been dishonest, and with someone who deserved nothing less than complete honesty.

And there was the other thing, the reality he'd been trying hard to avoid. But it was there, not just around him but inside him. He was Gerhardt's son. The son of a rapist, a sociopath who took advantage of patients he believed could benefit him. That man was half of Sully's genetic makeup. His skin, blood, bones, hair, all of it was at least partly made up of Gerhardt's genes. Emily might have been right: Inside, he was his mother's son. But the physical parts of him, those were at least partially Gerhardt.

He didn't want to be inside his body anymore, and it terrified him.

"You okay?"

Sully's gaze had drifted back down, and he lifted his head to look back up at Dez. This time, he only made it as far as the logo on Dez's T-shirt.

"Yeah. I'm fine."

He wasn't. His brother would see that as surely as he was standing here.

Dez didn't pursue it.

"Listen, there's another reason we came," he said instead. "Lachlan wants your help with his other ghost."

"Right. I'll do what I can. I'll come down and talk to him."

"We were thinking more along the lines of you coming with."

"Okay. But after that, I'll have to come back here."

For the first time in his life, he hoped for an argument from Dez. He realized as he stood here, drowning in self-loathing, he needed some sort of validation that he was more than a liar, more than a rapist's son, more than a man with the soul of a killer. Dez had always seen the best in Sully, and had been quick to remind him when he needed it. Dez had never let him down.

Until, with one word, he did.

"Fine."

5

CONVERSATION WITH LACHLAN was put on hold until they reached the mainland, boat nosed into a quiet spot on the shores of Riverview Park. Sully didn't breathe any easier when they hit land.

"I need to get the boat back to my friend," he said. "Find somewhere to hang out where no one will notice you, then send me the location. Not your apartment, Braddock. It's the first place Raynor will look. Now, give me a push back out."

Lachlan didn't wait for agreement, simply waited like a ship's captain for his impromptu crew to shove the boat from the shore back onto the water.

Sully watched him go before turning to scan the park. A few people were around, enough to convince him to draw his hood over his head. Dez followed Sully and Pax a few steps before spinning back to the river.

"What?" Sully asked.

"My SUV. The jerk's planning on driving my SUV."

"So?"

"So he's got a concussion. He's not cleared to drive yet."

"Well, you've got the keys, right?"

"Nope. I left all my valuables at his buddy's place. My keys, my wallet, even my wedding ring. Lachlan convinced me if we were going into The Forks, we should be going empty-handed, just in case someone tried to rob us."

Sully grinned. "I think you've been taken."

"Damn it."

"He'll be fine. How far is it to this buddy's place?"

"He's out of town. I'm thinking it'll be close to an hour before Lachlan gets back here."

"There are too many people around," Sully said. "And I guess we can't go back to the apartment. Any other ideas about where to hole up?"

Dez quieted in thought. When his expression registered he'd arrived at a possible solution, it also contained an element of reluctance. "Do you still remember the back door key-code at the Black Fox?"

"I don't want to go back there."

"Neither do I. But it's empty. We won't have to worry about anyone seeing you or looking for you there."

It was a good point, good enough to draw a defeated sigh from Sully. His years working there had largely been happy ones, the work honest and his boss Betty having become a friend. Then Betty was shot to death in the bar and Sully was nearly murdered himself. He hadn't been back since that last bloody confrontation with Lowell, and he wasn't eager to return now.

Dez couldn't be much happier. After all, he'd been the one to find Sully, unconscious in a tub filled with water and blood. But he was right. They needed somewhere quiet, somewhere out of the way. A shuttered bar was as quiet and out of the way as you could get in Kimotan Rapids.

Sully led the way, Dez falling into step beside him as Pax trotted along behind, occasionally distracted by the various scents along their path.

They walked in silence the few blocks to the back alley behind the bar. The rear door came into view, its image hitting Sully with a heavy and unpleasant dose of déjà vu.

He stalled, drawing to an abrupt halt in the rear parking area.

Dez had continued a couple of steps, but returned once he noticed he was proceeding alone. "Sully?"

"I told myself I'd never come back here."

"Me too." Dez shrugged. "But it's still our best option. Listen, we'll stay out of the bar area and we won't go upstairs." He nudged Sully with a solidly muscled arm. "Come on. We'll be okay."

THE DOOR to the bar area was thankfully closed, preventing Sully from catching a glimpse of the spot where Betty had died.

But here, just feet from where he sat at the base of the stairs, he'd unsuccessfully fought the gunman. The gunman he now knew was his own foster uncle.

Dez sat in a chair Betty always kept in the back area for propping open the door, Pax reclined and snoring lightly at his feet. The sound of traffic floated past outside, but here inside, they remained locked within their own world.

Sully lifted his eyes, gaze fixing on the top of Dez's head. He was slumped over in the chair, elbows on knees, hands cupped together in front of him. A man deep in thought.

Or trying hard to ignore the only other person in the room.

Sully wanted to say so many things, variations of apologies multiplying like rabbits inside his brain. But he knew Dez, knew he hated "sorry" on repeat. With no better way to repair their relationship, Sully looked for something else they could talk about.

He found it where he least expected it.

Until now, he'd done everything he could to avoid Gerhardt. Suddenly, an idea formed, one that might allow them to play one enemy against the other.

"Dez?"

Dez didn't look up. "Hmm?"

"This Lowell-Gerhardt thing. I've been thinking. Hackman

told us the two of them were in this together, at least insofar as the stuff at Lockwood with the drug. And they're both in that Circle. We know that now too."

"Yeah?"

"I'm wondering if the way to get Lowell might be to go through Gerhardt. He's in there like a dirty shirt. He has to be. And he's got to know who the guy in the mask is. Maybe he's another in."

That got Dez lifting his head, his eyes locking onto Sully's. "What are you getting at with this whole 'go through Gerhardt' thing? You're not thinking we're going to find something to pin on him to get him to talk, are you? I mean, I know what he's doing is really, really bad and even illegal, but sorry, man. Who's going to believe a bunch of diagnosed mentally ill people over him?"

"No one. That's not what I'm getting at. I meant we use him another way."

"Which is?"

"His son. I don't mean me. I mean his other son. The one who disappeared."

"The one who he believes was kidnapped from his backyard. He was trying to get your biological mom to find him before…."

"Before she died. I know. And he asked me about him a lot too. When I was in the Blue Room, he asked me every single time, at the start and at the end."

"But you never saw him?"

Sully shook his head. "Never. Maybe he wasn't taken and killed. Maybe he's still out there somewhere."

"Or maybe it doesn't mean anything. Could be you didn't see him because it was the wrong place, wrong time—you being in that room in those conditions."

"That didn't stop me from seeing all those other ghosts they wanted me to. Some people take other people's kids and raise them as their own, right?"

"Rarely. In my experience, most people who take kids are in it for something far, far worse."

"But not *all*."

"I guess not. It's a thought. Anyway, what are you suggesting exactly? How are you going to get Gerhardt on board without revealing yourself to him?"

"I haven't figured that out yet."

Neither of them spoke for a few minutes, but Dez broke the silence with a tentative question.

"You doing okay?"

"With what?"

"The Gerhardt thing. What I told you about him being... you know."

"I'm not mad at you, Dez. I already said."

"I didn't mean that. I meant, how are you doing with knowing, with what it means?"

"I don't know what to think," Sully said. "I hate him. I hate him so much it scares me. And I don't know what it makes me, to be born from that. From *him*."

"You're the same person you were before you knew. He's a sperm donor, Sully. Nothing more. You've got three true parents, and every one of them would have given everything to keep you safe and happy. Lucky risked her life to protect you, just like you're always risking yours to help others. You're your mother's son, man. Don't you ever forget."

Sully smiled, gratitude warming his insides. "That's a really nice thing to say, given how pissed you are at me."

"Hey, I can be pissed at you as much as I want. Doesn't make me care about you any less. And it doesn't change who you are, okay? None of this changes who you are."

"Maybe I can use it to get to Gerhardt."

Fire flashed in Dez's eyes. "No. No, Sully. He can't ever know about you."

"If he knows, maybe he'll talk to me. Maybe I can reduce the threat with him."

Dez stood, his size adding power to his argument. "Or maybe you increase it. You're not just his biological son, all right? You're evidence—not just of his warped experiments, but of the fact he raped a teenage patient. You can't reveal any of this to him, Sully. And you sure as hell can't reveal yourself. Don't you even think it."

Dez, an exceedingly large man at the best of times, looked like a grizzly bear when he got like this. Arguing with a grizzly never paid off.

Anyway, he'd made a solid point.

"Okay," Sully said. "I hear you. And you're right. It was a dumb idea."

"So you won't?"

"I won't. I'll figure something else out."

"*We'll* figure something else out," Dez corrected, before returning to his chair.

Sully studied Dez a moment. "Thanks, D."

"For what?"

"For having my back even when you'd rather pound it."

"We're brothers," Dez replied. "That means I can have your back and pound it at the same time."

Dez finished with a smile, one Sully gratefully mirrored.

The ease didn't last long. The sound of a vehicle driving through the back alley and stopping, the engine cutting, had them exchanging a look.

"It's too early for Lachlan," Dez said. He got up to crack the door open, bringing Pax to standing in the process.

He closed it almost immediately, face registering something between shock and rage.

"Who is it?" Sully asked.

The answer came out a growl. "Lowell."

Sully's stomach dropped out as he leapt to his feet. "What?"

"Get upstairs. Find somewhere to stay hidden."

"Come with me."

"No."

"Dez."

"I need to face him."

"If you're planning on confronting him, I'm not going anywhere. I won't let you do anything you're going to regret."

"My only regret is spending all those years looking up to the man who destroyed my family. Get upstairs."

"Not without you. If you're staying, so am I."

Dez growled, the sound as dangerous as it was frustrated. Sully braced himself for the unwanted reunion, for coming face to face with Lowell after two years in hiding.

As footsteps sounded in the parking lot's gravel, Dez at last relented. Giving Sully a shove to get him moving, Dez, with Pax immediately on his heels, jogged after his brother up the stairs.

The door to Sully's old apartment was partially ajar, the wood splintered along the lock where Dez had no doubt kicked it in the day he'd found Sully in the tub. Sully led the way inside, moving quietly as Lowell made entry downstairs. Bypassing the bathroom, Sully led them into the living room and signalled for Pax to sit.

Besides the heavy layer of dust, the room was more or less as Sully had left it—not helpful as he'd left following a fight to near-death with Lowell and Hackman. Yet there was no sign of a struggle save a hole in the drywall. No doubt Lowell and Hackman had righted the place before leaving, eliminating any potential notions of foul play. Sully remembered that day well. Not for the first time, he wished the blow to his head at the end of the attack had robbed him of a little short-term memory.

He left his own thoughts in the past as he focused on Dez. His brother was vibrating, tension wracking his body as they stood side by side, listening to Lowell making his way through the bar downstairs. Sully slipped his phone from his pocket, ensuring it was on silent, before nudging Dez to do the same.

Dez's hands shook as he flipped the ringer to silent and dropped the phone back into his pocket. "What's he even doing here?" Dez hissed.

Sully shrugged, stepped closer to Dez to answer. "He owns the place. Probably needs to check it every so often for insurance purposes."

They stood in silence a minute, maybe two, listening as Lowell's footsteps sounded below, a creak on the old wood floors. Water pipes kicking in told Sully he was right about Lowell's presence here. There was nothing to do but wait.

Waiting wasn't a skill Dez had ever fully mastered.

"I can't do this." Dez's voice was a low growl, teeth clenched around the words.

"You're doing good," Sully said, voice low.

"I'm not. I want to face him. I *need* to face him." Even through the whisper, Sully could hear the emotion.

"Not now. You'll get your chance, D, but wait until we have the upper hand."

"We have it now. There are two of us and one of him."

"You know where that leads. I don't want to go to prison. Lockwood was pretty damn close to one, and I can't live like that again. And I won't let you put yourself there either. Anyway, I confronted him once, and it almost killed me."

"Another reason we should deal with him now."

"It all leads to the same place. You know it as well as I do. If you act on what you're feeling now, it won't come out anywhere good." When the effect of that argument proved negligible, Sully tried a different tactic—one he knew his brother couldn't ignore. "Kayleigh deserves a father in her life, Dez. Don't let Lowell take that too. Your daughter's more important than revenge."

"Don't you fucking do that, Sully."

"You know I'm right."

Dez took a deep breath, but the low growl that followed suggested calm hadn't resulted. His hands balled into fists, and his eyes fixed on the wall in front of him as if wanting to punch through it.

The couch was within easy reach, and Sully pointed Dez toward it. Dez sat, hands white-knuckling his knees as they continued to listen to the sounds downstairs. It occurred to Sully Lowell might opt to run the taps in all the upstairs apartments as well. If so, they'd be screwed.

If Dez didn't calm down, Lowell would be screwed.

Sully sat next to his brother, daring to lay a palm on his shoulder.

Dez shook him off. "Don't."

Sully didn't try to repeat the move, nor did he say anything. Moments like this, words were neither necessary nor wanted.

Pax padded over, dropping his large head onto Dez's knee. It was the sort of comfort Dez wasn't as quick to push away, and he stroked the dog's fur while his breathing gradually returned to normal.

They sat together, the three of them, until the sound of the back door closing suggested Lowell had gone. Sully released tension through a breath, relieved Lowell seemed to have foregone the full check.

Sully's apartment didn't overlook the back alley, so he tiptoed into the hall, keeping close to the wall as he edged up to a window on the landing that would provide a view of the rear parking area. He got there in time to see a car drive off, Lowell behind the wheel.

Dez and Pax were standing at the doorway to the apartment when Sully turned.

"He's gone," he said, to which Dez gave a tight nod.

Dez took two steps into the hall, turned, drew back a fist and drove a punch through the drywall.

6

DEZ ANSWERED the rear door when Lachlan showed up twenty minutes later, signalling his arrival with a shave-and-a-haircut knock.

Dez was surprisingly pleased about the presence of an outsider. Sully had been hovering since taking care of his two split knuckles, watching him as if afraid he'd run out on a murderous rampage.

Sully's worry hadn't been entirely misplaced. Dez had never wanted to kill anyone, not really, despite having used the words in exaggeration. But never had he experienced a rage like this, one that curled around his insides like a parasite, sucking every good feeling from him and leaving only anger. Knowing he'd been just a few steps from the man who'd drowned his five-year-old brother, who'd murdered his father and all but destroyed Sully, it set off inside him a burning desire to act on his fury. He'd been able to picture it in his mind, beating Lowell to death with his bare hands. He was ashamed to think he'd enjoyed the mental image.

"Why the long face?" Lachlan asked through a smirk.

Sully appeared at Dez's left shoulder, fielding the question for his brother. "Lowell was here."

"Jesus. You two didn't kill him, did you?"

"No," Dez said, slipping his wedding band back on and pocketing the keys and wallet Lachlan handed him. "Thought about it. Thought about it hard. But no."

"So what happened to your hand?"

"Wall," Dez said. He stepped aside to allow Lachlan to enter.

"We didn't confront him," Sully explained. "We kept out of sight. He didn't even know we were here. Dez told me you wanted some help with your second ghost."

"Sure, but never mind that now. You've got me sold on your Lowell problem. I want to help bring the bastard down. Now, I know it's not going to be easy, but nothing's impossible. Sullivan, take me through everything you know."

Sully cast Dez an anxious glance before launching into it. Dez returned to the chair, hunched over to conceal most of his face as Sully took Lachlan through it, answering questions and providing detail, some of which Dez hadn't heard in full. When he finished, Dez's teeth were gritted and Lachlan was silent.

"Heavy stuff," he said at last. "The usual solution would be you going to the police and providing a statement to that effect. Of course, I recognize that isn't currently possible, and I can understand why—particularly now that you're wanted on the Montague homicide."

Dez raised his head at a growl from Pax and a sudden, sharp intake of breath from Sully, who glanced to his side and then quickly away.

"What?" Dez asked.

"Nothing."

"No. What?"

Sully sighed. "It's Montague. He's been on me since after the shooting. He blames me for what happened to him."

Dez repressed the shiver as his eyes went to the spot at Sully's side, empty to all save his brother. "He's here? Now?"

Pax was still growling, and Sully shushed him before answering Dez. "He didn't follow me inside Ravenwood. The place doesn't deal well with outsiders. But I saw him there the whole time, outside, waiting. I didn't notice him after we left, and I'd hoped maybe he didn't know and stayed behind. I guess he found me."

"Crap," Dez said. "You didn't kill him though. You had nothing to do with his death."

"He doesn't believe that. All he knows is I was an intruder in his home when the shot was fired. He thinks I'm involved."

"Why not go after the real killer?"

"He didn't see him. People don't become all-knowing just because they're dead. He's still limited to what he was aware of in life. I didn't see the gunman and neither did he. So he blames me."

"And he's stalking you in the meantime," Dez said. "That sucks." He spoke to the air next to Sully, too pissed off at life to care about his fears. "Hey, Montague, after everything you did, maybe you should consider you had it coming."

Two sharp barks from Pax coincided with a flinch from Sully, one that resembled a man about to get punched. "Dez, don't. You're just making him mad. It won't help. It *really* won't help."

It helped Dez, but given he usually couldn't see or experience the things Sully did, he sometimes forgot how severely they could impact his brother. No sense getting Montague riled up if it meant Sully paying the price.

"Okay, sorry," he said to the empty space. "You didn't deserve to be murdered. Justice is one thing but murder's another. But Sully didn't do it. He had nothing to do with it. You're targeting the wrong person. You want someone to haunt, go find Lowell Braddock. He deserves all the torment you can provide."

He waited a moment, watching Sully's face for a change.

"Anything?" he asked when Sully didn't comment.

"He's less pissed. But he's still here. Thanks for trying, Dez."

Great. It wasn't bad enough he was sitting here stewing over his uncle. They were now going to have to deal with the stalker ghost of a murderer to boot.

Lachlan had been unusually quiet during the exchange, and he chose that moment to speak up. "There's no way for Montague to find out more about the shooter for us, is there? I mean, he's uniquely positioned to be able to go places and do things none of us can."

"He wouldn't know where to start, and I don't know where to point him," Sully said. "Anyway, like I said, he blames me. In my experience, ghosts who've been murdered tend to be fairly one-track in their thoughts. The only way I'm going to get rid of him is to find the person who actually killed him and make sure they face justice. If he can see the person and hear them say they acted alone, that will probably be enough."

"Right," Lachlan said. "So all you need is for the assassin to come forward and provide a statement acknowledging everything he did and promising to plead guilty in court."

Dez snorted. "You really see that happening?"

"Nope. I'd say it's pretty obvious this was a professional hit. Someone paid a pro to take the judge down. And I don't think I'm reaching by saying it has something to do with this Circle."

"Maybe it was Lowell," Sully said. "He knows his way around guns. And it was his name Montague brought up to police. If word got back to him somehow, he might have decided he'd have to shut the judge up."

"You're suggesting a leak inside the department," Dez said.

"Not necessarily. Maybe someone went over to question Lowell about it, hoping he'd say something."

"Maybe," Dez said. "But it would have been a dumb thing to do, if that's what happened."

"Not every cop is as good as Dad was."

"Fair point. In that case, might be worth asking Raynor if he decided to jump the gun on that one."

"I can't see it," Lachlan said. "Every cop worth his salt, and even most of the dumb ones, know better than to confront a suspect without some evidence to back your play. Fallout could be a complaint against you to the department or sending your suspect underground. Either way, any chance at catching a smart criminal at something illegal could easily be diminished or eliminated altogether. And something tells me Lowell Braddock will make for one smart criminal.

"One thing's for sure. Much as I'd love to get my teeth into this whole who-shot-the-disgraced-judge thing, the police won't let us anywhere near that one. It's an open investigation, and one they're going to be loath to share info on. Plus, we'd be letting ourselves in for obstruction charges for trying to stick our noses in. We're better off focusing our efforts on the Lowell problem. If we can take him down, maybe we'll be lucky and solve Montague's murder at the same time—if you're right and Lowell was the one behind the gun. Does he have any ability to act as a sniper?"

"Like Sully said, he knows his way around guns," Dez said. "He used to take part in competitions here and there when he was younger. It might be he still heads out to the range to practice. Fast cars and extreme sports, that's Lowell."

"Smart," Lachlan said. "Really smart. He's behind several murders and attempted murders that we know of, and only one— Betty Schuster—involved a gun. He drowned his nephew, injected his brother with epinephrine and cut Sullivan's wrists. Avoiding a specific MO makes it harder to connect the homicides, or the person responsible—if the deaths were ever discovered to be homicides in the first place."

"I was thinking," Sully said. "If we want a way in with Lowell, the Circle might be the way to get there."

"If you're thinking undercover work, something tells me they're not going to be keen to let any of us in. It's a society for wealthy or soon-to-be wealthy men and women. Anyway, the last thing they'll want is a private investigator in their ranks, and you're supposed to be dead, so...."

"Not what I was getting at. I was thinking more along the lines of using someone already within their ranks."

"Such as?"

"Roman Gerhardt."

Dez sensed where his brother was going. "Sully, no. We talked about this."

Sully met his eye and shrugged. "Just wanted to put it out there for Lachlan, see what he thinks."

Lachlan's gaze flitted from Sully to Dez and back again, lifted eyebrows suggesting interest. "What?"

No getting around it, Dez explained his brother's earlier thought. "Sully reminded me Gerhardt has been intent on finding his kid, a six-year-old boy who went missing from his backyard. Gerhardt has been questioning psychic patients about it, but he's never gotten to the bottom of it. He mentioned to me a couple of years ago that a patient told him his son was with him or something. We now know that patient was Sully's birth mother."

"How long after the disappearance did Lucienne Dule come into his care?"

"Fifteen years, he said."

"Sullivan's twenty-four now, so add that to fifteen—you get something around forty years since the disappearance. I'll do some digging, see what I can find. It was before my time on the force, but I should be able to pull some strings and get us a look at the file."

"What's the point?" Dez asked. "Where are we supposed to go with this exactly?"

"I told you," Sully said. "We might be able to use this to our benefit. Gerhardt knows what Lowell is, and he's in a position to go to the police and have them believe him. It sounds bad saying it like this, but we can dangle his son's case like a huge carrot to get him to help us bring Lowell down. Trade info on the son for info on Lowell."

Lachlan pointed an index finger toward Sully and grinned. "Bingo."

Dez crossed his arms. "And as I already told you, I don't like it." He turned to Lachlan. "We can't do anything that risks exposing Sully."

"Who said anything about exposing him?" Lachlan asked. "Near as I can see, we're just two private investigators offering to solve the case for him. It's perfectly true I worked for a woman purporting to be Lucienne Dule, and I can tell him she mentioned having seen his son's ghost."

"Except it wasn't Lucienne. It was her crackpot sister you were dealing with. And since their mother was a patient of Gerhardt's, he's bound to know that."

Lachlan rolled his eyes. "I realize that, thank you. Moving on. I mentioned a couple of minutes ago how tipping off a suspect can make them go to ground. It can have another effect though. Sometimes it can trip a suspect up, get them making mistakes and taking chances out of panic. In Gerhardt's case, he's obsessed— understandably—with finding his son and laying him to rest. That makes him both highly driven and emotional, which is a good recipe for screwups. It also makes him more easily manipulated by anyone with information he'll see as helpful. If I had a nickel for every time a poor, grieving mother paid some fake psychic for supposed information on her missing child, I'd be a wealthy man. Parents will leave no stone unturned, and I normally wouldn't play on that sort of grief. But this is Roman Gerhardt, a man we know isn't above torturing defenceless patients to achieve his ends. My sympathy level is lessened significantly. If we can use this to our advantage, why wouldn't we try?"

"He won't talk to me," Dez said. "He hates me, and he knows how much I hate him."

"He'll talk to you if you have information he wants. I can't hide the fact you're working for me, Braddock. There will be times I'll need you to check into certain things on your own, and it'll raise his suspicions unnecessarily if he hasn't been made aware of you ahead of time. We'll just have to nip your joint dislike in the bud."

"So that's it?" Dez asked. "We're doing this? I don't get a say in the fact we're about to open one massive can of worms?"

"Every investigation is a can of worms, Braddock. You know that."

Dez rubbed at the back of his neck. Going after Lowell was one thing, and it was something he was increasingly eager to do. But poking at Gerhardt to do it felt like a line they were safer not crossing. Sully would have to be involved in this investigation. How long would it take before Gerhardt, naturally eager for involvement in the case, saw him? The loss of his first son was tragic, but discovering Sully of all people was also his son would no doubt result in a catastrophe.

And Sully's involvement in this was risky on a whole other level. If he got into this and found out he couldn't handle it, where did that leave them? Sully wasn't violent, far from it. But this was the man who had raped his mother and who had confined and tortured him. He'd confronted Lowell over Flynn and had nearly died doing it. If Sully fell into the chasm that ongoing proximity to Gerhardt would no doubt open, Dez wasn't sure he'd be able to pull him free. Not before his brother's life was forever shattered.

"If we're doing this," he said, "I'm keeping close to Sully. I'm not gonna risk this going sideways and something happening we can't reverse. He's already been traumatized because of Lock-wood. Last thing I want is him falling under the weight of a severe PTSD flashback or something else when I'm not around to hold him up."

"I'll be okay, Dez," Sully said. "I'm better prepared this time. Anyway, I need to face this. And at some point, I'll need to face *him*. It's the only way I'll find any peace. If we can get him to turn on Lowell, to provide info to the police, I won't need to be in hiding anymore. Best case scenario, he'd back my story and make it so I can provide a statement of my own, one the police might actually believe. If I had a way to come forward so people would believe me, we'd have him, just like that. After everything that happened to Dad and Aiden, you want that, too, don't you?"

"Of course I want that. But not at your expense. We find a way to take him down that doesn't destroy you in the process, I'm all-in. But Sully, this thing starts taking you down too dark a path, I'm calling it, you hear me?"

Sully smiled and Dez took some comfort in that, as well as in his following response. "I hear you."

7

THROUGH HEAVY SIGHS FROM LACHLAN, Dez ran a careful visual scan of his SUV, relieved to find no dings or scratches to suggest his concussed boss had lost track of the road.

"Happy now?" Lachlan grumbled.

"I'd be happier if you hadn't driven in the first place."

"I miss driving. As much fun as it is to be your backseat driver, I like not needing to rely on you for everything."

"Talk to your doctor. Get him to clear you. Please."

Lachlan seemed to find that funny, judging from the closed-mouthed chuckle that rumbled from his chest.

Dez wasn't keen to share in the joke. He had something on his mind, something he didn't think he could put off for much longer.

"Are you planning to talk to someone at the police department about getting you a look at Gerhardt's son's file?" Dez asked.

"Yep. I'll put in the call right away. Usually doesn't take my buddies long to dig things up for me."

"Good. Then I'm going to drop you off at home in the meantime. There's something Sully and I need to do."

"What do we need to do?" Sully asked as he let Pax into the backseat.

"We're about to start digging into some stuff we hope will lead us to taking down Lowell," Dez said. "We need to talk to Mom. She doesn't know any of this, and we need to fill her in before the pieces start to move."

Sully's shoulders slumped. "I hadn't even thought."

"Doesn't surprise me."

"What's that supposed to mean?"

"You know what it means."

Dez hadn't meant to start up another argument, but there it was. His emotions were all over the place these days, and the anger bubbling inside him was constantly threatening to boil over. Sully, close in both proximity and to being the source of the problem, would end up bearing the brunt of it unless Dez could get a handle on things.

That wasn't going to happen today.

"Boys, boys, play nice," Lachlan said. "Eyes on the prize. Whatever's going on between the two of you needs to be dealt with or put on hold. We all need to work together if we're going to get this thing sorted."

Lachlan had a good point, enough to get Dez to leave the argument alone and drop into the driver's seat. He held his tongue during the drive up to Lachlan's, Sully doing the same from the backseat. Anything else was an impossibility anyway, Lachlan having located a classical music station he decided he wanted to listen to on high volume.

By the time they reached Lachlan's house, he, at least, was in a good mood. "I'll give you a call once I get the file," he told Dez. "Keep your phone turned on."

"I always keep my phone on. Might be on silent from time to time, but I check it."

Lachlan looked like he had a retort burning a hole in his tongue but, thankfully, he held onto it. He settled for an inoffensive "See you later" before getting out of the vehicle and heading for the house.

Dez waited until Lachlan had let himself inside, in part because he expected Sully to get into the front passenger seat.

He didn't.

"You're not moving up?" Dez asked without turning.

"I'm fine back here."

Dez wondered how true that was, given Pax took up a large part of the seat and was rarely a still passenger, but he left it alone.

Dez sent a quick text to his mom, ensuring she was home before hitting the road. She used to have an office in the city where she'd counselled families in trouble, but she'd gone on stress leave after her own family situation took such a tragic turn. She was home most of the time now, a fact that was subject to change once she learned Aiden hadn't accidentally drowned in the creek out back. Whether she'd be able to stay at the acreage once she knew the truth remained to be seen.

It was nearly three quarters of an hour from here to the acreage, and Dez was content to make the drive in silence.

Sully, it turned out, wasn't.

"I know you're pissed at me, and I get it."

"You've got every right to be pissed at me too."

"Maybe, but I'm not. Anyway, it doesn't matter. We need to put all of this on hold, okay? Mom's going to need our support, and we can't give that to her if we're at each other's throats."

"We aren't at each other's throats. I'm mad, not homicidal—at least as far as the situation with you. Don't worry. Once we get there, I'm there all the way."

Sully remained quiet a few minutes but broke it with a further statement. "I didn't mean it the way it came out. About Mom, I mean. Of course I thought about it. I just didn't—"

"I know, okay? Honestly, it was the same with me. I got caught up in what I was going through, and I forgot she didn't know yet. I lost track of stuff outside myself. I'm sure it was the same with you. I shouldn't have said what I did to you."

"It's okay," Sully said. "I understand."

This time, the silence that followed was a little more comfortable.

THE SUV's tires crunched gravel as Dez crawled up the drive toward the house.

He'd tried to think through how best to tell their mom the truth but had yet to come up with the right words inside his own brain. Of all the people in the world he wanted to avoid hurting, she was up there near the very top of the list; what he was about to say would leave her shattered.

"Dez?"

"Yeah."

"I'll tell her, okay? I'm the one who held all this back. I should be the one to say it."

A wave of relief washed over Dez. Sully was no conversationalist, but he was better at calm and empathetic. "Thanks, man. I can't think of the words."

"Neither can I."

"You said them to me."

"And look how that turned out."

There was an argument to be made about the fact it wasn't the way Sully had said it so much as the fact he'd gone so long without saying it, but he left it alone. The last thing they needed right now was another argument. Breaking the news to their mom would be challenge enough.

She didn't make it any easier by answering the door with the beaming grin that formed the moment she saw them.

"I'll never get tired of this," she said as she let them in. "Seeing the two of you together again."

The reason was obvious as she enveloped Sully in a tight hug. Until only recently, she'd believed him dead. Dez's heart sank as he looked into his mother's face, the picture of contentment, like her world had been righted. He and Sully were about to shake it off its axis all over again.

She turned to Dez next, wrapping her arms around his middle, her head barely making it to his chest. He tried to meet Sully's eye but his brother was staring at the wall, the tight expression on his face suggesting he was deep in unpleasant thought. He could have been deciding on the right words or picturing their result. Either way, today's outcome wouldn't be good.

Dez suddenly regretted not waiting until Eva could be here with them. She was always better at this sort of thing.

Mara pulled away, at last giving Pax the playful head scratch he'd been waiting on. "You too, Pax. It's lovely to see you again, sweetie." She headed for the kitchen, Pax trotting along at her heels. "Come on. I'll put on some coffee."

Sully at last met Dez's eye, raised eyebrows and a grimace providing the answer Dez had looked for earlier. No, he wasn't looking forward to this any more than Dez was.

Mara busied herself with the coffeemaker while Dez slid onto one of the stools at the island, Pax settling himself into a puddle of fur next to him.

"So what brings the two of you by today?" she asked. "Or did you just want a visit with your mom?" She beamed up at Sully who'd circled the island to stand next to her.

"There's actually something we need to talk to you about."

She looked up at him, studied his face for a few seconds. "It's something I'm not going to want to hear."

He shook his head. "But it's something you *need* to hear."

Dez glanced behind him. The kitchen table was littered with its usual array of newspapers, flyers and magazines but was otherwise clear, the logical place to have this conversation.

"Maybe we should sit down," he suggested, receiving a nod from Sully in response.

"Good idea."

Mara glanced back at the coffeemaker. "Are you sure you don't want coffee first?"

"I'd rather just get this out," Sully said. "Is that okay?"

"It depends. You're not leaving again, are you?"

"No, nothing like that. And nobody's sick or dying. It's about something that already happened. About Dad and Aiden."

Sully's words proved sufficient to get her circling the island for the table where Dez pulled out her usual chair. The brothers gravitated to their old spots, leaving just one chair—their dad's —empty.

Or not so empty. Sully's eyes flitted to it, held there a long moment, long enough for a sheen of tears to form.

"He's here?" Dez asked, his voice breaking unexpectedly over the last word. His own eyes went to their dad's chair at the nod from Sully. It looked no less empty.

Never in his life had Dez wanted to see one of Sully's ghosts. Not until today.

"You see him?" Mara asked. For a moment, she smiled. Only for a moment.

Then she remembered.

"But Sully, you only see them if...."

She didn't finish. Sully met her eye and nodded.

"No."

"I'm sorry, Mom."

"No. It's not.... It can't be. He—It was a heart attack. He just had a heart attack. Like his father."

"You remember how Lowell said he injected Dad with epinephrine to try to save him?" Sully said. "The thing is, that's not really how it happened. Lowell did inject him, but Dad wasn't in any medical distress at the time. Lowell... he killed Dad, Mom. He did it on purpose. That's why I can see him."

"No, there has to be some sort of mistake, some misunderstanding. Lowell wouldn't do that. Not to his own brother."

Dez's gaze returned to the empty chair, willing himself to see. Hearing it out loud like this again, seeing the impact on their mom, he needed some comfort. They all did. Just to know, to be able to see his dad, even for a moment, it would be enough. Enough to be able to meet his eye one more time, to be greeted by his warm smile, maybe hear a word of encouragement if he was really lucky. That was all he needed. Just one second.

It didn't come.

Sully could see though. Given the way ghosts often appeared to him—looking very much dead rather than like the living person they'd been—maybe that was worse.

Sully was staring at the chair now. "You've never shown me how it happened. Show me now, so I can explain better." He reached out a hand. Often, if ghosts touched him they could more easily pass along their thoughts. "Dad?"

"What's going on?" Dez asked.

"He won't show me," Sully said. "I think he's trying to protect me."

"Sully, no," Mara said. "I don't want you to see that either. Stop. It's okay."

"But I need you to believe me."

"I do believe you. I have always believed you. You can see him, and he's obviously made you aware of why. That's enough for me. But I don't…. Why? His own brother? How could he do that? *Why* would he do that?"

Sully took a breath. Dez knew this was going to be the hardest part, and he thanked God Sully was here to do this. No way would Dez ever get the words out. He wasn't even sure he could get through hearing them out loud again.

"Mom, Dad isn't alone," Sully said. "Aiden's with him."

He paused, giving the words a moment to sink in.

They did, partway at least. "You see Aiden too?"

Sully held her eye, nodded slowly.

The remaining colour left her face, but she managed one more word, a question. "Lowell?"

Sully nodded again.

Mara's eyes filled with tears. Shaking hands came up to cover the bottom half of her face as a sob erupted. Dez slid out of his chair, knelt next to his mom and bundled her into an embrace, holding her there while she cried.

Sully, slumped in his seat with eyes downcast, held onto the rest of the explanation as Dez uttered useless words of comfort into his mom's hair. No way anything either of them said now was going to help the situation. Certainly, nothing Sully had yet to say was going to do anything but make this worse.

Dez stayed where he was until Mara regained control. She tried to stand, presumably to go for the tissue box, but Dez gently pushed her back down and retrieved it for her. She took one and blew her nose, and ended up needing a second.

"I'm sorry," came a quietly spoken apology from Sully. "I wish I didn't have to—"

"Don't," she snapped, the one word loud and crisp enough to draw the immediate attention of both her sons. "Don't you dare apologize to me. There's only one person who should be sorry, and it isn't you. The fact the two of you are having to put yourselves through this to tell me only makes me hate him even more." Her eyes went to Dez as he returned to his chair. The pain was still there in her expression, but a flash of heated anger had superseded it. "Have you confronted him?"

"No. I wanted to—still do—but no. Sully and Eva have been holding me back."

She nodded, eyes next going to Sully. "And you?"

"Um… I don't—I mean…."

Sully had evidently reached the part he was going to struggle with, so Dez took up the slack. "Yeah, he did. Two years ago. It's the reason he faked his own death and why he's still in hiding. That supposed suicide attempt, when I found him in his tub with his wrists slashed? That was Lowell too. Him and one of the orderlies from Lockwood. And when I managed to save Sully, Lowell had him committed instead, probably made sure they kept him drugged up in there so he couldn't say anything."

"Oh, Sully, no."

"It's okay. I'm okay now."

"Why would you have done that? Why would you have gone to confront Lowell by yourself?"

"I was angry. I wasn't thinking straight. Dad tried to stop me, but I was beyond listening. The only thing I could think about was beating a confession out of Lowell. I almost had him too. But then Hackman turned up."

"Why wouldn't you have taken Dez with you?"

"I didn't know," Dez said. "He didn't bother to fill me in until a couple of days ago."

"I didn't want to hurt anyone," Sully said. "And I didn't know what you would do. If I was angry enough to go after him, I knew you would be. Dad died confronting Lowell, and I almost did too. I couldn't let that happen to you. Either of you."

"It wouldn't have happened," Dez said. "I would have killed him first."

"Right. And you spending life in prison for killing that bastard was such a great alternative."

Mara laid a hand over one of Dez's to cut off his impending argument. "We know now. That's what's important." She turned back to Sully. "How long have you known?"

"About Dad? Since it happened. I saw him in the car with us on the way to the hospital. I didn't know the details at that point, but I figured it out pretty quickly."

"And Aiden?"

Sully's eyes flitted from Mara to Dez back to Mara, and then down to his lap. Dez's insides tensed. Another confession was coming.

"Almost as long as I've been here."

The reply had been mumbled, but Dez heard it nonetheless. "You mean since you were *seven*?"

Sully nodded, didn't look up.

Dez pushed away from the table and stood, anger heating up inside him all over again. "Christ."

A fresh sheen of tears formed in Mara's eyes. "How is he? How does he seem to you?"

"Do you really want me to talk about this?"

"Please, Sully. I need to know."

"He doesn't look physically hurt or anything. He's just dripping wet. What you need to know about him is he's stronger than you'd expect. He's come around a couple of times when it meant saving Dez. He looks out for him, and he does a great job of it."

Mara nodded, allowing a couple of tears to course unchecked down her cheeks. "My boy. My baby boy." She averted her eyes downward as a small sob erupted, but she held onto anything else, sniffling back emotion until she could meet Sully's eye once again. "Is he here too? With your dad?"

"They're together. They're almost always together now."

She managed a smile, her eyes drifting to the empty chair, searching it out. She held her gaze first at a spot that would have been Aiden's approximate height at his death, then moved it up to what would have been the level of Flynn's eyes had he been physically there to meet it.

"I love you both so, so much," she said. "I've never, not for one day stopped thinking about you." She glanced back quickly to Sully before returning her visual attention to her husband's chair. "They can hear me, right?"

He nodded. "Yeah. They're smiling."

"Both of them?"

"Both of them."

Mara took another long moment to study the space, as if hoping she'd see something herself. At last, she returned her eyes to Sully. "Why didn't you ever say anything during all those years? About Aiden, I mean."

"I always knew how broken all of you were about him. At first, I didn't know I only saw homicide victims, so I didn't realize what happened to him was anything but an accident. And at first, I was uncomfortable talking about the things I saw."

Dez tried to get a handle on his annoyance before responding. He knew he'd failed when his words came out sounding more accusatory than questioning. "You knew we weren't like your other foster families. You knew we wouldn't be assholes about it. You didn't think we'd want to know?"

"I tried, okay? At first, I didn't know how to talk about it. The idea of bringing it up to any of you made me really anxious. By the time I'd been here a year or so, I decided I'd try to tell you. But I didn't know how to say it without hurting you worse, so I talked to Lowell one day when he was over keeping an eye on me. I told him what I'd been seeing. I wanted to ask him to help me talk to you guys, but he kind of went crazy."

"What do you mean, 'went crazy?' " Mara asked.

"He accused me of lying, of seeking attention. He went off on me. Said I was making up this ghost based on information I'd learned from you. Said I'd only make things worse for you if I told you. I insisted, that I was really seeing Aiden. I described what he looked like when I saw him. Then Lowell hit me."

"Hit you how?" Dez asked.

"Punched me. In the head."

The anger already building inside Dez's insides bubbled. "Hard?"

Sully nodded. "Sent me across the living room. There was a bump after, but under the hair where it didn't show."

"Where was I when this happened?"

"You weren't there. I think you had a football tournament or something. Mom and Dad went to watch you, but I had a stomach bug, so you guys couldn't take me along. They called Lowell to come stay with me while you were out. After that weekend, he and I went out of our way to avoid each other."

Everything clicked in, Sully's lifelong distrust of Lowell. "So *that's* where it started. Why the hell didn't you tell us?"

"He told me if I said anything, either about Aiden or what he'd just done, he'd say I was lying. He told me I'd get sent back into foster care because no one would ever believe me over him. It never occurred to me he'd killed Aiden. For years, I just thought it was his warped way of trying to protect you guys from more pain. In a way, I could understand that, and it helped remind me to keep it to myself. This family is the best thing that ever happened to me. It was the first really good thing I'd ever known. I would have done anything not to lose it, even if it meant keeping secrets from you or dealing with Lowell. I knew how close all of you were to him. He was blood. I wasn't. I believed him. I didn't want to hurt you or to get sent back to foster care, so I did what he told me."

Any anger at Sully Dez had left dissipated. He returned to the table, laying a hand on his brother's head and giving it a gentle shake before sitting back down. "We would have believed you, Sull. I sure would have."

Mara extended a hand along the table, palm up. Sully met the invitation, placing his hand in hers. "We all would have believed you, kiddo," she said. "I'm so sorry you didn't know that."

Sully heaved a sigh, the sound of tension releasing. "I've held onto this for so long. I never thought I'd be able to say it out loud. I never knew how you'd take it."

"After all these years, how could you not have known?" Mara said. "Sweetie, you're my son. Not my foster son or my adopted son. My *son*. I love you with all my heart. Your dad and your brother always felt the same. If we had been asked to choose between you and Lowell, it would have been you. It would always have been you. You hear me?"

A tear wove its way down Sully's cheek, wiped away with the back of his hand. He nodded.

"Yeah, goes for me too, jerk-face," Dez said.

The childhood slight got the result he'd been after, drawing a burst of laughter from Sully.

Mara gave his hand one last squeeze, then stood and headed for the counter. "I think we need that coffee now. Then we need to figure out what we're going to do about this."

Dez got up to help his mom. "We're already working on it. Lachlan's in on it, and he's giving us a hand. We've got an idea, but I have to admit, I'm not a huge fan."

"What's the plan?"

"It involves Gerhardt."

Mara finished removing the lid from the coffee canister and dropped it a little heavily on the counter. "The maniac from Lockwood who tortured your brother? That Gerhardt?"

Dez offered her a tight smile. "Yeah. That one." He explained what they'd learned about the Circle and Gerhardt's apparent involvement with Lowell in the use of the experimental drug. "He knows Lowell's secrets because he was a member of this demented little club when Lowell was directed to kill Aiden. We've got a solid in with Gerhardt, one we can play on to hopefully get him to turn over info we can use to bury Lowell. His six-year-old son disappeared forty years ago, and he's never stopped trying to find out what happened to him. If we can find the boy, or if Sully can see him and get some answers, we can use that to get us what we need. Sully can't go to the police with what he knows, but Gerhardt can. What's more, they'll believe him, no question."

"He's got some pretty horrible secrets of his own to hide," Mara said. "I'm not so sure he'll be willing to go anywhere near the police."

"We're counting on it his son means more to him than the possibility of being found out," Dez said. "If he's obsessed enough to put his patients' well-being on the line to try to find the kid, I'm hoping he'll do whatever it takes if we can give him a way to get what he's been after."

Mara nodded, her expression suggesting she agreed with the argument. Dez sure did. If, God forbid, it was Kayleigh, he'd move heaven and earth to find her. The possibility of jail or job loss would be meaningless next to a chance at uncovering the answers that would bring her back to him. Mara, as a mother herself—and one who had lost a child to tragic circumstances—would understand.

Mara crossed her arms as she regarded Dez. "You mentioned you've got some reservations," she said. "What are they?"

This would involve another reveal, one which wasn't really Dez's to tell. He glanced over at Sully, waited until he met his eye and nodded his consent before turning back to Mara.

"We found out recently Gerhardt is Sully's biological father."

"What? How?"

"My neighbour, Emily," Dez said, explaining what she'd told

him about Lucky Dule's tragic stay at Lockwood and the manner of Sully's birth inside the institution.

Once he'd finished, Mara remained still and silent for a few seconds, processing, thinking. Then she returned to Sully at the table. He'd let his hair fall across his face in a way that told Dez he'd withdrawn somewhere inside himself, the way he often did during the discussion of painful subjects. Mara didn't say anything, just wrapped her arms around him. Sully remained frozen for a moment but then returned the embrace. A quiet sob sounded in his throat as Mara, still standing, folded herself protectively over him.

Another wave of guilt hit Dez as he recalled the abrupt, careless manner in which he'd thrown the truth at his brother. Sully hadn't spoken about the impact on him, other than the sadly expected questioning of his own character and soul given the nature of his genetic makeup. Now Dez could see just how much the truth had shattered Sully—a truth Dez had tossed out in anger as if it meant nothing.

Dez studied the tiles that made up the kitchen floor, one he'd helped his dad install a decade ago. It hadn't changed much in all that time, the soft pattern and colour barely faded by the sunlight that frequently bathed the kitchen. But so much else had changed.

Those had been easier days. He'd been in his final year of high school, looking forward to the possibility of following in his father's footsteps on the force. Sully had been fourteen, a kid whose dark past had been blessedly saturated by light, thanks to his place in a stable, loving family. Mara and Flynn had never truly gotten over Aiden's loss—an impossibility—but they'd found a place to put it, enabling them to move on with their lives. Most importantly, Flynn had been alive.

Yeah, a lot had changed. And there was no going back.

Even as badly as Dez wished he could.

Mara whispered to Sully, words Dez couldn't make out from his current position. He didn't need to hear to understand the gist of it, Sully nodding before finally releasing Mara and excusing himself to go to the bathroom. He kept his tear-streaked, emotion-fraught face down as he went, avoiding meeting his brother's eye —a move Dez took more as embarrassment over loss of emotional control than anger toward Dez.

Dez was angry enough at himself for both of them.

"He okay?" he asked his mom.

She returned to the coffee maker, spooning out some coffee into the filter Dez had placed inside the tank.

"He will be," she said. "He just needs to find somewhere inside himself to put this. But he'll come through. He's far stronger than he ever gives himself credit for."

Dez nodded, then decided his own confession was in order. "I was angry at him for holding back on the Dad and Aiden stuff. But I'm no better. I knew about Gerhardt for a while, and I didn't say anything to him. I wanted to protect him."

"I guess you can understand then why he didn't say anything to you," Mara said. "It says something about the two of you, that you'd want to keep each other safe from the pain of these things."

Dez dove forward before his mom got too heavy-handed with the compliments. "After he told me about Dad and Aiden and Lowell, I tossed it out at him, about Gerhardt. I feel like an absolute piece of shit over the whole thing. I let my anger control me. I did exactly what he was worried I'd do, only I took it out on him, not Lowell. It wasn't fair, and I feel like garbage for doing that to him."

Mara hit the coffeemaker's on switch, then took Dez's hands in hers. "If there's one thing I know about Sully, it's that he's very forgiving, particularly with the people he loves."

"That's not the point. I know he forgives me. He wasn't pissed with me to begin with. That's the problem. It would be easier if he hated me for it. That way I'm not the only one who's mad at me."

For a moment, Mara didn't say anything as she studied Dez's face. Then her frown turned to a smile. "You are every inch your father's son, you know that?"

"I wish. Dad was way more patient and calm than I am."

"Not by nature," she said. "He worked hard at it, to be that way. He had an explosive temper he had to try hard to control sometimes. In the end, giving into it is why he left us. Had he taken what he learned to his police colleagues rather than charging off to confront Lowell, he'd probably still be here. At the same time, I can't blame him for it. Had I known all of this back then, I would likely have gone with him—and not to hold him back either. You'd be visiting both your parents in prison right now."

"And now?" Dez asked. "How are you handling it?"

"Honestly? I haven't figured it out yet. Part of me wants to do exactly what your dad did and confront the bastard. The other part, the rational part, knows I can't because my family needs me. But most of me is just sad. We were happy once, weren't we?"

Dez nodded. "Yeah. We were."

"I have to hold onto the hope we can be again." She squeezed Dez's hands, watching his eyes as hers narrowed slightly with the promise of a command. "Don't be angry at your brother for holding out on you. And don't be angry with yourself either. We've made mistakes, all of us. As good people, we feel each and every one. Anger is natural, and you need to allow yourself to feel it. But direct it where it should go. Direct it at Lowell."

Dez forced one side of his mouth up into a half-smile. "Believe me, I intend to."

8

IT TOOK REMARKABLY little persuasion to get Mara to pack up a few things and come with them to Dez and Eva's. When they started to close in on Lowell, odds were he'd lash out like a trapped animal. A certain wisdom was found in the adage about safety in numbers, and Sully liked the idea of Mara, Eva, Kayleigh and Dez being in a position to have each other's backs.

Ordinarily, he would have stayed with them. But the situation was far from ordinary, and he was more likely than the others to be targeted once everything hit the fan. He hadn't said anything, but the moment the situation turned ugly, he planned to reveal himself to Lowell. If he could keep the killer's attention fixed on him, it wouldn't be honed in on anyone else.

They arrived at the house just as Kayleigh got home from school, and Sully, who had just set down Mara's suitcase in the living room, welcomed it as she flung herself into his arms.

"You're back!" she cried, squeezing his neck hard enough to restrict breathing as he knelt in front of her.

"Just for a bit," Sully said. "Your dad and I need to go do some stuff. He'll be back later though."

"What about you?"

"Not tonight, but I'll see you again soon, all right?"

"Promise?"

He pulled away far enough to look into her face. Her expression held an earnestness and more than a little worry. His heart sank with the knowledge he'd put it there.

He forced a smile. "Promise."

She gave him one last big hug before turning her attention to her father, hands on hips. "Aren't you eating before you leave? You have to eat."

Dez raised his eyebrows, then burst out laughing. "You sound more like your mom every day, you know that, kiddo? Don't worry. I'll make sure to eat."

Sully turned to Mara while Dez and Kayleigh chatted. "You going to be okay?"

"I'll be fine. It's you two I'm worried about. Don't let Dez do anything stupid."

"I won't." Sully debated whether to say what was on his mind. He didn't want to worry anyone, but decided they had plenty of reason to worry and to be prepared. "You know once we start closing in on this, Lowell's likely to lash out. We need to be ready —all of us."

"I'm more than aware. If he comes near anyone else in my family, I'll kill him." She stepped closer to him, as if realizing Kayleigh might be near enough to hear. "I need to help. I can't sit idly by while my boys are out there, endangering themselves. I need you to keep me in the loop."

"I'll do my best. But when things start rolling, they tend to move fast."

"Then take me with you."

"Mom...."

"Aiden was my son. Flynn was my husband. I have every bit as much right to be involved in this."

"I know you do. Come right down to it, you have more right than I do. But we also need to have someone here, keeping an eye on Kayleigh while Eva's away. If Lowell figures out what Dez and I are up to, he'll know Kayleigh's a weak spot. Given what he's done in the past, I wouldn't put it past him to think up a way to use her against us."

It might be a stretch, but then again with someone like Lowell, who knew? Really, all Sully wanted was to keep their mom out of harm's way. It was bad enough Dez was going into the trenches with him. He'd be damned if he was going to willingly put anyone else he cared about at risk.

Without knowing it, Kayleigh timed out her approach perfectly, tugging on Mara's shirt. "Grandma? Can you make your stew and dumplings?"

"It's a bit late to get started on that, sweetie."

"It's okay. Mom won't be back for supper, and I don't mind eating late." She put on her most winning smile. "I'll help you."

No way Mara could refuse that offer. "Okay. But I'm not sure your mom and dad have all the ingredients."

"Let's look."

With Kayleigh tugging at her hand, Mara allowed herself to be led to the kitchen.

Dez had gone off somewhere, and Sully spotted him a minute or so later, coming down the stairs with something in his hand.

"It's a portable charger," Dez said, placing it in Sully's hand. "I've got a second one I'm charging up now, but this one's good to go. It should be set for something like ten charges."

"For what?"

"Your phone, dummy. If you're insisting on staying at Ravenwood, you'll need a way to keep your phone charged. I don't like the idea of you being all the way over there with no way for us to reach each other. I'm thinking if you use this one until it starts running dry, then we can switch them out. I'll give you the other one while I recharge this one."

Sully pocketed the device. "Okay, thanks."

"Sure you won't consider staying here?"

"I'm sure. It's safer if I'm not around."

"Safer for who? Not you, obviously."

It seemed like a good time for a subject change. "Just so you know, Mom wants in on this."

"No fucking way."

"That's what I thought you'd say."

"If Lowell was willing to kill his own brother, he'd think nothing of going after her too. I don't want her in his crosshairs. Not for anything."

"I get it, but she's got a point too. Aiden was her son, and Dad was her husband. Would you be content to sit it out if it was Eva and Kayleigh?"

Dez blew out a tension-filled breath. "Maybe we shouldn't have told her yet."

"She had a right to know, Dez, same as you."

"When has that mattered to you before?" Dez asked. But this time, he combined it with a smile that told Sully he wasn't the same level of angry. He glanced back to the kitchen where Mara and Kayleigh were rifling through the fridge, looking for the items necessary for Mara's stew. "She *is* going to stay put, though, right?"

"For now, anyway," Sully said. "I think I managed to convince her to stay here for Kayleigh's safety."

Dez lost a shade of colour, and Sully realized his error. "Kayleigh? God, you don't think he'd—" It took Dez all of five seconds to think through his own answer, and for the blood to return full-force to his head with the resulting anger. "If that bastard comes anywhere near my family—"

"He won't," Sully said. "We won't let him."

"Damn right, we won't."

Time to divert Dez to a different track. "Have you heard from Lachlan since we dropped him off? He was trying to get that file."

Dez shook his head and pulled his phone from his pocket. After dialling, he waited only a moment before speaking. "Hey, did you…? I thought you were going to call once you…. Okay, fine. We're on our way." He disconnected and turned to Sully. "Lachlan got the file and he's digging through it now."

"He was supposed to call once he got it."

"You know Lachlan," Dez said, leading the way to the door. "He forgets stuff like including people when he gets his nose down on a trail. Let's go. Oh, and I'm thinking we should leave Pax here. The storage container's one thing, but I doubt Lachlan would be pleased to have a dog running around that art gallery he calls a home." Over his shoulder, he called, "See you two later. Look after Pax for a bit, okay?"

"Dez!" Mara hurried out to them. "What are you two doing?"

"Nothing much," Sully said. "We're going to look at a file Lachlan got his hands on. It's to do with Gerhardt's missing son."

Mara's eyes pierced Sully's, as if searching for something. "Are you sure you should be doing that?"

"If it will find us a way to get to Gerhardt or Lowell, then, yeah, we should."

"You know what I mean."

Sully smiled. "I'll be okay."

Mara appeared skeptical, proved it by training her focus on Dez. "You look after him, you hear me? Make sure he's okay."

Sully sighed. "Mom, I'm—"

"I'll watch," Dez cut in. "Don't worry."

"You two look after yourselves," Mara said as her sons beat a hasty retreat through the door. "I mean it."

SULLY, hood up, rang the bell at Lachlan's North Bank neighbourhood house.

The door opened to a mile-wide grin.

"This is shaping up to be one hell of an interesting case, boys."

He stood aside to let them in, then led the way into his art- and book-filled living room. The contents of a file were spread out over the coffee table next to a well-used notepad and half a mug of tea. Lachlan had pulled one end of the table up to the leather recliner he returned to now, enabling him to study the file in comfort. One side of the sofa remained within easy reach of the table's other end, and Dez sat there, leaving Sully to take a spot on the couch next to his brother.

They weren't alone. Justice Montague, blessedly absent after they'd left the Black Fox, had opted to make a reappearance now, hovering at Sully's other side.

Sully decided to ignore him. Nothing he could think to do would satisfy the man anyway.

"What have we got?" Dez asked.

"It's all in the file, but I'll give you the quick version," Lachlan said. "As you told me, David Gerhardt was six when he went missing from the backyard of his parents' old house—which, for our purposes, is rather inconveniently situated in The Forks. His parents told police he had a habit of wandering off, that he was an inquisitive kid who tended to forget the rules when something caught his attention. He was supposed to stay in the yard unless he was with an adult, but sometimes he didn't listen.

"The day he went missing—July 25, 1980—Dr. Gerhardt was at work, and his wife Eloise was at home with the kid. David was playing in the yard. Eloise had been out there, too, puttering around in the garden. Judging by the photos, they had a pretty nice little yard: a few trees, lots of shrubs and flowers, many of them big enough for a kid to hide behind. When David disappeared, Eloise checked behind all the bushes and flowers first, thinking maybe he was hiding, but nothing. Then she found the gate unlatched."

"Had she left David alone for a while or something?" Dez asked.

"The phone was ringing, and she went to answer it, she said. According to her, just a few minutes passed. When she came back out, the kid was gone."

Dez scratched at the stubble along his jawline. "Who was on the line? If this was an abduction, the phone call might have been a distraction to get the kid alone."

"I thought of that. So did the investigators at the time. Call was from her sister, though. Nothing suspicious there. A thorough area search was done in the hours following, and neighbours' yards were checked too. Nothing was found, nor did anyone see any suspicious people or vehicles nearby. Granted, it was a weekday and most of the neighbours were at work. Not many people were around to witness anything."

"Eloise didn't have an outside job?" Sully asked.

Lachlan shook his head. "Stay-at-home mom. Apparently, the not-so-good doctor thought it was the man's job to bring home the bacon. He liked the idea of having a woman at home to do his cooking and cleaning, bring him his slippers and pipe or whatever it is women were supposed to do in ancient times. Sounds like a real winner, this guy. You can only imagine the fallout after David went missing. No doubt Gerhardt blamed the wife."

"No doubt," Dez said. "Where'd she end up?"

"No one knows."

"Gerhardt said something about her having died."

"Maybe she did. Seems she was the subject of a short police investigation, too, a couple of months after David's disappearance. Gerhardt called in, saying his wife had taken some things and left a Dear John letter while he was at work. It said she was leaving him, but he suspected she actually planned to go off and kill herself. He told police she hadn't been right after David's disappearance, which is understandable. Police conducted a search, but there was no sign of her, nor was there any indication of foul play on Gerhardt's part."

"They checked?" Sully asked.

"I wouldn't say they pulled out all the stops, exactly—and there were fewer stops, given it was 1980 with no DNA capability —but they did look into the possibility, just in case. In the end, investigators simply chalked it up to a woman who couldn't handle life in that house anymore. Given she'd taken some clothes and toiletries, it was believed she'd run off on Gerhardt. And since no sign of her popped up on the grid afterward, investigators thought it likely she'd found herself a new life or a new man and started over, likely with a new name to boot." Lachlan plucked a photo from the scattering on the table and handed it to the brothers. "She was an attractive woman."

Sully scanned the picture, a family photo of the Gerhardts in happier days. His eyes went immediately to Gerhardt himself. He'd never seen a photo of him in his younger years, and Sully estimated his age in this picture to be near the age Sully was now. He searched the face and the form of the man, looking for similarities to himself, all the while hoping he'd find none. The fewer characteristics he shared with Gerhardt, the better.

"Sull? You with me?"

Sully snapped his gaze from the photo to Dez's face. "What?"

"I asked you a question."

"Sorry, I missed it."

Dez studied his face, and Sully did his best to appear impassive. When Dez raised an eyebrow, Sully knew he'd failed. Surprisingly, he let it drop. For now, anyway.

"I asked if you'd ever seen this kid or the wife anywhere before."

Sully returned to the photo, this time focusing on the other two people in it. Eloise Gerhardt was, as Lachlan had said, an attractive woman: honey blonde hair, perfect smile, pretty, petite figure. A little too much makeup, but given the photo had been taken in the late 1970s, that was probably to be expected. David sat on her lap, then a boy of about four years. He held a toy train in his hands and wore a beaming smile despite the fact his blond hair had been cut into one of those terrible chunky styles that were all the rage at the time.

Oddly, despite the fact Sully had never seen the boy during those sessions at Lockwood, there was something familiar in the face.

"I've never seen her," he said. "But I feel like I've seen the boy somewhere before."

"In Lockwood?" Lachlan asked.

Sully shook his head. "Not there. He never appeared to me in any of those visions they forced on me. It was somewhere else. I can't place it."

Dez spoke quietly. "It's not because he's... you know."

"My half-brother?" Sully finished for Dez, who shrugged and smiled apologetically. "No, I don't think that's it."

"You spent two solid years in The Forks," Lachlan said. "It's possible you passed by their old house. Maybe you saw his ghost there."

"Maybe." But Sully wasn't sure. He had a sense of the answer being something else, something he couldn't put a finger on. "Are you able to make a copy of this photo? I wouldn't mind having it with me. I want to give it some thought."

"I don't see why not," Lachlan said. "Just don't tell anyone. I'm not supposed to have the file, let alone be making copies of it."

"Hey," Sully said with a grin. "Who would I tell? Almost everyone I know is in this room."

"Good point," Lachlan said. "I'll make you that copy, and I'll give you the address to the old house. Maybe you could swing by there when you go back to The Forks, see if you notice anyone or anything around the place."

"No," Dez said. "It's bad enough he's at Ravenwood, but at least not a lot of people go there. If he starts wandering around The Forks, he's a walking target."

"I hate to tell you this, Dez, but I've walked around there before," Sully said. "I'm still alive. Anyway, I've always had Pax with me. He's a pretty powerful disincentive for anyone thinking I'd make a good victim."

"I still don't like it," Dez said. "If you check out this house, I'm going with you."

"I need you to come with me to talk to Gerhardt," Lachlan said.

"Why?" Dez asked. "I won't be much help. The guy hates me."

"While I'm sure he's eager for answers, I can't imagine he'll be in a hurry to trust a pair of P.I.s nosing around. He won't want us anywhere near his dirty little secrets, and he'll wonder whether we have ulterior motives. You'll be a good in."

"Right. Because me turning up on his doorstep is going to get us past his defences. He knows I hate him over what went down with Sully."

"He also likely knows by now you were with his buddy Hackman when he expired. Honestly, I'm starting to think our best tactic might be you going on your own to see him, get a look inside his house, see what you see."

"If Sully can get us some answers at the old house, it will give us an even better in," Dez said. "And if he's going, so am I."

Sully jumped in before his brother got too ahead of himself. "I'm not sure that's a good idea, Dez. I can get around The Forks okay on my own because I know how to look like I belong around there. You—"

"Hey, I can scruff myself up just like you can."

"You don't even own the right clothes."

"We can stop by one of the secondhand shops in Riverview. They've got a lot of nasty-looking junk no one will ever buy. You can give me a makeover."

"I still don't think it's a good idea."

"I don't care what you think," Dez said. "You're not going alone. And before you bring up Pax, I was going to say I kind of like the idea of him acting as guard dog for Mom and Kayleigh while we're not there. That dog barely trusts anyone, and I like that. He'll eat Lowell for breakfast before he'll let him hurt anyone in that house."

Sully had planned to go back and get Pax before heading back to The Forks. The dog wasn't just protection, he was a companion, a good friend to help him stay calm and settled in a place where calm was hard to come by. But he also saw Dez's point. Sully would never find peace again if anything happened to anyone else he loved, especially if he hadn't done everything in his power to protect them. If loaning them Pax would help keep them safe—

and he knew it would—he was willing to make the temporary sacrifice.

"Are you planning to go there now?" Lachlan asked.

"I'm not planning to be there once the sun sets," Dez said. "That's for sure."

Lachlan appeared to be thinking, and judging by the tight expression on his face, his thoughts weren't taking him anywhere good. "I hate to say it, but I'm not sure I'm up to the trip. Taking a boat out and sitting on the shore is one thing, but venturing in there is another. I'm not in the best shape of my life at the moment. If we were to run into trouble, I'm not sure I'd—"

"It's okay, man," Dez said. "We've got it cased. What are you going to do?"

"Keep digging through this file for a start. And I'm going to get us Gerhardt's current home address as well. If I get it soon enough, I'll take a spin past, see what I can see. You can get a good feel for a man by checking out his home." He leaned forward in his chair, fixing first Sully and then Dez in a pointed look. "I know I'm not your father, and I'm not trying to be. But I'm going to insist you take every precaution while you're in The Forks. Don't take any chances. If you feel like things are going south, get out fast. It might prove useful to check out the old house, but it isn't worth your lives. You understand me?"

In Sully's peripheral vision, Dez smiled. Sully felt his own lips turning up in response to the unusual display of concern from Dez's boss.

"Thanks, Lachlan," Dez said. "We'll be careful. Don't worry."

"Hey," Lachlan said. "I'm a man with a concussion and a doctor with a stick up his ass. It feels like all I'm cleared to do is worry."

9

BY THE TIME they made it back to the island upon which The Forks had been built, evening was on the verge of closing in. Sully sensed the worry wafting from Dez.

They'd stopped at a few secondhand shops first, not all of them carrying clothes large enough to fit Dez's larger-than-normal form. As it stood, there hadn't been much to pick from.

Sully fought the grin as he checked out his brother for the hundredth time. Dez was kitted out in a worn pair of camouflage pants, a T-shirt with a goofy logo he had promptly concealed beneath the zip of a slightly-too-small hoodie and a trench coat that somehow managed to be a little too big on him. He'd found himself a cap too, one he'd tugged further over his features each time he passed someone remotely respectable on the Riverview-neighbourhood streets.

"I look like a cartoon," Dez complained as he finished pulling their rented rowboat onto the shore. He straightened up and lifted the bottom seam of his outer jacket. "Does this look like blood to you?"

Sully peered at the suspicious brown-red stain and shrugged. "Maybe. If it is, it's old."

Beneath the brim of his cap, Dez's eyes widened perceptibly. "What if someone died in this coat?"

Sully laughed.

"It's not funny," Dez complained.

Sully patted his brother on the chest, then went to haul the boat farther up the shore to where he could conceal it in the trees. Dez gave him a hand. The other boat—the one Sully usually used —was still there, hidden in the greenery. They'd rented the current one at the Kimotan Rapids Rowing Club from a guy who seemed suspicious of them, and there would be hell to pay if they didn't get it back to him by the end of the evening.

"We've got three hours before the club closes," Sully said.

Dez wiped his hands on his pant legs. "You really need to reconsider this whole not-coming-back-with-me thing later. That guy already looked like he wanted to report us to the police just because of the way we looked. If I turn up without you, he's going to think I killed you and buried your body somewhere."

Sully chuckled. "That blood stain won't help."

"Shut up."

It was quicker cutting through the mansion rather than going all the way around, so Sully went for the back door. Dez grabbed his arm.

"Can't we go around? I don't want to go back in there."

"It's quicker," Sully said. He leaned closer, whispering the next part in Dez's ear. "Plus I'm hoping to shake the judge."

Dez turned wide eyes on Sully. "He's here?"

Sully didn't look back, but he could sense Montague behind them, a short distance back. No way he wasn't there, having ridden over in the rowboat with them. "He's barely left my side since he was killed."

"We need to find a way to get rid of him."

"One problem at a time. He won't come in the house. I've figured out that much."

Dez didn't look sold, but the options for a guy who hated

ghosts weren't great: haunted house or stalking spirit. In the end, Dez chose the house, leading the way to the back door.

"I hate this," he said as he went.

Sully did his best at a reassuring smile before nudging past Dez to open the door.

They'd taken just two steps inside—the door closed behind them and Montague left, scowling, in the back garden—when the whistle of something cutting through the air had Sully ducking. Noisy Ned, unfortunately, had grown wise to their tricks and had aimed lower this time. Sully grunted in pain as something caught him hard in the left hip. He looked down to see a small but solid paperweight hit the floor and roll.

"Damn it!" he shouted. "It's me!"

He and Dez stalled in the rear entryway, waiting. When nothing else sailed through the air at them, Sully decided he'd gotten his point across.

"You okay?" Dez asked. "That thing hit you pretty hard."

Sully rubbed at his hip. "Yeah. At least I know Ned's on the ball."

"How about you-know-who? Did we lose him?"

Sully took a quick glance, spotted the furious ex-judge glaring at the house from the backyard. "He's still outside. I won't know if we've lost him until we're out the front."

Sully led the way through the house, Dez a hovering presence at his right shoulder. Thankfully, they reached the front entrance without further problems.

With no immediate sign of Montague, the brothers walked through the large, overgrown front yard and down the long drive leading to the main road. Sully had ventured this way a few times, but could count the trips on one hand. Several times in the winter when the river had not been quite frozen enough to safely cross, he'd been forced to resort to taking stuff still left at the nearby shuttered shops. He'd been fortunate Ravenwood sat on the end of the island, farthest from the majority of the homes and businesses. Few people ventured out this way, and those who did found little to hold them here. A handful of smaller stores were in this area—those that hadn't been utterly destroyed by the violence of the flood—and while they'd been burgled like everything else, there was still a decent supply of goods.

He hoped, with temperatures dropping, people would be less likely to venture out of doors as the evening closed in, enabling him and Dez to make their way unbothered to the Gerhardts' old property.

Dez checked his cellphone screen. "It's probably about a half-hour walk from here. We'll have to make it a quick search if I'm going to get the boat back before close."

"In The Forks, you need to do everything quick," Sully said. "By the way, commit the map to memory. You don't want to be flashing electronics around here."

Dez nodded, gave his screen one last long look before handing it to Sully to do the same. Map committed to memory, Dez returned the phone to one of his many pockets and joined Sully as they passed through the large gate separating Ravenwood from the main road.

The roadway had once been well-maintained, paved and manicured for the benefit of the ultra-rich who lived on this side of the island. The flood and the subsequent years of abandonment had left the pavement cracked and outright broken, creating places for grass, weeds and even small trees to sprout. The ditch made for an easier walk, and Sully kept them there, the treed sides providing a good place to duck into should the need for quick concealment arise. Sully hadn't told Dez, but a notorious local street gang had turned one of the nearby mansions into its stronghold, meaning it wasn't uncommon for several members at a time to drive along here, between their house and the busier sections of The Forks. The gang had checked out Ravenwood initially, before being chased out by Ned.

Usually, if gang members were on the road, Sully had some forewarning in the sound of an approaching engine. If he heard anything like that, he'd tug Dez into the bushes and deal later with the fallout from the required explanation. If Dez found out Sully's nearest neighbours were the inner circle of the Red Jacks, he'd use any means necessary to get Sully back to the mainland with him at evening's end—force included.

"I didn't really like The Forks when it was the way it used to be," Dez said. "But this is actually kinda sad."

"Kind of ironic too," Sully said. "The rich chased the poor out of here constantly, and now the poor own it."

"What's left of it, anyway."

They fell silent as they maintained a brisk pace west, past the island's largest properties.

Dez commented as they moved past one spot, the property all but obscured by the trees that had grown in. "That's where Paul Dunsmore lived, isn't it?"

"Yeah. There's nothing left now, though. The house was completely washed away."

"Jesus," Dez muttered.

Sully knew where his brother's thoughts had gone. Four years ago, Sully had been trapped in the house with Paul, Bulldog and Bulldog's niece. Only because of Dez and Eva's timely arrival and some ghostly assistance were they all able to make it out alive. The fact the entire house had been taken by the flood sealed just how close they'd come.

They left it at that, and Sully kept his focus centred on the houses coming into view ahead where they lined the road. There wasn't much left of these places, most too badly damaged by the flood waters to provide adequate shelter. They'd have more to worry about once they turned north and headed deeper into The Forks where the former businesses and numerous other homes stood. The damage had been lessened to those on higher ground when compared to buildings near the river's edge—making them more attractive to those in need. Sully opted to steer them away from the main roads upon which most businesses were situated, taking them through residential areas instead. There, they cut through overgrown yards, avoiding the more open streets wherever possible.

They passed a few people, those who, like Sully, had sought a place farther from the crime and drug scene plaguing the west side of the island. The people here were either in a similar predicament to Sully's—forced to avoid the outside world—or they were addicts who needed to be close enough to their dealers but wanted to avoid the unpredictability and frequent violence within the drug scene itself. Like their surroundings, these people were a wreck, an abandoned part of this city left to fend for themselves.

Dez was right. It was sad.

Dez remained a rigid bundle of tension at Sully's side until, at last, they reached the Gerhardts' house.

"That's it, right?" Dez asked as the two of them stared at the large two-storey Victorian. "I can't make out the numbers on most of these places."

"Looks like the one we saw in the pictures back at Lachlan's, but everything looks a lot different after the flood." Sully peered closer. Lots of buildings in The Forks had been tagged with graffiti, but the stuff marking this building was different. These weren't gang tags; they were personal. *Deranged Doctor. Psycho Shrink.* A variety of curse words. These were the markings of people who'd been to, and escaped, Lockwood.

"Check out the tags," Sully said. "We've definitely got the right house."

Dez squinted as he read. "Oh. Yeah."

"Listen, we'll have to watch our step going in, and not just because of the possibility of squatters. Most places on the island are badly water damaged, with rotted-out floors and everything. Stay close to the walls, or better yet, wait outside while I look around in the house."

"No way," Dez said. "We're not separating. Where you go, I go. Like you said, we can stick close to the walls, just in case." He returned his gaze to the house, and Sully smiled as he spotted the predictable shudder. "God, it looks like the setting for a horror movie."

"It's just a house. It'll be fine."

With Dez following, Sully stepped up to the gate, left askew and prevented from closing by a young tree that had sprouted. Sully squeezed past and waited for Dez to do the same before approaching the wraparound veranda.

"Would have been a nice place in its day," Sully said.

"Yeah, sure," Dez said. "Let's just get this over with, okay?"

Maintaining the lead, Sully stepped cautiously onto the planked veranda. Several boards had snapped farther down where vandals had likely tried to stand to spraypaint the exterior, and he moved even more lightly as he crossed to the partially open front door.

With Dez at his heels, Sully pushed the door all the way open, allowing light to enter the dim interior.

The inside of the house was dark enough to suggest curtains had been drawn. Whether by the last owner before they left it the night of the flood or by squatters, they had no way of knowing.

The house stank of mildew, mould and urine, the latter suggesting the vandalism wasn't limited to paint. The over-whelming odour provided another very good reason to make this search a quick one.

Sully hugged the short wall separating the entryway from the living area. Across from him stood a staircase, one that looked to be in one piece. With any luck, the structural damage was kept to a minimum, at least compared to other places in The Forks. Taking a few steps into the room, Sully observed a creak to the floor, but not the spongy feeling suggesting rot had taken hold.

"I think it's safe right here, but watch your step," he said.

"I'm planning on it."

Sully entered first what looked to be a sitting room to the left before moving to an open kitchen behind that. From here, through a gap in the curtains, showing a dust- and grime-covered piece of window, Sully could just make out the backyard.

Dez moved to Sully's right side. "That's where they think he was taken from. Do you see anything?"

Sully crossed to the pane, tugged back the fragile material and scanned the area. It was heavily overgrown, and one of the large elm trees had toppled, covering much of the ground beneath. If there had been places to hide back then, there were even more now. From where he stood, there was no sign of a small child's ghost.

"I don't see anything from here," Sully said. "We can go out there, though. Could be I just can't see him yet."

"Let's cover the house first. I'd rather get that part over with."

Sully patted Dez's abs and moved around him, rifling a few drawers and coming up with nothing but rusted cutlery, pots, pans and small appliances. What paper they found had been waterlogged to the point of illegibility.

From there, they walked past a pantry and the door to the basement—"We're not going down there. Forget it," came Dez's pronouncement—before ending up in a dining room. Passing through, they pushed a sliding door into a formal lounge and, from there, back to the entry hall.

Photos once lining the walls had been knocked off and now cluttered the floor with countless other pieces of rotted and vandalized debris. Nothing to see here. They'd have to go upstairs.

Sully scanned the ceiling, taking note of sagging plaster and more than a few protruding boards. The main floor seemed sound enough, but rainwater might have seeped through the compromised roof throughout the past few years, compounding the water damage on the upper floor.

"I think you'd better stay down here," Sully told his brother. "You outweigh me by close to eighty pounds. My weight will be enough up there."

"Maybe you shouldn't go either."

"We came here hoping to find some answers. It's possible David's still around here somewhere. Sometimes kids go back to their old rooms, or it might be I'll see him in the backyard from a higher viewpoint. Just let me...."

He trailed off as his eyes drifted to the stairs. A small blonde woman stood there, a series of ghastly stab wounds to her chest, neck and face, marking her as dead. Her eyes met Sully's and held, widening as she recognized him as someone who could see her.

She shot forward, reaching him in a fraction of a second. He flinched, took an involuntary step back. Sometimes, in their excitement, spirits forgot the rule of personal space, and he gave himself a more comfortable distance from which to communicate.

Before he could open his mouth, she had, her fast-moving lips forming silent, unreadable words.

"Hold on," he interrupted. "I can't hear anything you're trying to tell me."

"Oh, God," Dez said. "You found a ghost."

Sully glanced over at his brother, who was peering at the space where Sully had just been looking. "It's too tall for a kid, though, judging by where you were looking."

"It's not a kid. It's a woman. She's been stabbed repeatedly."

"Any idea who?"

"I've got every idea," Sully said. Her face was a little messed up but he'd recognized her once she'd gotten close enough. "Eloise Gerhardt."

SULLY RUBBED HIS FACE, let his heart settle.

"Not the ghost we were expecting," Dez said. "I remember Gerhardt saying something about his wife having died, but.... Jesus, Sully, what if he murdered her?" His question, one that would inspire horror in most people, had instilled in him a small, hopeful smile.

Sully raised his eyebrows. "You want to tell me why you think that's a good thing?"

"Hey, if he killed his wife, that's not only a way to bust that asshole for something serious, it might also give us a way to really crack open this whole thing with Lowell. If Gerhardt's going down for something as serious as murder, he'll have no reason to guard anyone else's secrets—especially if he offers up info the same way Montague said he would."

Sully hadn't thought to cut in before Dez finished the statement. Now it was too late. Montague, summoned by his own name, reappeared as his usual intimidating presence at Sully's shoulder.

"Damn," Sully muttered.

"What?"

"Montague. He just found me again."

"Aw, shit. Sorry, Sull. You think he heard me?"

"I guess he did."

"How? We're a decent hike away from where we left him."

"Yeah, but I think saying his name triggers it somehow."

Dez's brow rumpled in thought. "How does that work?"

"No idea. I don't understand the whole ghost travel thing. I just have to work around it." Sully did his best to ignore Montague, returning his attention to an increasingly desperate-looking Eloise. "Like I was telling you, I can't hear you, but I can usually see things if you'll show me. Touch my hand and try to think of what you want me to see."

He held up his fingers. Immediately, her hand met his, ice biting into flesh. He grunted as pain—her pain—seized his chest, neck and face. But it was more than that. The intensity of heartbreak, loss and desperation hammered into him hard enough to steal his breath. He gasped, struggling to breathe beneath the weight of her emotions. Images formed, zipping past him in a way that reminded him of those books he and Dez used to like as kids, where you flipped through really fast to make it look like the cartoons inside were moving. Nothing held inside his brain, pictures flashing bright and indecipherable as they spun past. Fire ignited inside his skull, the pain now his own.

"Sully, stop! Stop!" Hands were on him, pulling his hand back by the wrist and pinning it to his side. Instantly, the pain stopped, and Sully discovered he'd somehow ended up on his knees on the floor, a worried-looking Dez next to him. "What happened?"

"She's intense," he said. "Like, really intense. She's frantic to have me help her, but it means she's just firing stuff at me at a pace I can't process. My brain felt like it was melting."

"Well, don't do that again." Dez gave Sully a moment to collect himself before continuing. "She lost a child, Sull. I can't begin to imagine the way that affects a parent. Loss to death is one thing, and it's nightmare enough. But to *not* know…. God, I don't even want to think what that would be like."

Sully nodded. He didn't have kids of his own, but he had

Kayleigh. It wasn't impossible to picture the horror of the kind of loss Eloise had suffered, and the excitement of finally finding someone she believed could help.

He lifted his head but found her gone from her place before him. Scanning the room, he spotted her back on the stairs.

"I'm sorry," he told her. "It was too much to process. Maybe if you try to focus on just one image?"

But she seemed to have a different idea. She lifted a hand, moving it in an indication for him to join her.

"She wants me to follow," Sully said for Dez's benefit.

Dez helped Sully to his feet. "Let's go."

They'd taken just a few steps up, Sully in front, when Dez's foot broke through a stair. As he fell forward, he managed to catch himself, preventing a face plant.

"You all right?" Sully asked as Dez pried his foot out.

Back on solid footing, Dez checked his ankle. Sully noted a couple of scrapes, but nothing serious. "Fine," Dez said.

"You'd better wait down here. I'll try not to be long."

Dez sighed. "That's probably a good idea, unless you want to be dragging my carcass back to Ravenwood." He caught Sully's wrist as he made to follow Eloise. "Don't let her touch you again, all right? If she wants to point you toward something, fine, but keep it there."

"No problem," Sully said.

While Dez returned to the main floor, Sully climbed the stairs.

The upstairs hallway sagged in places, the ceiling broken above. Nearer the end of the hall, pieces of board, brick and whatever had been in the attic had settled into a large pile on the floor. Thankfully, Eloise didn't take him that far, leading him instead into a room off to the right.

It was a little boy's room, its train and airplane wallpaper peeling and faded by weather and light but still visible. A shelf above the bed held a toy train, the kind a small child would play with. A bookshelf across the room contained numerous books, all of them for children.

Sully knelt to scan the titles. Eva had been big on reading to Kayleigh as a young child, and Sully had been handed the duties several times. More than a little familiar with kids' books as a result, he still didn't recognize any of these. He pulled a few out and cracked them open to check the years. All, he noticed, dated from the nineteen seventies or earlier.

Sully turned at an icy touch to his shoulder, one that was withdrawn almost as soon as he felt it. Eloise stood near the door, pointing to something on the yet-hidden back side of it. Sully straightened and joined her, pushing the door shut far enough to see behind it.

A child's door-mounted hat and clothing rack hung there, a sweater and a baseball cap on its pegs. Each peg was placed beneath the car of a train, with each of those cars emblazoned with a letter that, together, spelled out a name.

DAVID.

Sully met Eloise's eye. "He still lived here. Your husband, I mean. He lived here until the flood."

Her expression, wistful as she gazed at the name on the rack, tightened into one Sully could only describe as disgust. It seemed Eloise shared his dislike of the psychiatrist.

Sully had questions, but Eloise left the room before he could ask them. He followed her to a room directly across the hall, one that had clearly been the master suite. Eloise gave no indication of interest in any particular spot, rather eyeing the space as if in wistful remembrance. Sully kept an eye on her as he explored the room, peering at a pair of family photos, searching the bedside drawers and scoping out the walk-in closet. Signs of Eloise were still very much present here, her image showing in the photos and her clothing still taking up a corner of the closet. The room's decor, too—very much nineteen-seventies style—suggested Gerhardt had touched little since his wife had disappeared. They might have been estranged, and he might well have bullied her out the door, but there was no indication he'd killed her.

Then again, Sully had seen regret in killers more than once. It might be Gerhardt lived with such a regret, that his memories of Eloise remained fond, despite whatever had passed.

Sully faced the spirit, seeking out her eyes. "Did he do this to you? Did your husband kill you?"

He wanted a yes, wanted it so badly. Even if it turned out he could pin nothing else on Gerhardt, he'd be satisfied if he could nail him on even this one crime.

But Eloise shook her head. No, her husband hadn't killed her.

"If he did something to you, you don't owe him anything. You can tell me the truth. Did he do this?"

Another head shake.

"Who, then?"

She opened her mouth as if to speak, but closed it almost immediately, as if recalling he wouldn't be able to hear.

Bracing himself, Sully once again held out a hand. "Show me."

Eloise took a step forward, slowly raised her fingers to meet his. A light touch this time, fingertips to fingertips.

It didn't matter. Images fired into Sully's brain, rapid-fire memories rendered nonsensical to anyone but those who were there. David laughing. A backward glimpse of the house. A flash of trees. A vehicle interior. An unfamiliar room. The back of a woman's head.

Sully pulled away when the fire relit inside his brain. As his senses returned, he discovered he was back on his knees on the abandoned home's dusty floor, Eloise in front of him with regret written on her face. He didn't need to hear the words to know what she wanted to say.

"It's all right," he said. "I'm fine. We'll find another way, okay? I'll find a way to help you."

The dresser stood next to him, and he reached up to its surface, using it to draw himself to his feet. A little unsteady, he leaned against the dresser and spotted something inside a decorative bowl: a set of keys.

A large set of keys.

They might fit the house, but there were far too many for just that. Most notably, several of the keys were the old skeleton types, the kind you'd only ever fit to locks from the turn of the century or before.

A word formed in Sully's brain, spelling itself out in black letters: Lockwood. The night of the flood had been terrifying, the evacuation hectic. With the island's destruction imminent, homeowners had grabbed their most important items and fled, each desperate to be as close to the front of the line as possible. What Gerhardt had considered his most treasured possessions was anyone's guess, but clearly his work keys were not among them.

They might not have served a purpose to the psychiatrist on that awful night, but they might prove plenty useful to Sully. He dropped the keyring into the inside pocket of his outer jacket, then returned his attention to Eloise.

"I'm sure you've tried to find your son since you've been in spirit form. Have you found out anything? I know we're having trouble communicating, but maybe you could just nod or shake your head for me if I ask questions. Could we try that?"

She nodded, and Sully readied himself to start the questioning.

A series of loud noises and shouting downstairs—shouts that weren't Dez's—snapped Sully's attention away from Eloise. More than one voice was audible. Far more than one, shouting something that sounded very much like a gang name.

"Shit," Sully said, dashing from the room and to the stairs. Dez's voice came now, limited to grunts and yells as he took on a fight. Sully flew down the stairs, turned the corner into the sitting room to his right.

He counted five.

All of them with metal bars or knives.

Dez was good in a fight, but not against this many. He was already stumbling, blood on his head suggesting he'd taken a hard blow.

"Hey!" Sully shouted.

The distraction gave Dez the chance to rally, to land a solid, knock-down punch to one man's face, then start battling a second.

It also brought two of the gangsters rushing at Sully. He deked left as one sliced at him with a knife, managing to avoid the blade while placing himself in a position to punch the second man in the face. A second knife swipe, this one aimed at Sully's gut, barely missed its target. He managed to pull his abs back just in time, limiting the severity of the resulting injury. The knifeman was already delivering another strike, and Sully ducked away from that one too.

This time, though, he collided with one of the other men. Sully found himself effectively pinned as the man caught him in a bear hug from behind. Judging by the feel of him and the strength in his sizeable arms, he approached Dez-proportions.

Already, the knifeman was moving back in. Sully got his legs up in a double kick, taking a cut to the calf but managing to catch the assailant on the chin. The knifeman fell back, blade skirting away and sliding beneath the sofa.

A glance to his side had Sully's heart thudding even harder. Dez was being piled on by the remaining three guys, the one he'd hit earlier now back in the fray. Two were beating on him with pipes.

As Dez finally dropped beneath the weight of the attack, a third man retrieved his knife from the floor.

Panic seized Sully.

He was about to watch his brother die.

A flash of movement—the arrival of several new presences—drew Sully's attention for a second. Flynn and Aiden, hand in hand, had appeared out of nowhere, joining the ever-present Montague in the sitting room. Eloise was nowhere to be seen, and Sully didn't care right now where she'd ended up. His eyes had gone back to the horrifying scene, his brain churning through every worst-case scenario as he screamed at the men to stop.

Desperate to help Dez, he pulled hard against the man holding him. He managed nothing more than a slight shifting and subsequent tightening of the restraining arms.

Flynn moved closer, stretching out fingers to touch Sully's face.

The memory blasted into his mind, the battle between himself, Lowell and Hackman in his apartment above the Black Fox. His partial possession by Harry Schuster. The extra power he'd drawn from the ghost's energy inside him.

Flynn pulled back, returning Sully to the here and now. His father's eyes shifted meaningfully to Montague.

The rage inside the judge. Added to Sully's own, it might be enough.

As he had at Hackman's apartment, the day he'd pulled the spirit of Nora Silversmith into himself, Sully focused in on Montague.

Instantly, the judge's glower changed, narrowed eyes widening as he was towed forward.

Sully could feel him fighting it. But need and desperation drove Sully, made him stronger than any spirit. With Dez's pained grunts spurring him on, he completed the process in seconds, absorbing Montague's spirit and energy.

He felt it inside him now, the intensity of Montague's fury. The man's thoughts formed inside Sully's brain, but he swept them aside, focus entirely on Dez.

The gangster with the knife pushed aside one of his crowbar-wielding buddies, preparing to deliver his own blow to Dez.

He was laughing. Like killing an innocent man was nothing more than a cheap form of entertainment.

Rage built, Montague's own turning Sully's into a lit stick of TNT. He vibrated with it, unreleased tension and fury.

And power.

Power he'd never felt.

He exploded.

The arms around him released like those of a child as he pulled free of the hold. He flew at the knifeman, tackling him hard to the floor before he could deliver a blow to Dez. The big guy was already moving back in, but Sully regained his feet in time to grab and throw him into a chair that toppled beneath his weight.

Sully's eyes went to Dez's, found him staring up at him wide-eyed. But it wasn't the worry Sully saw. It was the blood.

His brother's blood.

It was gasoline on a fire.

It overwhelmed him, the intensity of a hate so deep he knew it couldn't be fully his own. He drew on it, let it take over. There was power in it, and he gave into it gladly.

Five men came at him now. All of them. Wielding knives and metal bars.

None of it mattered. They didn't matter. They were nothing.

He was everything.

The world around him went red, his senses limited to the feel of his fists delivering blow after blow; of flesh shifting and bone breaking beneath him; to the cries of pain from the men. He revelled in those, drank in the smell of their blood as they one by one fell before him.

Through the crimson mist, he watched one flee, then a second. Two were on the floor, unmoving. The last of them was in his grasp, neck constricted beneath Sully's tightening fingers. He could envision it now, the man's head popping off like a pus-filled cyst, squeezing until it separated completely from his body.

"Sully, stop! Sully!"

He knew Dez's voice. Knew and didn't care.

All he cared about was the man kneeling before him, bulging eyes staring with sheer terror into his.

It had been years. Lifetimes since he'd held the fate of another man in his own, since he'd watched death close in at his bidding.

He would enjoy this. Every blessed second.

"Sully! No!"

He felt it the moment they entered, the red-haired man and his son, sharing space inside this body. They were light to his dark, light that gradually filled every space, every nook and cranny.

A memory flashed, a smoke-scented child seated in a police interview room while the red-haired man knelt before him.

Offering to give him a home.

His first real home.

"Sully, please!"

Dez. That first day at school. Taking on an entire cafeteria and Sully's bullies, warning anyone to mess with his new brother was to mess with him too.

"Sully!"

Light filled him, drowning out the hate, the rage.

His fingers released, the man previously encased within his grasp falling, gagging, to the floor next to his two moaning friends.

Sully next released Montague, who instantly fled. He watched him go and allowed himself a moment of amazement at finally being rid of his stalker.

"Sully?"

He turned, found Dez standing next to him. Sully tried for a smile, but it was lost to blackness as consciousness faded.

11

Dez wiped another trail of blood from his forehead before it could drip into his right eye.

He needed his vision, every iota of his senses he could muster as he ran. It was bad enough he couldn't hear much above the pounding of the pulse in his ears, anxiety and physical exertion intensifying the flow of blood. His heart thudded out a manic rhythm, one borne less of the run and more of what he'd just experienced.

Sully, draped over his shoulder, stirred with returning consciousness, but Dez ran on. He didn't see anyone around, and he doubted anyone would be crazy enough to follow after what had just happened, but he wasn't about to bank on it. The men who attacked them hadn't, thank God, had guns. But who was to say they didn't have friends nearby who did?

"Dez," came a movement-rattled voice from the other side of his shoulder. Dez ignored Sully for now, making for a thick grove of trees next to a badly damaged house. Branches whipped at his face as Dez dove into the bushes, taking the two of them to what he hoped would be temporary shelter. When a quick scan revealed no sign of any pursuers, Dez set Sully on his feet.

Sully's hands bunched up the front of Dez's jacket. "Are you okay?"

"I will be. Bunch of meth heads. Goddammit."

"Are you sure? You're bleeding."

Dez swiped at his head again. The back of his hand was already sticky, coated with his own blood. He'd been momentarily stunned after taking the blow, but he hadn't lost consciousness. He wasn't dizzy, wasn't faint, and he wasn't tired or confused. No sign of a serious head injury. The rest of him hurt, and he knew bruises—some of them deep and ugly—had to be forming, but nothing felt fractured. Small blessings.

"I'm fine. How about you?"

Sully gave up an obvious visual inspection of Dez to lift his own shirt. A bloody furrow had been left across his abdomen, and the lower left leg of his jeans was stained red.

Dez checked the abdominal wound before kneeling to look at the calf. "You could use a few stitches."

"Won't be happening," Sully said. "I've got butterfly bandages back at Ravenwood. They've come in handy in the past."

Dez dropped Sully's pant leg and stood with some difficulty. On the way up, he noticed his brother's torn and scraped knuckles, and his thoughts returned to what he'd just seen.

His quiet, mild-mannered brother, completely out of control and in possession of a strength Dez would have struggled to equal on his best days.

"Sully? What happened back there?"

"Not here," Sully said. "Let's get back to Ravenwood."

They kept conversation to a minimum, Dez keeping his focus entirely on their surroundings and on any potential signs they were being followed. They reached the gates of Ravenwood without any further issues, and Dez breathed a sigh of relief as they passed through onto the property.

He was aware of the oddity of the situation, the fact he was grateful to be returning to a haunted house. Everything was relative, and he'd take Noisy Ned over a group of murderous, meth-binging gangsters any day.

Even so, Dez stuck to Sully as he went to get his bag from the hidden passage in the basement. Ned hadn't come at them upon their return, but Dez wasn't satisfied he, without his brother, wouldn't make for a good target.

Bag retrieved, the two of them headed for the lounge at the back of the house.

Sully dug through the bag until he produced a bottle of disinfectant and bandages.

"The pharmacies were probably among the first places to get raided," Sully said, wincing as he dabbed at his injuries with alcohol wipes. "The good thing is people were mostly just after the drugs. The place on this side of the island still had a few first aid supplies left. Not much, but enough to hold me."

Dez applied the bandages while Sully pinched the skin of his abdomen, then his calf together. They then did the same with a couple of bleeding injuries Dez had sustained. "We should be doing this back at my house. This place isn't exactly sanitary."

"Dez."

There was meaning in the tone, and Dez looked up to meet Sully's eye. "Come on. You're not seriously planning on staying here? Not after all that."

"I have to—even more so now than before."

"What does that mean? Look, if Raynor comes looking for you at my place, he'll need a warrant to enter. Good luck applying to a judge for an arrest warrant on a dead guy. Anyway, he hasn't made a move yet, so why would he now?"

"That's not the only problem. You saw what I did back there. I'm not...." Sully trailed off, looking up and away. A sheen of tears formed, just visible in the waning light from the dusty window.

Dez stood. "You're not what?"

"I'm not safe to be around. I'm not *good*."

"What the hell are you talking about? Honestly, man, all the years we've known each other, and the few fights we've been back to back in, I can't say I've ever felt safer around you than I did half an hour ago. I mean, hell, man. You saved my life."

"You don't get it."

Dez crossed his arms. "So explain it to me."

Sully finally met his eye, a challenge in the way they narrowed. "You going to tell me what just happened didn't freak you out?"

Truthfully, yeah, it had. It had scared the hell out of him. "No. It didn't."

"Bullshit." Sully dropped onto the fainting couch, lowering his head into his hands and running fingers through his hair. He'd lost the tie sometime during the fight and his hair hung loose now, dropping into its familiar curtain around his face as soon as he released it.

Dez sat gingerly next to him, wary of the capacity of the water-damaged couch to hold both of them. It held, and Dez sat forward, too, elbows on knees as he tried to see around the hair.

"What's bullshit, exactly? You think because you went a little nuts on those guys, you're a bad person?"

"It wasn't all me. It was Montague. I used him."

It took Dez a moment to puzzle through that one. "Like drawing on his energy, or do you mean like a possession?"

"The latter. Only he didn't possess *me*, Dez. I possessed *him*."

This time, Dez really did require an explanation. "What?"

"You remember Nora Silversmith? I pulled her off Hackman the day she killed him, but it was more than that. I pulled her into myself. And I did the same thing with Montague. I could hear their thoughts, feel their emotions—because I sucked in their energy. I didn't use it that day with Nora, but I did this time. And I used it once before, with Harry, the day Lowell and Hackman tried to kill me. Back then, I didn't know how to hold onto it, how to work with it."

"And you do now?"

"I don't know how I know. I just do. Like an instinct."

"Okay. Wow." Dez considered what he'd just been told as he searched for the right words. It didn't take him long to realize there were no right words, not for this. Nothing he could come up with, anyway. "Well, it can't be that bad, right? I mean, you used it to protect me, and yourself."

"That's the way it started. But it's not how it ended. He's there, Dez, inside me, and he's strong."

"Who? Montague?"

Sully shook his head. "No, I released him. He took off. I doubt he'll be back."

"So who do you mean?"

"The hangman."

"He's a past life, Marc and Raiya figured. Souls evolve, remember? They grow."

"But maybe they don't really change," Sully said. "I'm not like him, not the way I am now. But when I drew those two spirits into myself, I lost who I am. I became him. But maybe it's more than that. Maybe I became *me*."

"Come on, Sully."

"I'm the son of a rapist. I'm half-bad, even in this life. Why wouldn't I be the kind of person who does the things I did to those gang members?"

Frustration turned to anger, had Dez grasping fists full of his brother's jacket and turning him to face him. "Because that's not who you are! I know you. I've known you most of your life. You aren't Gerhardt, and you aren't this hangman. You're you. You're who you choose to be. That's all. And don't forget, you stopped it. You didn't kill anyone today. The hangman would have."

"Yeah, you're right, he would have!" Sully shouted back. "And *I* would have. I wanted to. I wanted to so bad, I could smell the blood. I could picture it in my head, what it would look like, what it would feel like to do it. I didn't stop myself, Dez. It wasn't me. I would have kept going."

"So why'd you stop?"

"Dad and Aiden." The answer, quietly spoken, had Dez

releasing Sully, allowing him to turn back into the shelter of his hair. "It was Dad and Aiden."

"How?"

"They possessed me, too, I guess. I could feel them, all their light. They were stronger than the hangman, stronger than me. That's why I stopped."

Emotion hit, bringing a lump to Dez's throat that had him gasping out a breath. "Are they here? Now?"

Sully looked up, then lowered his head before answering with a nod.

Dez smiled, eyes going to the spot Sully had been looking at. "Thanks, guys." Then he turned back to Sully, draping an arm over his shoulders. "Hey, here's the thing. I don't know who you would have been if you hadn't ended up coming into our lives. But what I do know is that it doesn't matter. You've got the life you've got, and I'm pretty sure that's enough. I've met a lot of screwed-up people who have done bad things. Most of them aren't bad. They're just messed up, and they don't have stable people to help them get past their problems. Most of what they do is because they use booze and drugs to medicate the pain. The monsters they become when they're drunk or high, that's not really who they are. I think, in a way, it's the same with you."

"Except it *is* who they are," Sully said. "Booze and drugs, they just remove walls. Those people you're talking about, the people who get violent, it's because the chemicals tap into something that's already there. They're angry to start with. The alcohol, the drugs, they just free it or intensify it. It's probably the same for the assholes who attacked us at the house. If they weren't on whatever they were on, they probably wouldn't have done what they did. But it doesn't erase the anger they're probably carrying around. That's what I'm worried about, that I'm carrying something around inside me that's like a time bomb. The Dules said their men fall to evil. I almost did."

"But you didn't."

"Not because of a choice I made. It was only because someone stopped me. It's getting stronger, Dez. I can feel it. Raiya told me my abilities would grow. What if next time, Dad and Aiden aren't enough?"

"If you don't use this whole spirit possession thing, it won't be a problem, right? That much you can decide for yourself."

"I didn't use it either time because I wanted to. I used it to try to save people. And if, in the future, I have to choose between losing myself to evil and saving someone I love, I'll pick the latter every time."

Dez blew out a breath, then moved his hand to ruffle Sully's hair before dropping it.

"I don't understand anything about what you can do," he said. "But I understand this much: You're not partly bad because of who supplied the sperm to create you. You're all good because of the people who care about you. And you're good because of who you are at your core. Everyone's got some bad in them, Sull. I've been fighting myself to keep from finding Lowell and beating him to death. It doesn't make me a bad person. It makes me human. For once in your life, you need to stop being so hard on yourself. You're in a bad place right now, and you're going through a lot. Maybe it makes you more susceptible to that part of yourself. That's normal."

Sully didn't say anything right away, which relieved Dez. He'd expected further argument. He waited, listening to the sound of the evening breeze outside, until Sully spoke again.

"I wasn't sure you'd forgive me after what I kept from you. I don't know what I'd do if you weren't in my life."

Dez patted Sully's back. "And you won't ever have to find out."

He'd left his wedding band and keys behind some books on one of the shelves, and he stood to retrieve them. He checked the time on his phone, discovering it was a little past seven thirty.

"It's getting dark out," Sully said. "You should get going. You need to get the boat back to the club."

"I don't want to leave you here."

"You have to."

Sully stood, leading the way through the house and to the cellar stairs.

"Why this way?" Dez asked.

"Once the sun goes down, it's safer than going outside. Too hard to see anyone who might be hiding out there. This gets us right up to the river without being seen."

Dez followed Sully into the cellar, over to the sliding shelf and through the tunnel until they reached the hidden grate. Back outside, the spot in sight where they'd hidden the boat, Dez turned back to Sully.

"Please, come back with me."

"I can't."

"Damn it, Sully." Dez paused, then drew his brother into a hug. "You be safe, you got that?"

"I will."

Dez released Sully, but his eyes remained fixed on the darkness behind his brother. The house was back there somewhere, concealed in shadow and overgrown vegetation. It was impossible to say what else—or, more specifically, who—might be hiding in the dark. They'd barely survived a brutal attack by a bunch of tweaking gangsters. The reality was The Forks was crawling with people like that.

The other reality was that Sully was completely alone now, not even Pax here to watch over him. Sure, Noisy Ned had proven himself a decent alarm system, and Sully could definitely protect himself if he had to—as long as he saw the danger coming. Dez wasn't sure how much faith to put in a poltergeist when it came to ensuring Sully was looked after.

Dez had just two real fears in life: ghosts and being helpless to protect the people he loved from harm. He had zero control over the first, but he could do something about the second. And the latter fear outweighed the former by a ton.

"You know, I could make you come back with me," he said.

"You could," Sully agreed. "But you won't."

"No, I won't. So I guess that means I'm staying too."

"Dez, come on."

"Honestly, I'd rather Kayleigh not see me when I'm all banged up like this. And it's a long way back from here to my place. And—"

"And you're reaching." Sully's features were barely visible now, just the dimmest outline in the dark. Even so, Dez could make out the smile.

He added one more valid argument. "Look at it this way. If I go home, I'm just going to be lying awake all night, worrying about your ass."

"Here, you'll just be up all night, worrying about all the noises."

"Better that than the alternative." He turned Sully toward the hidden boats. "Come on. Let's get the boat returned and then come back and get a fire going. We're going to freeze our nuts off, standing around out here."

"You're not going to take no for an answer on this, are you?"

"Nope. You're stuck with me. Let's go."

12

DEZ POKED THE FIRE, flipping over a log to expose the flame beneath to the air.

He searched for calm in the crackling of the blaze. As long as he kept it roaring, it helped to drown out some of the other noises in the house.

He'd woken Sully twice already, believing he'd heard the sound of intruders. Sully had assured him they weren't the sort of intruders who could hurt them and went promptly back to sleep.

It hadn't made Dez feel any better. The difference between human bad guys and ghosts was minimal when it came to his nerves.

He'd given up on trying to sleep, relegating himself to fire duty and overall watchdog as the night ticked slowly past. His body ached from the beating he'd taken, a large, painful lump having formed on his head where he'd been clobbered by the pipe.

He'd gotten up an hour ago, keeping a musty quilt pulled up over his head like a cloak as he watched the fire.

He checked his watch. Almost twenty minutes after three. Being October, several hours remained before daybreak.

Crap.

Dez jumped at the sound of a scratch from the other side of the wall. At least, he hoped it was the other side. Nothing was on this side.

Nothing visible, anyway.

He'd heard the same sound earlier, and had awoken Sully to ask about it. The answer hadn't been encouraging. Just a ghost, he'd said. One of the women. No, Sully had never seen her, but he had a sense of her. Yes, she was annoyed they were here, but she'd tolerate them. Go to sleep, Dez.

Well, sleep wasn't happening, Sully.

Dez stared at the wall another few seconds as the scratching moved in the direction of the door. From his spot on the floor, Dez turned, facing that side of the room. His eyes darted along the wall, movement everywhere as the flames cast their dancing light upon it. He slid closer to Sully, hand hovering in preparation to wake him should the need arise. Dez's eyes, wide and unblinking, focused on the door, awaiting the moment it flung itself open. The scratches were still moving that way, edging ever closer.

Now they moved to the door itself.

His eyes shifted to the knob. It was unlikely he'd see it turning from here, given it was round, but he was pretty sure it was rusty enough to make a noise should she try to open it.

Please, don't let me hear that sound, he thought.

His hand lowered onto Sully's arm, preparing to shake him awake.

Then the moaning started. Dez had heard a similar sound before, when he'd been with an accident victim as they died. Death moan.

Crap.

Dez shook Sully's arm.

"What?" he grumbled.

"Do you hear that?"

"Hear what?"

"The moaning. It's right outside the door."

Sully lifted his head from the nest of his pillow and bundled covers. He was silent a moment, listening. Then he dropped his head back down and shut his eyes. "I don't hear anything."

Dez sighed. "Of course you don't. You can't hear ghosts, can you? But apparently, I can. And it's right outside."

"I can hear the scratching, if that helps convince you you're not crazy."

"I wasn't worried about being crazy. I know what I'm hearing is real. How is it you can hear the scratching but not the moaning, anyway?"

Sully shifted the covers, burying most of his head beneath them, just his face exposed to allow his groggy answer. "I don't know. Probably the usual problem with me not being able to hear them speaking. It's different when they interact with the environment. I don't know why, and I don't care. Can you try and get some sleep?"

"With the Woman in Black standing outside the door waiting to kill us? I don't think so."

"She's not going to kill us. The only one with the ability to cause us any harm is Ned, and he's not going to."

"But she doesn't want us here, right?"

Sully opened his eyes to meet Dez's gaze. "No, she doesn't. But she's not the boss of us, okay? They need to accept if they're going to stay on earth that they need to share their space with the living. I'm not letting her or any of the others tell me what I can and can't do in my own world. Neither should you."

Dez's eyes darted to the door, then back to Sully. "If you're suggesting I should tell off a ghost, you're crazy."

"I'm not suggesting anything, except that you should try to get some sleep. If there's any real danger, Ned will let us know in no uncertain terms."

Dez glanced back at the fainting couch. It was on the other side of the large fireplace, too far to reach without moving from his current spot on the floor. He stood and approached it, then tugged it to the other side of the fireplace, right next to a set of chairs Sully was using as a bed.

Once Dez had lain down and tucked himself back in, he found Sully smirking at him.

"What are you doing?" Sully asked through a smile.

"Shut up."

Sully chuckled but didn't say anything more. The scratching didn't stop.

Metal creaked—the sound of the doorknob.

"Sully?"

"Don't worry, it's one of her usual tricks. She's never actually opened the door."

"What if she does tonight?"

Sully didn't answer right away. When he did, it wasn't any kind of reply Dez had been expecting.

"Remember when Mom and Dad took us on that road trip west? We went through the mountains and stopped at that place made entirely out of pop bottles?"

"What the hell does this have to do with ghosts?"

"Nothing. That's the point. You used to prattle my ear off when we were kids until I went to sleep. I'm returning the favour."

"You really think it's going to help?"

"It helped me."

"You were seven."

"Still helped. Now shut up and let me talk."

Dez smiled. "Thanks, man."

He lay there, eyes closed, forcing his brain beyond the night noises and into the past. Eventually, caught between memories and exhaustion, Sully's voice and sleep drowned out the spirit at the door.

***

DEZ AWOKE TO A LOUD RING.

He patted the air, searching for his bedside table where he kept his phone charging. The search came up empty, and he opened his eyes to find out why. Morning disorientation fogged his brain, and it took a moment for him to piece it back together.

Ravenwood. The most haunted house in the city.

He'd survived the night.

The scratching from last night was gone; daylight streaming into the room had washed away the nighttime terrors.

Sully was gone, too, but the fire was still crackling lightly, suggesting he'd rekindled it recently.

A chill hung in the air, one that made the idea of getting up even more unpleasant. His phone had stopped ringing, and he had yet to remember where he'd put it. He'd called Eva and Mara last night, letting them know he'd be spending the night with Sully. It could be one of them was checking in, and they'd be worried if he didn't respond quickly.

His visual sweep of the room ended as the door opened to reveal Sully, plate in hand.

"Was that your phone?" he asked.

"Yeah," Dez said. "Can't remember where I put it."

Sully scanned the room until his eyes settled on a spot above the fireplace. Dez followed his brother's gaze to the mantle and watched as Sully plucked it from its spot there. Dez accepted the phone as Sully returned to his length of chairs, sitting on one and swinging his legs up onto the others.

"Who was it?" he asked.

Dez checked his missed calls. "Eva. Probably wanted to make sure we're still alive. What you got there?"

"Breakfast," Sully said, placing the plate next to Dez where he could see and reach it.

Dez wrinkled his nose. The contents of a can of salmon, a few pickles and a small pile of mushy strawberries from a tin. "Dude, that's gross."

"Hey, it's survival. How do you think I've kept myself so svelte the past couple of years?"

"I'm getting the picture. Please tell me that stuff didn't come with the house."

"It didn't. I picked up a few things at a late-night convenience store before coming back here a few nights ago. Figured I'd need some supplies."

Dez hated canned fish, but he accepted one of the pickles before calling Eva back.

"How's everything going?" she asked as soon as she answered.

"We survived the night," Dez said around his crunching. "How's everything there?"

"Fine. Pax is pretty mopey, though. I think he misses Sully."

"Don't worry. I'll bring him by soon. They can reunite. Sully's mooning over Pax too."

Sully gently slapped the uninjured side of Dez's head.

"I'm not sure it's such a great idea for Sully to come by here," Eva said. "Raynor was by at the crack of dawn. Probably thought he'd catch us by surprise. He's looking for Sully. Said he really needs to talk to him."

"Talk to him how?" Dez asked. "Like an informal chat, or a formal police station interview room kind of talk?"

"He didn't say anything about an interview, but he definitely wants to speak with him about the Montague homicide. Investigators are getting desperate to piece it together. They've made no arrests and they've got no suspects—and you can bet your ass the press is all over it. There was a story on the news last night about the fact the case is still unsolved, and it's been front-page news since it happened."

"Damn. Did Raynor mention the words 'obstructing justice' at all? 'Cuz I guess that's kind of what we're doing."

"Yeah, well, so is he, and he knows it. That's why he's getting desperate. He can't expose Sully without outing his wife at the same time. I bet he's hoping Sully will come forward willingly and fix everything."

"Yeah, well, that's not happening," Dez said. "Not yet, anyway."

"Dez?" Sully said.

Dez hadn't put his phone on speaker, and he put his hand against the mouthpiece to allow him to speak to his brother. "What?"

"I'll meet with Forbes, okay? If it will help convince him I'm not responsible for the murder, it might help them solve this thing sooner."

"He's well aware you're not responsible," Dez said. "But you're still a key witness. You're the only other person who was there when it happened. Raynor's not the only one who will be interested in what you have to say. If you meet with him, I'm afraid he might haul you in. There's enough to arrest you on suspicion, at least until they clear some stuff up."

"So I'll phone him," Sully said. "That's safe, right?"

Dez shrugged, then returned to the conversation with Eva. "Sully says he'll phone him."

"I doubt that will satisfy Forbes, but it's better than nothing," Eva said. "Make sure Sully's prepared for questioning first, though."

"I think he's already prepared," Dez said. "But I'll walk him through whatever I suspect Raynor's going to ask."

"Everything okay with the two of you?" Eva asked. "We haven't really talked about it."

"Yeah, everything's fine. We sorted it out."

"Good. I'm proud of you. And about everything else, with Lowell, I mean. Let me know how I can help. And your mom too. Don't leave us in the dark on this."

"I won't. Thanks, babe."

"Later, Snowman. Love you."

"Love you too. Hey, uh, just so you know, I kind of got beat up yesterday."

"Beat up how?" Eva's voice was tight, as Dez had expected. He'd debated not telling her, but he'd be seeing her later today, and he didn't want his injuries to come as a shock.

"Nothing broken, but I'm pretty banged up. Sully and I got into a scrape with some gangsters at a house in The Forks."

"The Forks?"

Dez grimaced. He thought he'd told her. "I mentioned we were staying there, didn't I?"

"You told me you were staying the night with Sully. I assumed you meant at your apartment. Damn it, Dez. The Forks?"

Dez spoke fast. "The house is actually fairly safe. It comes with its own poltergeist guard. It's the rest of the island that isn't so good."

"Damn it, Dez."

"I'm sorry. I thought I said."

"You didn't. You think if you had, I would have been so quick to let it slide?"

"Okay, point taken. We'll come back over today, all right? Could you forewarn Mom and Kayleigh for me, that I've got some bumps and bruises? I don't want anyone freaking out over it."

"I'll mention it. Anyway, I'm likely to add a few when I see you. Be careful—or more careful than you have been."

"I will. Sorry, babe."

"We'll discuss it later."

She hung up without another word, and Dez exhaled through pursed lips as he tucked his phone into his pocket.

"She's pissed, huh?" Sully asked.

"Uh, yeah, you could say that. Guess we'd better track Lachlan down next."

"Yeah, but maybe we could do that from the boat. In my experience, it's best leaving in the early morning or late at night. Less chance of someone being able to see. If anyone catches wind I've got a boat hidden away here, it'll be gone before I know it."

"Ned won't watch it for you?"

"Ned stays in the house, at least as far as I'm aware. This place is all he cares about."

"Okay, well, if you're thinking we should bail now, I'm all for it. The sooner we get out of this place, the happier I'll be."

WHILE DEZ ROWED, Sully called Lachlan but, at Dez's insistence, waited on the call to Forbes. Dez wanted to ensure his attention was undivided when his brother made the call, enabling him to shut things down quickly if Forbes tried any tricks.

Sully put Lachlan onto speaker, allowing Dez to hear the conversation from both ends.

"Find anything useful at the house?" Lachlan asked.

"Death," Dez said. "We almost found death."

Sully provided a better explanation. "We were jumped by some gang members tweaking on something. We got a little banged up, but we'll live."

"Speaking of which, I haven't checked your cuts today," Dez said. "Remind me to take a look when we get to shore. If they get infected, we'll have some serious decisions to make."

"I'm sure there's a story there, but I'd rather hear if you found anything of use to our investigation," Lachlan said.

Dez snorted. "Thanks for your concern."

"Hey, you're well enough to gripe at me, so you're clearly all right. Now talk."

"I saw Eloise," Sully said. "She's appearing to me as quite young, and she's got some pretty bad injuries. She showed me their son's room—and it was very much still their son's room. Gerhardt had to have been living there at the time of the flood. He never left, not until he had no choice."

"Could be he was attached to memories in the place, or hoped his kid might find his way back there," Lachlan said. "Or it could be he was sitting on top of evidence he didn't want to leave for someone else to uncover. I've seen it before. Had a case once where a guy killed his wife and buried her in the basement. Lived there for thirty-odd years—right on top of her—to make sure no one found out."

"We didn't have time to give the place a real thorough search," Dez said. "And I doubt we'll be able to. I'm not sure how those guys saw us go in there, but they swooped in on us pretty quick. It could be they're set up in a place nearby. Until we know for sure, we can't risk going back, not without a full-scale tactical team at our backs."

"I did get one other thing out of it," Sully said. "I grabbed a set of keys from the master bedroom. I can't say for sure without checking, but they look to me like they might be for Lockwood."

Dez raised his eyebrows. "You didn't tell me that."

"I forgot. Things went sideways fast after I found them, and we've both had plenty of other stuff on our minds since."

Lachlan offered a, "Hmm," but didn't add to it immediately. Dez was too focused on his increasingly sore body to bother trying to figure out what Lachlan was thinking. His injuries roared at him as he continued to row, and the shore, though only another couple of minutes away, felt miles off.

"I'm wondering," Lachlan said at last. "Might there be value in our sneaking into Lockwood? The place is a fortress. If I had something to hide, better to keep it there than at home. He runs the place, after all, and he's well-respected by most around there. Others fear him. I can't imagine many would cross him by digging through his personal property."

"Given he left his keys behind at the house, some locks were probably changed," Dez said.

"To his office and personal filing cabinets, certainly," Lachlan said. "But not the ones for the main building. They would've just given him copies of those."

"Yeah, I realize that. What I was getting at was that anything useful to us would likely be kept in his office. Only he and maybe the cleaning staff would have keys, and I'd actually be shocked if he allowed the cleaners a way in. Guy like him, he'd probably do his own dusting before allowing anyone a chance at catching wind of one of his dirty little secrets."

"There's a good chance that's not where he keeps his dirty little secrets," Sully said. "The Blue Room is in the old, unused part of the institution. Hardly anyone has keys to that wing, and no one's allowed in. Seems to me that might be the logical place to keep anything he doesn't want found."

"You have the keys to get in there?" Lachlan asked.

Sully pulled a large keyring from his pocket. Even from here, Dez could see what appeared to be a series of older keys dangling from the ring. "I might, yeah."

Lachlan went quiet again, and Dez waited for the inevitable: the request he didn't feel either he or Sully could meet.

"I'm thinking we might need to take advantage of this find, boys," Lachlan said a moment later.

"As in sneak into Lockwood and search the place?" Dez asked. "No way."

"Only the abandoned wing," Lachlan said. "Not the rest."

"Same thing, and answer's the same. No way. I'm not allowed near the place, and it's got all kinds of cameras up. And Sully— well, that's obvious, isn't it?"

"I'm not saying the plan is perfect," Lachlan said. "Hell, I don't even have a plan yet. I'm just saying we should keep it in mind as a possibility. It might be there are answers we won't find anywhere else."

"My worry is we'll find a lot more there than answers," Dez said. "And it could be the answers we get aren't ones we'll want."

13

SULLY HELPED Dez tug the rowboat to shore and conceal it within the bushes.

The first time he'd done that, he'd fully expected to return and find it gone, but so far, no one had happened onto it.

This stretch of riverbank was relatively free of pedestrian traffic, close to nothing but the main road above and the old warehouse district behind that. The part of the warehouse area closer to Kimotan Rapids' core had been converted into bars, night clubs, condos and trendy businesses, but this side didn't possess the same sort of ambience. Some of the buildings were still in use, but many had been abandoned.

Regardless, it was a fairly quiet area, perfect for stashing rowboats you'd need later.

Also perfect for phone calls to suspicious police detectives.

Dez, though, seemed to have other ideas. He'd left his SUV parked behind one of the abandoned businesses, and Sully imagined he was anxious to ensure it was both still there and in one piece. Sully trailed Dez to the vehicle and watched as he gave it a visual once-over.

"Everything where it should be?" Sully asked as he and Dez dropped into the front bucket seats.

"Seems to be. Kinda thought I'd get back to find it gone. I need to invest in a steering wheel lock"

"It would have come in handier as a weapon at the Gerhardt house than in the vehicle."

Dez nodded and slipped the keys into the ignition.

"Dez? I should call Forbes."

Dez sighed. "Right." He dug out his phone and laid it on the dashboard between them. "Listen, I'm going to make it clear I'm here with you. That way I can—"

"No," Sully said. "If he starts thinking like I'm obstructing justice, and you're a part of it, he could get your private investigator's licence revoked."

"Uh, newsflash. I don't have a licence. Not yet. I'm just helping Lachlan, technically."

"Okay, so it could keep you from getting one down the road then. Same thing. I don't want him knowing you're here."

"All right, but I'm staying while you talk to him anyway," Dez said. "If things head somewhere I don't like, I'll make a cutting motion and you end the call."

"Right, but I should use my own phone then, not yours."

Dez didn't respond other than to re-pocket his phone.

Sully removed his own. "Any other advice?"

"He might try to trip you up by asking you the same questions in different ways. People who are lying sometimes have a hard time repeating their stories without flubbing something up."

"That's great because I won't be lying. Forbes knows why I went there, and I had nothing to do with Montague getting killed, so I've got nothing to hide."

"Except you broke into the house of a murder victim, pretended to have a gun and threatened the guy into talking."

"I made an edit of the audio using your laptop, and I took out the threat part. I was going to start a fake email account and send it anonymously to Forbes, but I guess there's no point now. He knows it was me anyway."

"*Suspects* it was you," Dez said. "I didn't confirm anything."

"Come on, Dez. Forbes is a lot of things, but he's not as stupid as Lachlan likes to say. He knows me well enough to recognize me on a surveillance video. I'm not starting this off by lying to him about that."

"If he knows for sure it was you in there, he can't sit on that information," Dez said. "He'll be obstructing the investigation if he doesn't reveal what he knows."

It was a good point, one Sully hadn't given enough consideration to. With Forbes, ensuring his wife's secrets remained untold would only go so far. He was a husband, but he was also a police officer with serious ambitions to reach the top of the ladder someday. Forbes was caught between a rock and a hard place, and Sully wasn't certain he wanted to take a chance at finding out which side the cop was willing to break apart first.

"I know what to do," he said.

"What's that?"

Sully dialled without answering his brother's question. He just wanted this over with before his anxiety got the better of him.

Forbes answered his cellphone almost immediately. "Raynor, Major Crimes."

Sully put the call onto speaker for Dez. "It's Sully."

"Give me a minute."

Sully waited, listening to the sounds of movement in the background. Half a minute passed before Forbes spoke again. "Wanted to get somewhere quiet. Where are you? I need to speak with you."

Dez waved a hand around in a wild gesture of "no"; Sully didn't need the advice. "I can't. You know that."

"I can't keep pretending I don't know anything about the tape. I know it was you in Montague's house that night."

"I don't know what you're talking about."

"Don't bullshit me, Gray. I'm not an idiot."

"I'm not trying to bullshit you. I'm just calling to tell you I'd be happy to help with your investigation, but not until I can come out of the reeds. I can't risk my life, and I can't risk my family's. You can't ask me to do that."

"A man is dead."

"Several people are dead, including my dad. I think this all comes down to the same thing. Montague knew something about Lowell and the Circle, and he tried to use it to buy himself a deal. If word got back to Lowell, there's no doubt in my mind he either took that shot himself or paid someone to do it."

"Is he capable of pulling off a hit like that himself?"

"He's trained in firearms. I didn't have him pegged as a sniper, but I haven't exactly spent much time around him. If I were you, I'd start checking it out. Find out which shooting clubs he uses, and if he's certified in sharpshooting. After that, start checking into any former Armed Forces members or police officers with sniper backgrounds. Could be one of them's running an underground murder-for-hire gig."

"We're already checking into that angle, given what we're looking at here—the Army/SWAT thing, not the Lowell Braddock thing. No one's really treating Montague's supposed info on Braddock seriously, at least insofar as his murder goes."

"Why not?"

"Come on. The head of a major pharmaceutical company turned assassin? Does that sound plausible to you?"

"It does, and you know it."

Forbes sighed heavily. "All right. I know what you told me, and I believe you. But if I bring that forward without something to back it, I'd be laughed out of the room."

Sully met Dez's eye. Dez shrugged, then nodded agreement at Forbes's suggestion.

"What if I told you I can get you the info you need to get people to take you seriously?" Sully asked.

"What sort of info?"

"I can't tell you yet, but I can get something to you. I just need to know you'll cover for me. If you drag me in there, you'll not only put lives in jeopardy, you'll prevent my being able to help put all of this to bed. And you do need me, Forbes. There are elements at play here no one but me can get at—namely witnesses no one else can interview."

"Because they're dead." Forbes had always been good at stating the obvious. "Damn it. Okay. Okay, I'll buy you a little more time. But you'd better be close to something."

"We're closing in on Gerhardt. My hope is if we can promise him the thing he wants the most, he'll give us Lowell on a platter. If he does, I'll send him your way."

"You really think he'll talk? Hell, if you could get Lockwood's chief psychiatrist to talk, people would have to take it seriously."

"I'm hopeful," Sully said. "Just give me some time."

"I need something soon," Forbes said. He paused, and Sully sensed he was about to switch tracks. "Did you have anything to do with Montague's death?"

"I didn't kill him, and I wasn't connected to anyone responsible for the shooting. I promise you that."

"Okay. I guess that'll have to be good enough for now. Do what you've got to do, but keep me looped in, you hear me? I can't wait around forever."

"I'm not asking you to. Our time is limited on this too. If we can't get Lowell soon, I'm afraid more people will get hurt. Work things from your end, and tell me what you find. But play it cool, okay? If Lowell thinks police are closing in on him, he'll lash out. It's what he does. Don't get caught in his crosshairs."

"I can handle him."

"My dad was one of the strongest people I've ever known. He thought he could handle Lowell, too, and he's dead. Don't underestimate him. We need you on our side here, and I'd rather be able to communicate with you alive than dead."

"All right, all right. Call me with updates. If I find anything I think you can help with, I'll call you. I can reach you at this number?"

"For now. If I need to switch out phones, I'll get you my new number."

Sully disconnected without a goodbye. He replaced the phone in his pocket, then met Dez's eye and grinned. "How'd I do?"

Dez raised his eyebrows. "Good, actually."

"I'm like a really cool confidential informant now, aren't I?"

Dez smirked. "The only time you're cool is when you're standing outside in winter, but as far as the confidential informant angle, you're doing all right. Now let's get back to my house for a shower and change, and so I can check your injuries and get some ice on mine. After that, we'll figure out where to go next."

"I've got an idea," Sully said. "There's one person who knows Lockwood almost as well as Gerhardt. Emily might be able to help—and if it involves taking down Gerhardt, she'll definitely want to. One suggestion, though? Maybe we should skip your house and go to your apartment instead."

"I want to go home, Sull."

"Mom's there. The second she sees us looking like this—"

"Crap. You're right. My apartment it is."

SULLY HAD CHANGED his clothes back at Ravenwood, but he gratefully stood under the spray of Dez's shower while Dez made himself a proper breakfast from whatever was left in the fridge and cupboards.

They traded places, Dez first ensuring Sully's injuries weren't turning colours they shouldn't be. Seemingly satisfied on that count, he closed himself in the small bathroom while Sully ate the eggs, bacon and toast Dez had left for him on the counter.

While chewing, Sully's eyes drifted to the remains of the coffee table propped up against the wall, then the short note he'd written Dez before leaving, still on the counter where he'd left it. That had been only a few days ago; Sully had anticipated it would be months or even years before they reached the point they'd come to now. He'd underestimated his brother more than once. Not only had Dez not gone after Lowell, he'd found a way to forgive Sully far sooner than expected. The past few years, Sully had complained Dez didn't give him enough credit for being able to take care of himself; only now did Sully realize he hadn't given his brother the credit he deserved either.

Dez stayed in the shower long enough to soak up the rest of the hot water. By the time he returned to the kitchen, Sully had finished eating and was washing the dishes in lukewarm suds.

Sully looked back at Dez, relieved to find him less pale than when they'd arrived. "How you feeling?"

Dez grabbed a towel and started drying. "I took a couple painkillers and had a good hot soak, so I'm feeling like a human being again. You?"

"Sore but okay."

"Let me know if things get worse. God knows where that knife had been before it ended up in you. There's all sorts of bad stuff you could wind up with."

"Thanks, Doctor Doom, but I'll be fine." He handed Dez a plate.

Dez dried it and placed it back in the cupboard. "Listen, I've been thinking. Given Raynor's not likely to come at you now, you should stay here. It doesn't make sense, you going back to The Forks. This is closer, it's safer and it's more practical. Plus, you've got running water and electricity. And the best part is, you're neighbours with Emily, not Ned or that other ghost whose main skill is finding ways to keep people from sleeping."

"Dez, you're back home with Eva and Kayleigh now. There's no point holding onto this place, is there?"

"Until things are sorted out, there's plenty of point. Like I said, I'd love it if you'd stay here. Anyway, if Eva gets sick of me again and gives me the boot, it's good to know I've got a place to crash." Dez grinned, and Sully responded with a smile of his own.

"Thanks," Sully said. "I'll think about it."

"What's to think about?"

"I just need to make sure the risks don't outweigh the benefits."

"I'm looking forward to the day when the riskiest thing we need to worry about is whether to eat the chicken that's been sitting in the fridge for a week and a half."

Once the dishes were done, they headed across the hall.

Emily answered the door, glasses-magnified eyes wide as she peered up at them. "I thought I heard someone go into your apartment, but I couldn't get up fast enough to see anything but your back, Desmond. Both of you? Does this mean everything's all right between the two of you again?"

Sully all but buckled under the weight of Dez's hand as it settled firmly on his shoulder and gave it a shake.

"Yeah," Dez said. "We're good."

Emily gave a little sigh as she beamed. "Thank goodness. Come in. That calls for tea and coffee cake."

Sully grinned. Emily's coffee cake was another great reason to move back into Dez's apartment.

Five minutes later, the three of them were gathered around her table, Dez devouring his second piece of cake while Sully picked more politely at his.

"I was certain things would work themselves out with the two of you," she said. "I haven't met many siblings closer than you are."

"Yeah," Sully said. "We're lucky." He glanced at his brother in time to see the rest of the cake disappear into his mouth.

"Another piece, dear?" she asked.

"Uh… I really shouldn't," Dez said. The smile that formed a moment later said otherwise.

With Dez tucking into his third piece, Sully launched into the reason they'd come. "We wanted to talk to you about something you might not like discussing much. Dr. Gerhardt."

He watched her for signs of discomfort, but didn't see anything obvious. Nothing to indicate this topic of conversation would cause her any great distress. "Yes?"

"We're looking into what happened to his son."

"David."

"Right. Were you working at Lockwood when he disappeared?"

"I was. It was a terrible time."

"I know you described what a horrible person Gerhardt was later on," Sully said. "Was it because of what happened to David?"

"He was a horrible person even before that. Don't get me wrong. He was a fine doctor, and he was always very good with most of the patients and their families. But he could be a tyrant as a boss, and he treated many staff members like his servants. He utterly debased us over minor mistakes. Major ones—well, you can imagine. A young nurse once put the wrong medication into the cups. She caught it in time, thankfully, but one of the other staff members told him about it. He pulled the nurse aside and tore a strip off her, screamed at her that she was completely incompetent and a failure, and that there was no room for people like her in his workplace. She ran off in tears. I never learned what became of her after, poor dear."

"And his family? Do you have any idea whether they might have been treated like that too?"

Emily offered a dry smile. "One thing I've learned about people like him. They're very good at putting on a good front where they believe it counts. He's always been able to charm the right people, and he's also been an excellent advocate for the staff in terms of helping to ensure competitive pay and excellent bene-fits. Some staff there, the ones who never had a run-in with him, they'd defend him with their dying breath. If you asked them, they'd tell you any staff member who's complained was simply sucking sour grapes. To answer your question, he always showed his true colours when he believed he could get away with it. I suspect his family might have suffered the same sort of wrath he otherwise reserved for weaker staff."

"Did you ever hear any talk about what happened to David or Eloise?" Dez asked.

"Nothing about David. No one so much as breathed his name

afterward for fear of upsetting the doctor. Everyone simply saw it as a terrible tragedy, and I know sympathy for Dr. Gerhardt increased significantly for a time. When Eloise left him, and no one heard from her again, some people did talk. Some said she ran off after he'd beaten her. Some said she committed suicide because he blamed her for their son's disappearance. Others said he killed her."

"Did you know her?" Sully asked.

"A little. I'd see her at functions now and again, and I spoke to her when I had the chance. She was a lovely woman, doted on their little boy. David was so happy around her. Two peas in a pod. She put on a pleasant face around her husband, too, but I don't know. I always suspected something was off." She tipped her head to the side. "Hard to say now, of course, whether I'm recalling what I truly thought then or simply imposing what I know now. He tried to have me killed, after all, once I attempted to confront him over your mother. I have hated precious few people in life, but I do hate him."

"We're trying to figure out a way to solve what happened to David and Eloise," Sully said. "The thing is, I've seen her."

"Alive?"

"Dead. Definitely dead."

"And the fact you can see her means she was murdered, doesn't it?" Emily asked.

Sully nodded. "I saw her in their old house, in The Forks. She was—"

"Not a good idea to go to The Forks, dear. Not anymore."

Dez snorted and shook his head. "I keep telling him."

Sully nudged his brother and continued with what he'd been trying to say. "She was beaten and stabbed. While I was at the house, I also found some keys. I think they're to Lockwood. He must have left them there when he evacuated before the flood. We're wondering now if there's some way we'd be able to get in to use them. The problem is, I obviously can't be seen there, and Dez isn't supposed to be around there either."

Emily's face scrunched up a little as if in thought. A moment later, widening eyes and an open-mouthed grin told Sully a light-bulb had gone off. "As it happens, I might have a solution." She stood, using the table edge as support, and shuffled to the side of the fridge. Pulling something from beneath a magnet, she returned with the card to the table and laid it in front of Sully. "Lockwood homecoming. One hundred and fifty years since they opened the institution. Every living person who's ever worked there has been invited, and it will be open to families of patients too. I went to the one hundred and twenty-fifth, and I remember they had the gates open to visitors. Patients considered dangerous or a flight risk were kept inside locked areas of the institution, so access to the grounds wasn't considered a problem. A lot of people showed up, and I'd expect the same for this reunion. Parts of the institution will be open for tours—Dr. Gerhardt's way, no doubt, of showing what a great job he's doing. I'd expect you'd be able to blend easily enough into the crowd."

Sully peered doubtfully at his mountainous brother. Emily conceded the point.

"Or *you* could, anyway," she told Sully.

Sully expected Dez would have something to say about that, and he wasn't disappointed. "I don't want you going in there without backup."

"I'd go with him," Emily said. "Don't worry."

"No offence, Emily, but I was thinking more of someone who could fight off any orderlies who might identify Sully."

"Oh, I won't be going without a little backup myself," she said, tapping the side of her nose.

"What backup?"

"Messers Smith & Wesson."

Dez had just taken a mouthful of tea, and Sully smirked as he watched his brother struggle to swallow. Once he had, he stared at Emily with wide eyes. "Your handgun? You're going to go armed to your reunion?"

"The chief psychiatrist had me hit by a car, and when he failed to kill me, threatened me into a life of silence. Damn right, I'm going armed."

Dez shrugged. "Guessing they won't be running anyone through metal detectors."

"Like I said, the security risks will be kept inside. Staff won't be anticipating any major problems with the guests, and I won't give them any unless they're keen to start something first."

Dez grinned. "I wish you were my grandma."

Sully scanned the invitation for the date. "This is tomorrow."

"It is. Will you be ready?"

Sully delayed his response, waiting for his heart to stop thudding like a marching band bass drum. After everything he'd gone through, he'd vowed never to go anywhere near the place again. He was fast coming to the realization he would have to break that promise to himself.

"I'll have to be," he said.

14

DEZ KNEW Lachlan wasn't going to stay quiet for long. The expected call came while he was still at Emily's, stewing about his brother's planned return to Lockwood.

"What's up, Lachlan?" he asked upon answering his vibrating phone.

"We need to interview the psychiatrist. And I'd like to get on it now."

"We've got a lead," Dez said. "My neighbour has a way in to Lockwood tomorrow. It's open for a reunion thing. She and Sully are going."

"Maybe that's our way in, too, then," Lachlan said. "We could go there to speak with the doctor about the case."

Dez liked the idea of being nearby should Sully need him, but recent memory dampened his enthusiasm for the plan. "Gerhardt told me I'm not allowed back there."

"What's the worst that can happen? He boots you out again? Big deal. Anyway, I'll tell him you're my associate, and I need your help on the investigation. If he's truly interested in finding his son, he'll accept whatever help comes his way. That should include you."

"He doesn't trust me."

"He's a father searching for his missing child. Trust doesn't factor into it. Desperate parents will go to any lengths to find answers, and often that includes trusting in every two-bit shyster who comes forward. By comparison, you're pretty damn reliable."

Dez was happy to concede the point. He checked the card Emily had laid on the table. "Reunion starts at two tomorrow. Casual dress. I'll pick you up at one-thirty." His gaze moved between Emily and Sully. "You two will go at the same time?"

"I think we're all better waiting an hour or so," Emily suggested. "Place will be busier by three or four."

Dez nodded. "Emily says—"

"I heard her, junior. Good idea. Pick me up at two-thirty then. In the meantime, I'd like you to swing by my office. I've got someone else we should speak with. Fill you in when you get here."

Dez agreed and disconnected the call. "I guess we've got a plan," he said to Sully and Emily. "I need to head over to Lachlan's office. He wants to talk to someone."

"Who?" Sully asked.

"He said he'd fill me in."

"Does he need me?"

"He didn't say."

"All right," Sully said. "I'll head out to The Forks and grab my stuff. If I'm going to be staying at the apartment here, I'll need it."

Dez frowned. "Wait a bit, and I'll go with you."

Sully met Dez's worry with a soothing smile. "I'm just heading to Ravenwood, that's all. I don't even have to go in, really. My stuff's all down in the tunnel. I can be in and out in ten minutes."

"Okay," Dez said. "But do us both a favour and pick up Pax first, huh? I'd feel better knowing he's there with all his teeth. Oh, and don't mention to Mom about your injuries."

Sully rolled his eyes. "Like I was going to say anything." He turned his attention to Emily. "Sorry to ask, but would I be able to borrow your car? I'm not driving it into The Forks or anything, just to where I stashed the boat. I'd call a cab to take me, but they probably wouldn't want Pax in there."

"Of course you may, dear," she said. She stood and retrieved her keys from a basket on the counter nearest the door. "Just don't get pulled over. You don't have a licence."

Sully accepted the keys. "I may not have a licence at the moment, but I'm still a way better driver than Dez."

Dez smacked him.

LACHLAN WAS his usual picture of impatience when Dez arrived.

"What took you so long?"

"Traffic was nuts. It's right before the weekend. Lots of people have EDOs today."

"Whatever."

"So where are we going?"

"Nowhere," Lachlan said. "He's coming to us."

"He, who?"

"Paul Dunsmore. I think you know him."

Paul. Son of Reynold Dunsmore, president and CEO of Dunsmore Developments. Dez and Sully had dealings with Paul four years ago while searching for Bulldog's missing niece. Nice enough guy, had even come to Sully's funeral. Plus, he was rich—a point that would run in his favour with Lachlan, ever on the lookout for lucrative cases.

"I know him a little," Dez said. "What's he want?"

"Nothing. I asked him to come."

"Why?"

Lachlan's face cracked into one of his all-knowing smiles. "I've been doing a little asking around about this Circle you boys told me about. I've known Paul a while, and figured his family was just the sort who'd be welcomed into a fold like that. When I contacted him, he said he knows about it and would be happy to share."

Dez's heart thudded. "He's a member?"

"Has been for a while, I understand. And he didn't sound too enthusiastic about it."

Lachlan stopped talking as the sound of footsteps on the floorboards outside the door reached them. A moment later, a knock sounded.

Dez answered to find Paul there, watched as the man's gaze travelled upward until his eyes met Dez's. Paul grinned and reached out a hand to shake.

"Desmond Braddock. I haven't seen you since—" He stopped abruptly. Dez read it in his expression, the realization he'd just stepped into an awkward topic. The last time they'd seen each other, of course, had been at Sully's gravesite.

Dez pumped Paul's hand warmly, seeking to ease away the man's discomfort. "Good to see you, man. Come in. Have a seat."

"What are you doing here?" Paul asked. "Not that it's not great to see you."

"Desmond works with me," Lachlan said. "I didn't think you'd mind."

"Of course not," Paul said. He crossed the room, settling into one of Lachlan's armchairs. He waited until Dez took the one next to him before asking, "How are you doing?"

"Okay, thanks," Dez said. "You?"

"Fine, but I meant…. You know what I meant."

Paul, like most of the rest of the world, had no idea about Sully's being alive. As much as Dez liked Paul, it was a truth he wasn't prepared to share.

Then again, Dez didn't want to start the conversation with a lie, either.

"Oh," he said, with a shrug. "You know."

"Yeah," Paul said, finishing with a pat to Dez's shoulder.

Lachlan cleared his throat, drawing their attention to him. "You're probably wondering why I wanted to know about the Circle, Paul."

"Actually, what I've always wondered was why no one wants

to know more about it. Most people have never heard of it, but those who have never seem to question it."

"Bunch of wealthy men and women," Lachlan said. "They're rarely what you'd call 'the usual suspects,' are they?"

"Fair enough," Paul said. "I guess the question should be why people aren't more suspicious when rich, powerful people get together to pool their resources. I'd definitely question what's going on. I have, actually."

"But you're a member, aren't you?" Dez asked.

"My parents are founding members and they brought my brother and me in. We really had little choice in the matter, given we're all co-owners of Dunsmore Developments." He shrugged. "I try to have as little to do with the Circle as possible. I attend meetings as required, but I stay out of decision-making. My parents are majority shareholders in our company, anyway. They make all the big decisions for us—which includes anything to do with the Circle. Personally, I wish it didn't exist, but that's just me."

"We know a little about the Circle," Lachlan said. "But we'd love to know more. What can you tell us?"

"It's been around quite a few years. Decades, actually. It started off pretty small, just a few pissed-off, rich, white men who couldn't get into the Masons or something like that. Since then, it's grown to more ridiculous proportions.

"In essence, it's become a mini-bank. Members invest when they find someone they believe will go places. It's an incestuous little group, everyone sitting on everyone's boards or acting as investors in each other's companies. My father, in particular, has dropped money into countless ventures." He met Dez's eye. "That includes your uncle. My father had a fair hand in LOBRA's establishment, and he put up a significant amount of capital to help Lowell set it up back in the day—construction, hiring, research, everything. It was costly, you can imagine, but my father saw something in him."

Paul returned his gaze to Lachlan. "Usually the way these

things work, deals are made based on risk and promise. If you've ever watched *Dragon's Den*, you'll get the idea. Prospects petition existing members, offering a portion of their company or profits in exchange for start-up funds or something else they need to get their business off the ground or booming. Depending on the risk involved, members might seek a greater return. There are opportunities down the road for owners of successful ventures to buy out investors, should they want a greater share of control in their own companies."

"What if they aren't successful?" Dez asked.

"Some people are simply turned away at the start. But for those whose ventures fail after significant investment… well, nothing comes for free, does it? Those members are usually kicked out, and they're left on the hook for whatever they owe. I've seen people literally destroyed, forced to declare bankruptcy or revert to fraud to repay what they owe. You remember that Kay O'Hanlon affair a few years back?"

"Multi-million-dollar fraud," Lachlan said. "She was a member?"

"Failed member. The fraud was intended as a way to repay the Circle."

"I didn't hear mention of the Circle during that investigation. She did say she owed investors, but that was it."

"It doesn't pay to mention the Circle by name. They guard their secrets well. As it stood, she owed them money. If she'd brought them into it by name, she would have owed them her life."

"Hang on," Dez said. "The Circle would have had her killed?"

"I'm not suggesting they're *all* a bunch of killers. Most wouldn't have the stomach for it. But some people, as you're well aware, are prepared to do anything to hold onto what they have. If the Circle breaks, they all fall. What makes them strongest also makes them weakest. Because they are all in each other's back pockets, if one of them goes down, the chances of him or her taking others down are high. And if they go, more follow. It's like a house of cards."

"Harry Schuster," Dez said.

Paul's head snapped toward Dez, his eyebrows lifted. "What?"

"Sorry," Dez said. "Harry Schuster. He was a member of the Circle who was committed to—"

"I know who he was. I didn't know his involvement in the Circle was well-known."

"It isn't," Dez said. "I found out about it by chance during an investigation a while back. There's some suspicion his health problems and subsequent death in Lockwood weren't altogether natural."

Paul nodded. "He knew things. A lot of things. Enough to worry most members. He was valuable to them, but they feared him too. Because of the way his brain worked, the whole psychic thing or whatever you want to call it, he could foresee where the biggest successes would come. But he also knew where the bodies were buried. It was only a matter of time before something happened to him."

Dez leaned toward Paul. "Do you know what happened to him?"

"Only that he suffered a fatal stroke while in Lockwood. I've always suspected there's more to it, but I have no proof. And good luck to anyone else looking to prove it."

Lachlan sat forward behind his desk, lifting steepled fingers to his chin. "What are your thoughts on Lowell Braddock?"

Paul glanced from Lachlan to Dez and back again. "Are you really asking me that? Now?"

"I am."

Paul's eyes darted back to Dez.

"It's okay if you've got issues with him," Dez said. "I've found out some stuff about him. Made me realize he's not who I thought he was."

"This is strictly between us, I presume," Paul said. He inclined his head toward Dez. "I'm trusting you with what I say here. If any of this gets back—"

"It won't," Dez said. "I've got no loyalty to him anymore." He considered it briefly, decided on some quid pro quo to invite honesty from Paul—but nowhere near full quid pro quo. Dez still had people to worry about, and if it turned out Paul reported back to Lowell, he didn't want to think about the ramifications. "Sully told me Lowell and the head orderly from Lockwood tried to kill him. When they failed, they got him committed. Lowell was present for experiments they conducted, experiments using LOBRA drugs."

"Christ," Paul said. "But you don't have proof?"

"No, and I don't know we'll find any. Nothing people will believe anyway."

"And you'd like my help to find some."

Dez's thoughts hadn't travelled there yet, simply wondering what Paul already had for information. This new possibility was a hopeful one.

"Would you be willing to?"

"I can try," Paul said. He turned another few inches in his chair so he faced Dez more fully. "Here's the thing. I liked your brother. Sure, he pegged me for a killer once, but he also saved my life with all that ghost stuff he could do. He was a good man. Harry, troubled as he was, was a good man too. I'd hate to think how many more good people have been bowled under by the rich and the powerful in this city. You know I've always done what I could to help fix the parts of this community my family and others like them have broken. I will do what I can now."

He returned to his previous position and rubbed the palms of his hands over his legs as if to rid them of sweat. "It won't be easy, but I'll try."

"No one wants you to put yourself at risk here," Dez said. "That's definitely not what I'm asking."

"Risks are inevitable." Paul said. "Given your family history, you know that better than most." He paused, but his mouth remained slightly open as if he was merely searching for the right words. Dez waited him out.

"You asked about Lowell," Paul said. "And you told me what he did to Sullivan. I said most members of the Circle don't have the stomach for murder. Lowell isn't one of them. I have no proof —and I have no doubt you'd have to search long and hard to find any—but I believe Lowell is behind what happened to Harry. Lowell and Roman Gerhardt. I know that must sound outlandish—"

"It doesn't," Lachlan cut in. "We're aware of what they did to Sullivan in Lockwood— him and other patients who shared similar gifts. Our understanding is the drug developed at LOBRA was being tested on patients with psychic abilities. We have also learned the experiments weren't exactly a heavily guarded secret within the Circle. At least one other member—Prescott Montague —knew about it, and he's since been permanently silenced. We also know there was a man present at the experiments, someone Sullivan described as wearing a mask."

Paul nodded. "What you're saying sounds like something a fellow wearing a tinfoil hat might come up with. But all of it makes perfect sense. I can't say I was in on any of this regarding the experiments, but I very much believe what Sullivan reported was true. More than that, I believe I know the identity of the man in the mask."

Dez unconsciously straightened in his chair. "Who?"

Paul offered a sad smile. "My father. It makes sense. He's a heavy investor and a significant shareholder in LOBRA. I'd have to double-check the numbers, but I believe he holds a forty-one percent share in the company, with Lowell maintaining fifty-one percent and other Circle members the remainder. My father is effectively Lowell's partner. Nothing would happen without his say-so, and I also know he's a very hands-on kind of business-man. He's not content with reports. He needs to see for himself. If LOBRA is testing a drug, and they're using Lockwood patients to do it, my father would be involved. No question."

"Why the mask?" Dez asked.

"Well, it's not exactly legal what they're doing, is it? If they were found out, it would ruin him—all of them." A corner of Paul's mouth quirked up, surprising Dez. "I can't believe I'm saying this out loud, but I'd actually love to see that happen."

Paul looked from Lachlan to Dez and back again. "Thank you for letting me know. I'll keep my ear to the ground and pass along any information I get. But you need to give me a little time. I'm going to start liquidating some assets and getting as much as I can out of the company. If I'm going to be in part responsible for taking down Dunsmore Developments, I'd like to ensure I've got something to live on when the dust clears."

He stood. "I need to get back, but I'll keep you both informed."

Dez and Lachlan stood too. Across the desk, Lachlan extended a hand, which Paul shook. "Thank you for agreeing to help us, but as Desmond said, don't put your life at risk over this. The last thing either of us wants is you ending up where others have."

"That's where we differ," Paul said. "The last thing I want is to stand idly by, allowing others to end up that way. If there's anything I can do to make things right, I intend to."

He tipped an imaginary hat and bowed his head toward Dez and Lachlan. "Gentlemen. Good day. I'll be in touch."

He left the office, closing the door behind himself. Dez listened to Paul's footsteps fading away on the stairs before turning to Lachlan. "What do you think?"

Lachlan's face broke into a Cheshire cat grin. "I think we're well on the way to cracking the case of the century."

15

Sully had only intended to go as far as the basement side of the tunnel where he'd stashed his duffel bag and Pax's extra food.

Then he remembered he'd left Dez's portable cellphone charger upstairs, in the back parlour. Hoisting his duffel bag up and over one shoulder and tucking the bag of dog food into the crook of the opposite elbow, Sully left the passageway and headed for the basement stairs.

He hadn't stopped to get Pax as Dez had suggested, wanting to avoid their mom until he'd returned from The Forks. She'd have questions, and he'd feel better tackling them if Dez was with him. But he found himself wishing he had the dog at his side as he gained the main floor to find the house eerily quiet.

There were two kinds of quiet in Ravenwood: the natural kind you'd find in any empty house, and the gathering storm kind of quiet. This was the latter, a silence so deep you could have heard a pin drop. No creaking floors, no scratching, not even the sound of wind pressing against the remaining windows.

It got like this just before Ned unleashed his fury on an unsuspecting intruder.

Sully decided he'd make this quick.

He headed for the parlour and searched the bookshelves and

the mantle for the device before recalling he'd used it to charge his phone next to his makeshift bed last night. It was still there, on the floor next to the chairs, and he picked it up and pocketed it before turning for the door.

A clamour from the front hall drew him up short, the clang of something heavy and metallic, the sound of glass breaking, something heavy impacting on a wall or table.

Hurricane Ned had begun.

This time, the intruder wasn't Dez.

Sully scanned the room until his eyes settled on the wrought-iron poker laid across the brick base of the fireplace. Having placed his bag and the dog food quietly on the floor, he grabbed the poker in a two-handed grip and stood to one side of the door-way. The door was open, and he didn't try to close it, the creak likely to give him away. Standing motionless, he held his breath and tried to slow his rapid pulse to allow him to better hear an approaching enemy.

Another clatter from the hall, another heavy object thrown, wood on wood this time.

It was followed by a high-pitched squeak. Female not male. No second voice, nothing to indicate more than one human presence.

Curiosity got the better of him. He peered around the edge of the doorframe but saw nothing in the short hall. He'd have to make his way toward the entrance hall to see anything.

Keeping the poker hefted baseball-bat style, Sully left the room, putting his back to the wall and edging alongside it, foot over foot as he inched forward.

Another solid throw by Ned resulted in a louder shriek this time. It was close, close enough he thought he'd probably be able to see the woman if he peered around the corner.

Keeping his weapon at the ready, Sully peeked into the entry hall.

What he saw had him lowering the poker and leaving his place of concealment.

"Quit it!" he called out to Ned. "She's not a threat!"

He'd first met Phoebe Waters two years ago in Lockwood, back when he was just a visitor looking for answers regarding Harry Schuster. Like Emily Crichton, Phoebe was tiny and had large glasses that magnified her eyes, contributing to her nickname, Snowy the Owl. But Sully had learned there was more to Snowy's moniker than mere appearance. She had a certain wisdom to her, an all-seeing aspect that made her different from many other patients inside the institution. She'd been a friend of Harry's, not just because her ingrained empathy drew her to the desperate man, but because she was like him. Snowy had a gift, the kind of gift that had made her a target to men like Gerhardt and Lowell.

The time Sully had spent as a patient there was mainly lost to the haze of drugs, but he remembered Snowy talking to him in those in-between moments when his family or Ara weren't there. He couldn't always respond, but her presence had been a comfort —a far more substantial comfort than what she was clearly experiencing now.

Snowy was, he believed, somewhere in her late sixties, although it was possible her time at Lockwood had aged her prematurely. Regardless, she had achieved a yoga-like posture on the floor, curled up on herself like a turtle as she anticipated further ghostly attacks.

"Sully?" she asked, voice quaking from within the helmet her arms had created around her head.

"It's okay, Snowy. He usually listens to me."

"Usually?"

Sully chuckled, hoping the sound would ease her anxiety, before approaching her and offering a hand. She peered up at him, one large eye visible through a space at her elbow's crook, then slowly extended the arm to take his hand.

Having helped her to her feet, Sully guided her through the house to his room. He waited until they were inside to encase her in a gentle hug.

"I can't believe it's you," he said. "I thought you must be dead."

"And I assumed *you* were," she said. "It wasn't until recently I learned otherwise. I *heard* you, when you went to Dr. Gerhardt's old house. Terrence and I, we've been staying in a house near that one, and I knew you were there."

The word "heard" for Snowy meant something different. She had the ability to read thoughts. It wasn't perfect, she'd once told him, but it worked very well with other psychics, those whose minds were already more open. It was how she'd been able to communicate with Harry and to complete the rudimentary drawings giving voice to his visions when he no longer could on his own.

"I'm sorry we didn't come to your assistance," she went on. "We saw those men enter, and Terrence went to help, but he came back a minute later and said you had it well in hand. He was impressed, and he doesn't impress easily."

"Terrence?" he asked.

"I'm sorry, you didn't know, did you? Terrence Waters. You met him, I understand, around the same time you met me. He was medically discharged from the Armed Forces, and he managed the army surplus store. He told me you helped him with his friend, the one who was killed in the explosion. Terrence is my son."

"What? Seriously?" Sully considered the information. "I always figured something must have happened to you in Lockwood, but it was Terrence, wasn't it? He helped you escape."

"He has skills that come in very handy. I'm sorry we weren't able to help you too. It needed to be a 'quick extraction.' His words. There just wasn't time."

"You don't need to explain. I understand. Where is he now?"

"Outside, keeping watch near the front gate."

"It would be great to see him."

"He won't come in here. Ghosts spook him too much. I don't share that fear—except for the one I've just met."

"He has that effect on people. How'd you know I was here?"

"After you and your brother left the Gerhardt place, Terrence and I tailed you back here. I'd hoped to speak with you, but Terrence talked me out of it. Your brother is nephew to Lowell Braddock, the man who forced my son into hiding. It was what brought him to break me out of Lockwood when he did. He's convinced Lowell tried to kill him, and he said he was a walking target. He decided starting over somewhere else would be necessary, but he didn't want to leave me behind."

"He's a good son."

"He is. Anyway, I've been working on him since last night and finally convinced him to let me come back to talk to you."

"Good timing," Sully said. "I'd actually just been packing up to leave. I'm going to stay at Dez's place in Riverview."

"You're certain that's safe?"

"I can't say this is safe either. The threat of break-ins and attacks like the one last night are always there."

"But on the outside, there's Lowell," Snowy said. "You know what he is. I'm sensing that from you."

"I do know what he is," Sully said. "But he thinks I'm dead, and I doubt he even knows where Dez's apartment is. I'll be fine there. Anyway, if I stay at Ravenwood much longer, Dez will be the bigger threat. He'll kick my ass."

"I wasn't thinking of you staying here alone. I meant for you to come back with Terrence and me. You could stay with us. It would certainly give Terrence a break if he didn't feel he has to keep a constant watch."

"I'd be happy to help, but with what I'm working on now, there's a good chance the end result will mean all of us can leave The Forks forever and go back to our real lives."

Snowy fell silent, and Sully sensed her mind working away. It was a little creepy, her picking away at his private thoughts, but he reminded himself he had nothing to conceal anymore.

"There's a reunion tomorrow at Lockwood," she said. "You're planning to attend."

"I'm trying to—"

"I know what you're trying to do, and it's admirable. But it might also be stupid. Why would you go back there?"

"The answers I need might be there. Anyway, I have to deal with what happened at Lockwood. The sooner I do that, the stronger I'll be to handle Lowell when that fight comes."

"What if it goes the other way? What if you can't handle the memories of the torture you endured?"

Sully shrugged. "Maybe it won't go so well. But my brother will be nearby and so will a couple of friends. I won't be alone."

"One thing about trauma, Sullivan. When we're trying to find our way through it, we are always alone. Do you really think it will be worth the risk? Are you so certain Dr. Gerhardt will buckle to your demands if you solve what happened to his son?"

"I'm hoping so. What about you? You've had the opportunity to look inside his mind, haven't you?"

"I tried once or twice," she said. "But he's a closed book to me. He's built walls a mile thick, and short of drugging him, I can think of no way to penetrate his mind. Nor would I want to. There's a real darkness inside him, and I've been trying my hardest to stay away from the dark. We both know where his thoughts run, Sullivan. No need for a mind reader there."

"I guess I was really wondering whether he killed his wife. Did you know her? Eloise, I mean?"

Snowy shook her head. "She was before my time at Lockwood. I was there perhaps a decade, long after everything happened with his family."

"A decade?" Sully asked. "I didn't know it was that long. How did you deal with it, with the Blue Room?"

"I wasn't taken there that often, actually," she said. "A gift like mine wasn't going to prove useful to the doctor and, quite frankly, I made him anxious. He didn't need a person who read minds. I would be of little use to him unless he could place me next to someone he believed held some answers. With what you can do, you're far more valuable. You'd be able to see his son in the afterlife."

"All these years, all of his torturing psychics to find answers, and he's never gotten them. Why?"

Snowy's brow furrowed. "I don't know. It might be, though, there are some answers we're never meant to receive. What about you? I can tell there are answers you're still seeking. You're wondering about Harry, about the vision he had that led to the little Braddock boy's drowning."

"I was told Harry foresaw Aiden bringing down this group called the Circle. Do you know anything about that?"

"Harry thought about it frequently. He never got over it, that his prophesy was used to justify the murder of a young child."

"Why did he say it then? Why not keep it to himself?"

Snowy's responding smile was a sad one. "He didn't often have a choice in what he said. His prophesies would come while he was in a trance-like state. When he was still at home with his wife, he was known for wandering around the neighbourhood, muttering things. Some people believed he was sleepwalking because he was so unresponsive. Betty used to visit Lockwood, and we'd talk. She told me she'd finally had to lock the bedroom door at night and nail the windows shut to keep him from getting out. It got especially bad after his first stroke. She also used to hear him talk about the vision he called 'River Boy.' Whenever he thought too hard about it, he'd end up depressed for days. Betty didn't know the whole story, and Harry, in one of his lucid moments, begged me never to tell her. He didn't want her to know he had a hand in such a cold-blooded crime."

"Betty and their son assumed Harry's vision was him looking back into the past, but it wasn't," Sully said. "He predicted something far earlier, something big enough to lead to the murder of a five-year-old kid."

"He foresaw the downfall of the Circle. It was another recurring vision of his. Whenever it would enter his mind, he'd mutter the words, 'second son,' over and over."

"And you saw the vision?"

Snowy nodded. "I saw what he saw: a man, his face in shadow, standing over members of the Circle. A few of them were dead, some injured, others were pleading for their lives. It ended with the survivors in prison cells. You can imagine why an image like that would cause panic."

"What does it have to do with this second son thing?"

"The prophesy was that the downfall would be brought about by the second son of a member of the circle. You can imagine the pandemonium that must have created. How many members back then would have had more than one son? How many must have looked at their children and wondered?"

"But Aiden wasn't the son of a member," Sully said. "He was Lowell's nephew."

"Did Lowell ever have children of his own?"

Sully shook his head. "No."

"So maybe he viewed Desmond and Aiden as his own children. I don't know. Whatever it was, Aiden was considered a threat, and a big enough one that the council ordered his death."

"So Harry must have zeroed in on Aiden then," Sully said. "I can't imagine the council ordering everyone to kill their kids. That would have been insane, and it would have attracted a hell of a lot of police attention, even if the deaths had been made to look like accidents."

"I know Harry did foresee something more specific as to the identity of the second son. But I don't have all the answers. You'd need Harry for that, and he's gone."

"Maybe I can find him."

"Maybe. But I doubt you'll get him to talk about it. Like I said, he carried a great deal of shame over it. It was only because of the strength of my gift that I was able to see inside his mind, even without his willing it."

"I'll do my best," Sully said. "My abilities seem to be getting stronger too."

"I can't go with you to Lockwood," Snowy said. "But Terrence and I will be here if you need help down the road. Please let us know."

"I will. Thanks." Sully checked the time on his cellphone screen. He'd decided not to risk driving Emily's car. One taillight was burned out, and getting pulled over was not an option. Dez might be done by now with whatever he was doing with Lachlan and could pick him up.

"You need to go," Snowy observed. "I should go too—if you wouldn't mind seeing me to the door. I'd rather not be alone here after all that activity a few minutes ago."

Sully led her back toward the front door and returned her subsequent embrace.

"It was good to see you," she said. "You take care of yourself, and make sure to call on us if you need help."

"I will," he said. "Thank you."

She released him, but continued to hold him in a narrow-eyed gaze.

"I understand your need to find answers and a way out of this half-life you're living," she said. "But be certain the truths you are after are ones you can handle."

She left without awaiting a response.

16

DEZ WAITED in the rear parking lot of a defunct business in the warehouse area, keeping to his spot behind the wheel as he waited for Sully.

A few minutes passed, and Dez was considering calling his brother again when he finally saw him jogging over from the direction of the riverbank—without his dog.

"Where's Pax?" Dez asked as soon as Sully had put his belongings in the back and dropped into the passenger seat.

"I couldn't take Emily's car because of the taillight," Sully said. "And I decided I didn't want to be anywhere near Mom and her questions until you were there to help me field them."

"You realize the questions are only going to be worse once she sees me, right?"

Sully's discerning gaze covered Dez's face before drifting to the rest of him. "You don't look as bad as you did last night. The swelling's gone down on your head, and your eye's not as black as we thought it might get."

Dez checked out the eye in the rearview mirror. "It's still black underneath," he said. "Mom's going to ask."

Sully smirked. "I could go in first, sneak out some of Eva's makeup for you. Bit of foundation, maybe some lipstick and mascara, you'd be a whole new you."

Dez was about to backhand Sully in the gut when he remembered the injury. He settled for a light smack to the back of his brother's head.

"If you're finished being a dipshit, I'll fill you in on the meeting Lachlan and I just had," Dez said.

"Who was it?"

"Paul Dunsmore. You remember Paul. You almost drowned in his basement."

Sully rolled his eyes. "Yeah, I remember. How is he? What did he tell you?"

"He's good, and he had a few interesting things to say." Dez filled Sully in on the meeting, detailing Paul's involvement in the Circle and the man's thoughts on Lowell. "He's willing to give us a hand, be our eyes and ears inside the Circle."

"Is that safe?"

"Probably not, but nothing feels safe to me anymore. One thing in his favour, anyway: His father is among the founding members, and being one of the richest men in town, he holds some clout around there. Any murderous Circle member would think twice about going after Paul if it means upsetting his father."

"Okay, so—"

Dez cut in. "Hang on. One more thing you should know. The masked man in the Blue Room you talked about? Paul thinks it was his father."

Sully's head snapped fully toward Dez. "What?"

Dez nodded. "Paul says his father is basically Lowell's partner, and that he's been investing heavily in LOBRA from the start. He said Ray Dunsmore is a hands-on kind of guy. He would have wanted to be there to see the experiments in action."

"Hackman told us all he knew about the guy in the mask was that he was an investor," Sully said. "What Paul told you makes sense. And if it was Ray Dunsmore, I get the mask thing. What they were doing was wrong on multiple levels. If anyone found out what he was involved in, he'd be finished."

"I know. It does make sense—as much as anything makes sense to me anymore. How about you? You get everything out of Ravenwood?"

"Yeah, and I got more than I bargained for. I ran into Snowy."

"Snowy? You mean the Lockwood patient who looks like an owl? The one you thought died there?"

"Yeah. It turns out her son helped her escape. Terrence Waters, the guy who—"

"I remember him," Dez said. After the playground fight with the war vet, Dez would have a hard time forgetting. "He's her son? Did you see him too?"

"No, he was apparently keeping watch outside. Anyway, he had to go into hiding because of Lowell."

"Because of the break-in at the Black Fox?" Dez asked. "He thinks Lowell wants to kill him over that?"

"Probably more that Terrence can point police toward Lowell in Betty's murder," Sully said. "And Snowy told me Lowell already tried to kill him."

"How?"

"I don't know. I didn't get to talk to him. He wasn't all that eager to have Snowy speak with me in the first place, given our family connection to Lowell. I think I managed to convince her there's no love lost there."

An idea occurred to Dez, one he wasn't sure he wanted to put out there. He did anyway. "I was thinking, you know how police are looking into the possibility of the judge killer being ex-military?"

"It's not Terrence," Sully said. "He told me once he doesn't have it in him to kill anymore, and I believe him."

"He's also a man who was under significant threat from a member of the Circle."

"Yeah, but a different member," Sully said. "It was Lowell he was worried about, not the judge."

"I know. I'm just saying it's something we should keep in mind."

"Okay, I hear you." Sully paused, and Dez could sense something within the silence—something Sully wasn't sure how to say. "There's something else Snowy told me, about the prophesy Harry had that led to what happened to Aiden. I think we need to talk to Mom about it. Do we have time to go over there now? She's still at your place, right?"

"Should be, yeah. What about this prophesy? What did she tell you?"

No way Dez was waiting until he was all the way home before hearing the details. Not when it came to this.

Sully didn't argue the matter. "Harry called it 'second son.' The prophesy involved the second-born son of a member who takes down the Circle. Harry saw the man standing over Circle members, some dead, others injured. The survivors ended up in prison."

"And this man, that was Aiden?"

"Possibly. The man's face was in shadow. Harry couldn't identify him."

"Hold on. So Harry didn't know who the guy was, but Lowell killed Aiden anyway? What, just in case?" The thought of it, of Lowell holding his little brother under the waters of the Kettle Arm, all because of some goddamn prophesy—let alone one without any real detail—got his stomach knotting and blood boiling.

"Snowy said Harry zeroed in on Aiden later on, but she didn't have any more detail than that."

"It's a good thing Harry's already dead," Dez growled. "If he wasn't, I'd fucking kill him."

"No, you wouldn't," Sully said. "Anyway, it wasn't really his fault. He couldn't control the things he saw or the way he voiced them. He was basically in a trance when they came. Snowy said he felt really guilty the rest of his life because of Aiden."

"Good."

"Dez."

"Okay, okay. But he's still the starting pistol in this whole thing. If it wasn't for him getting this thing going, Aiden would still be alive."

"Harry might have seen what he did, but it was Lowell who chose to act on it. Orders or not, he made the choice."

"I know that, Sully, all right?" Dez had snapped the words, and he ended by taking a deep breath, searching for calm in a world that had stolen it from him. "Sorry. It's not you I'm angry with."

"I know. I get it."

Dez blew out one more breath, but the tension abated only a little, his fingers still tight enough around the steering wheel to make his knuckles sore. "Guess we'd better get going."

"I was thinking," Sully said. "Harry could still be around somewhere. If I can find him, I'm hoping I can get more detail on those visions. Maybe he could even show them to me."

"But you haven't seen him for a couple of years, right? You thought maybe he and Betty crossed over or whatever."

"Maybe they did. Maybe they didn't. I won't know until I look."

"One thing at a time," Dez said. "Let's deal with the Gerhardt mess first. If we're going into Lockwood tomorrow, I don't want our attention divided."

Sully nodded. "I hear you. Okay, we'll deal with the whole prophesy thing later. Maybe we should hold off then on talking to Mom about it."

"Probably a good idea. But we can't really hold off much longer on going back there." He unfolded the driver's side visor, scanning his reflection in its mirror, as if he might look different in this one than the rearview. He didn't. "Damn."

Dez met Sully's eye. "What you said about Eva's makeup? Maybe I really would look good in foundation."

"Ow."

"Stop being such a baby."

Dez did his best to sit still in the SUV's driver's seat as Eva applied what she'd called concealer to his under-eye area. Sully had gone inside Dez and Eva's to keep their mom occupied, and Eva was thankfully on a day off. She was also much cooler about Dez and his injuries than his mom was likely to be.

At last, Eva sat back to check out her work.

"How's it look?" Dez asked, not sure he wanted to see.

"Much better." Eva smiled coyly at him. "You look really pretty, actually. Wanna get in the backseat?"

Dez quirked up the side of his mouth and moved in for a kiss. He succeeded in a light lip-lock, but found himself shoved back when he tried to deepen it.

"Don't," Eva said with a smirk. "You'll smear your makeup."

Dez growled and turned to check out his reflection. It didn't look as awful as he thought it would. Honestly, he could barely tell he was wearing makeup. The best part was the black eye was barely noticeable now. Eva had also touched up the lump on the side of his head, a bruise on his jawline and a few scrapes on his knuckles. It wasn't perfect, but he was nowhere near as startling.

"Thanks, babe. That looks pretty good, actually."

"I know," she said. "I'm the best."

Eva slid out of the SUV and Dez joined her, taking her hand as they crossed the driveway toward the front door. "I'm bringing Sully upstairs to check him out next," Eva said. "Keep your mom busy."

"I already checked him. I would've taken him to the hospital, but that's not possible. Besides, it all looks good for what happened to him."

"Yeah, well, I don't trust your judgment. With guys, as long as things aren't oozing green pus or spurting blood across the room, you figure everything's okay."

Dez shrugged. He figured he'd been careful enough, but no sense arguing with Eva. He'd only end up paying for it later.

They found Sully and Mara in the kitchen, Pax sitting flush against Sully's thigh as if to show he wouldn't allow any further separation.

Eva plucked at Sully's sleeve as an indication to follow. "Come here. Something I need to talk to you about."

Sully turned slightly panicked eyes on Dez as he stood from the table. It was clear he thought he was in trouble. Dez smirked, not about to tell him any different.

With Sully and Eva gone, Pax at their heels, Dez joined his mom at the table.

"What happened to your eye?" she asked.

Dez huffed out a breath. "It's fine."

Mara reached out for his face, and Dez sat back to avoid a touch that would smear anything. "It's fine, Mom."

"Okay, but I'd still like to know what happened."

"Got in a bit of a scuffle. No big deal."

Mara sat up a little straighter. "With Lowell?"

"No, we haven't gone anywhere near him. Don't worry."

"Sully told me you two are planning on going to Lockwood tomorrow."

Dez's stomach dropped. "He told you that, huh?"

"I didn't give him much choice. Something was clearly on his mind, and he's never been very good at lying to me. I pulled it out of him."

"Yeah, we're planning to go. It's a good in for us. Sully was going to go anyway. The way we've arranged it, I'll be there too."

"If they'll let you in."

"The front gates are open during the day, and they'll definitely be open tomorrow. And my understanding is they're having most of the events on the grounds, not inside. It's supposed to be fairly warm tomorrow, so it should work out."

Mara sat forward. "I meant the doctor isn't likely to allow you to stick around once he sees you. And he *will* see you. You're hard to miss, even in a crowd."

"I'm going with Lachlan. Once Gerhardt realizes why we're there, he should prove more cooperative."

"I think you're missing a very good opportunity," Mara said.

"Which is?"

"Me. No offence to you, kiddo, but I think it's far more likely Gerhardt will talk to me than to you and Lachlan, don't you think? I'm a mother who's buried two sons. I understand better than anyone what he's been through. It could be what you really need here are kid gloves. And you, Dez, don't own any."

"I don't like the idea of you going in there."

"Tough. I don't like the idea of the two of you going in there, but you are anyway. Face it, I might well be the best chance you have for getting answers out of that man."

"You sure you can, you know…?"

"Hold it together around him?" Mara smiled. "Dez, if you can manage to keep your cool, I certainly can—even as much as I would like to throat-punch that asshole."

Dez let loose a laugh. "That, I would pay to see." His amusement fell away abruptly. "Are you sure about this?"

Mara folded her arms. "I'm sure my boys are going into a dangerous situation as a means to catch the man who killed my other son. That's all I need."

Dez studied his mother a long moment, then nodded. She'd never been weak, but he'd also never seen this level of determination in her either. This was a new Mara, one who wasn't about to back down to a potential threat. What was more, she had a right to be there, too, front and centre when Lowell finally went down for what he'd done to Aiden.

"Okay," he said. "But you stay close to me."

"You, Sully, Eva and Kayleigh—you're the most important people to me in the world," she said. "If there's a threat to any of you, close to you is exactly where I intend to be."

17

DEZ BARELY HAD time to find himself a comfortable spot on the sofa when his phone rang. Discomfort only grew as he saw Lachlan's name on the call display.

"I swear, he knows the second I sit down," Dez told Eva, next to him on the couch. He punched the talk button a little harder than necessary. "Yeah?"

"Crusty?"

Dez checked to make sure his mom and Kayleigh weren't in earshot before voicing his thoughts. "I feel like I've been beaten by a bunch of nut jobs with heavy, blunt objects. Oh, wait, I was."

"Done with the sarcasm?"

Dez sighed. "Yeah."

"Okay. Then if it wouldn't be too much trouble, I'd like it if you'd drag your delicate carcass over to my place. I've got some info you're going to want to hear."

"Can't you tell me over the phone?"

"No point, because I'm going to need you to drive me somewhere. And bring the psychic."

Lachlan hung up without allowing a response, and Dez simply tucked the phone back into his pocket before gently rubbing at his eyes.

Eva slapped at his hand. "Stop touching your eye. You're going to irritate it."

"The rest of me's irritated. Why should my eye get left behind?"

HE FOUND Lachlan on his sofa, the contents of a file in front of him on the coffee table.

"Christ, Braddock, you look like hell," he said by way of greeting once Dez had let themselves in.

Dez ignored the comment. "Maybe you should start locking your door. You know, considering the reason for your concussion and all?"

"I always keep it locked," he said. "But I knew you were coming and when, so I opened it for you. No sense me standing by the door like some loyal golden retriever until you got here."

No doubt Lachlan's logic made sense to him, and as far as Dez's boss went, nothing else mattered.

"What did you want to see us about?" Dez asked.

"Speaking of 'us,' where's—"

"Here," Sully said, emerging from the entryway. "I just had to take off my boots. They were kind of dirty, and I didn't think you'd want bits of riverbank on your rugs."

"Good call. Sit down."

Lachlan waited until the brothers had taken up spots on either side of him before launching into his find. "I know we basically agreed with the original investigation that the phone call to Eloise didn't mean anything, but I thought I'd take a closer look anyway. You might recall it was her sister who phoned her, taking her out of the yard and enabling David's disappearance. The sister's name was Mariel Kisbey—Kisbey being her maiden name. She was quite young at the time, just nineteen."

"Okay?" Dez said. There was a point here somewhere; Lachlan just wasn't always great at getting to it quickly.

"I did some internet digging, and I found her obituary. By the time she died, you'll be interested to know, she'd gotten married. Married name was Mariel Echoles."

Sully beat Dez to it, his raised eyebrows showing all the surprise Dez felt. "Marc's wife."

Lachlan grinned. "Bingo."

Dez shrugged, then winced as the movement pulled at a sore spot. "Weird connections aside, what's that got to do with anything?"

"Maybe nothing," Lachlan said. "Maybe everything. I don't know. All I do know is we haven't found our answers yet, and any good investigation leaves no stone unturned. Investigators at the time looked at the possibility of family involvement, but they ruled it out very quickly—maybe too quickly. I think we should visit your friend Marc, see if he knows anything."

Dez found himself pinned in an imploring gaze from Sully, who then addressed Lachlan directly. "Um, maybe it would be better if Dez and I went to talk to him ourselves first. He really loves Mariel, and he's bound to be protective. If he gets the impression you're accusing her of anything—particularly something this serious—he'll probably shut down on you."

Lachlan pressed his lips together. He wasn't fond of the suggestion, that much was clear. But he was thinking about it, which said something about Sully's power of persuasion. Not easily would Lachlan agree to sit out a witness interview he'd personally deemed necessary.

Maybe it also said something for his faith in Dez and Sully to do the job that his lips turned up into a slight smile. "Okay. You have a point. But don't beat around the bush on this. I know he's your friend, but he might have answers we need. You have to get him to share what he knows—even if it means getting a little forceful."

Lachlan handed over a copy of Mariel's police statement and the subsequent report before letting the brothers go on their way.

"I'd imagine that's why you didn't want Lachlan coming

along," Dez said once the brothers were back in the SUV and on their way to the university. "I don't get the impression 'getting a little forceful' with Marc is the way you want to play this. Good call, by the way."

"That was part of the reason, but not the only one," Sully said. "Lachlan doesn't know about Marc's empath abilities, and I'm not sure Marc would want to share. Plus, let's face it, Lachlan's personality being what it is, his aura has to be all sorts of colours that would put Marc off from the start."

It was a good point. Marc's ability to read auras allowed him to see right into a person's soul at first glance. Lachlan was a good person, but he could also be a complete dick and a huge bully when he chose to be—which some days was quite often. Marc wasn't likely to spill any secrets to a man like that, much less about a deceased loved one.

Marc wasn't in his office when Dez and Sully arrived on the floor housing the Sociology department, allowing them a little more time to go through the documents Marc had provided. Sully had read them aloud on the way over, but Dez had never been the best at processing information that way. Seated in a pair of chairs outside Marc's closed door, Dez took the statement and the report from Sully and read them over himself.

"They're short," Dez said. "But it looks like investigators ticked the right boxes back then. They even noted she appeared distraught—about what you'd expect from a young woman whose nephew's gone missing."

"I didn't see anything to suggest she knew something." Sully paused, fingering the wooden cross hanging around his neck. It had been a gift from Marc, one not lightly given since it had belonged to Mariel. Sully had his hood up, but Dez could see enough of his face to recognize tension along the jawline. That and the way he was toying with the cross suggested he didn't want to say what he was thinking. He did anyway. "But I'm not sure there's anything here to prove she didn't know anything either. I mean, people with a guilty conscience could be distraught, too, right?"

"Do you really think Marc would have married a woman who had a hand in hurting her own nephew?"

"No, I don't. But maybe the answer's something else."

"Or maybe the answer's what the police thought at the time," Dez said. "That she had no knowledge of the disappearance."

Sully nodded, the hood moving with the motion. "You're right. That makes the most sense. Don't tell Marc I said anything."

"If I were you, I'd take a breath and try to put it out of your head," Dez said. "The second he sees you, he'll know something's up, whether or not you say anything."

Another nod, then the two fell into silence as Dez folded and tucked the documents into his jacket pocket.

Another fifteen minutes passed before the elevator doors opened down the hall to reveal Marc approaching with leather briefcase in one hand, coffee mug in the other and a stack of books and papers balanced precariously along his forearms. He looked stressed, but his eyes lit up the moment he saw Dez and Sully waiting for him.

"Boys, good to see you." Marc reached them, jingling a set of keys on one finger while meeting Dez's eye. "Help me out and get the door for me, will you? I didn't think ahead when I left my office. Essay turn-in day. You can guess how I'll be spending my weekend."

Dez carefully extracted the keys from Marc's overtasked hand and unlocked the office door. Inside, Dez and Sully helped the professor unload his burden onto his cluttered desktop.

Dez scanned the top of one of the papers. "Witchcraft, huh?"

"More specifically, the persecution of women and societal outsiders condoned during the witch trials. Interesting topic. I'm just not sure I'm in the mood to read over this class's offerings. Not the brightest bulbs, if you catch my drift."

"Love to help, but witches aren't really my thing," Dez said. He recognized his foot-in-mouth comment as soon as it had escaped, Marc being a practicing Wiccan. "Present company excluded, of course."

Marc chuckled, then slid into his chair. "Naturally. What can I help you two with? I can see something's on your minds."

Sully shut the office door, then took one of two other chairs. That left Dez the other, which first required relocating a few books from the seat to the desk.

"We're looking into something as part of an investigation," Sully said. "It's about a missing kid."

"Oh no," Marc said. "I didn't hear about a missing child. What happened?"

"It's not a new case," Dez said. "This one dates back forty years. Actually, it's Roman Gerhardt's son we're trying to find answers about. We've just learned Gerhardt's wife was Mariel's sister."

Marc had been leaning forward, his expression one of interest. Now he sat back in his chair, the springs squeaking beneath him. An expression crossed his features for a fleeting moment—worry or fear, Dez believed—but it was gone quickly, replaced by what would be best described as an inscrutable poker face.

Apparently, Sully had caught it too. "Marc?"

Marc's eyes snapped onto Sully's. "Why are you doing this? After everything you went through at that man's hands, you're putting yourself back into the fray? Why? What do you think you're going to get out of this?"

"Answers, if we're lucky," Sully said. "We're getting really close to being able to move on some major players and expose their dirty secrets. Gerhardt might be the key, if we can give him what he wants."

"His missing son," Marc summed up. "You want to expose another human being to a monster like that? What for?"

"We don't even know David's still alive," Dez said. "Let's be honest, most people who take children aren't planning Disney trips. It could be all we find is a body he can bury, but at least it would give him some sort of closure."

"He doesn't deserve closure. We all know what kind of man he is, what he does to innocent, helpless people. Monsters like him are exactly why it's so crucial to teach the subject I do. People like that made the witch trials possible, and if you think it couldn't happen again, you'd be very wrong. What he's been doing in Lockwood, that's a form of torture."

"If it turns out David *is* alive, we wouldn't hand Gerhardt a bunch of info on him just like that," Sully said. "We know better. But here's the thing: We're trying to take down something far bigger than Gerhardt or David or either of us. Gerhardt could be the key, and we're going to have to weigh everything we do against the big picture."

"What are you trying to do, exactly?"

Marc was doing exactly what Sully had expressed a fear about. He was shutting down, closing in on himself. Yet he was their friend, and he was no doubt asking questions because of that existing relationship. If they could give him satisfactory answers, maybe they could elicit a few from him as well. Because one thing was very clear: Marc did indeed know something. And he wasn't keen on sharing.

Dez and Sully gave Marc a full rundown on what they were working on, providing details of the Circle, of Lowell's crimes, of Sully's blood ties to Gerhardt and of their forming plan to deal with all of it. When they'd finished, Marc's poker face had crumbled. Still, he remained silent.

They gave him a minute or two, and Dez watched as thoughts played out in the narrowing of eyes and the deepening of forehead lines.

"You truly believe you can shut down Lockwood?" he asked at last.

"Our goal isn't to shut it down," Sully said. "It does good work for a lot of the patients, ones who aren't psychic anyway. It's just Gerhardt who needs to go."

"To hell, preferably," Dez added.

"And you think Mariel knew something," Marc said.

"We don't think anything," Sully said. "We're just asking the question. She called Eloise at the exact moment David was taken. It's possible a kidnapper was waiting behind the fence for an opportunity, and one simply presented itself when Eloise went to answer the phone. But we need to check into every possibility, including that Mariel was providing an opportunity on purpose."

Marc released a long sigh, one suggesting a difficult truth was about to be revealed.

"What I'm about to tell you is something I swore never to reveal," he said. "I promised Mariel as she lay dying. I'm only saying this so you can make an informed decision as to how best to proceed, given all that's involved." He leaned forward, into arms folded atop his desk. His face lowered, concealing much of his expression. Maintaining the position, he took a long, deep breath and let it out in a shaky exhale. His eyes remained fixed on his cupped hands as he spoke. "When I first met Mariel, I was certain she was the most beautiful human being I'd ever set eyes on. Her aura was incredible, an array of bright colours that told me she was as lovely inside as out. But there was something else there too: a muddy spot that told me she was carrying something unpleasant, something that came from deep guilt or regret or pain. I asked her about it a few times over the course of our marriage as it never disappeared, but she wouldn't speak of it. She kept saying she'd tell me one day, when she was ready. That day came as she was lying on her deathbed."

He stopped, lifting a hand to press at the corners of his eyes where tears had begun to form.

Sully's voice pressed into the silence. "I'm sorry, Marc."

Marc glanced up, catching Sully's eye. "I know. It's all right." He took another deep breath and continued, this time maintaining his gaze on his visitors. "Mariel aided in the kidnapping of her nephew. But it isn't what you might think. There was no malice in it, only love. She adored that little boy with all her heart. All of the family did. Everyone but his father, that is. I can't imagine Roman Gerhardt having it in him to care about anyone. Even this obsession with finding the child, it's not about love. It's about control. As far as he's concerned, that child was *his*, his property, his possession, and someone took that from him—and in doing so, prevented his plans for the boy. Don't ever mistake his feelings for anything honourable."

"Was he abusive?" Dez asked. "Was that why Mariel wanted to get David away from the situation?"

"He was a jerk, all right, and he was verbally and emotionally abusive to both Eloise and David. As far as Mariel knew, he never raised a hand to them, but abuse of any kind is abuse. It's something far bigger, something that wouldn't make sense to many people."

"It has to do with the Circle, doesn't it?" Sully asked.

Marc nodded. "Mariel was in university at the time, and she befriended a young man named Harry Schuster."

"Hang on," Sully said. "Harbinger Harry? You didn't tell me that when I came to you with the possession stuff two years ago."

"I didn't think it pertained, and I've explained to you why I've kept this secret. Anyway, Mariel told me she was out for a walk one night and encountered Harry on the street. He appeared to be in a trance. The friend she was with thought he must be sleepwalking, but Mariel suspected differently. Her friendship with Harry had come to include a shared interest in Wicca. Perhaps sensing she was someone who would understand, he told her about his gift of prophesy and how the visions came to him. When she saw him on the street that night, she recognized he was in the midst of that type of trance. Her friend was spooked about the whole thing and left, but Mariel stayed and guided Harry home. He talked the whole way, muttering out a prophesy about a second son. He mentioned the name Gerhardt, and said Gerhardt's second son would have to die to protect the Circle."

"And she bought it, just like that?" Dez asked. "She helped to arrange a boy's kidnapping from his parents over something a guy muttered on the street?"

"I know how it sounds, but there's more to it. When Harry and

Mariel first met, he appeared stunned. He apologized and told her to ensure her mother didn't drive on the night of October thirteenth. Mariel didn't heed the warning, thinking it sounded crackpot. The night of October thirteenth, her mother was going to visit her parents out of town. A drunk driver crossed into her lane and hit her, head on. She was killed instantly. Mariel didn't doubt him again."

"Okay, but we've looked at the file, and we didn't see anything about David having any siblings," Dez said.

"Actually, there was another boy. Gerhardt and Eloise's first son was named Leo. She was almost full term when she suffered a miscarriage during a fall. Some have said that's when Gerhardt started to go wrong in the head, but Mariel told me otherwise. He's always been wrong. We're all aware of the existence of sociopaths, and most people argue it's a mental disorder, at least as far as the ones born that way. But I've always wondered whether it's something else. Most people are born with a soul; I suspect sociopaths are not. I met Gerhardt once. The aura around him, the only way to describe it is like staring into a black hole. There's nothing there. No colours, not even the muddy ones you'll often see in people who have done bad things. There's only one explanation I could come up with."

"Maybe that's why Snowy couldn't read him," Sully said. "There's nothing there. If her connection to people is through the soul rather than the mind, that makes sense."

"For most people, there is a connection between mind and spirit. Not for people like him." Marc's eyes bored first into Sully's, then Dez's. "Now, perhaps, you can understand why Mariel felt it necessary to do what she did. The second son prophesy put at risk the futures of some very ambitious men, Gerhardt included. Someone like him, there's no doubt in my mind he would have found a way to protect himself, even at the expense of those closest to him. The thought of killing one's child makes no sense, not to people like you and me. But to people like him, people who place nothing above the importance and preservation of oneself, everyone else is expendable. If what Harry said was taken seriously—and I have reason to believe it was—David was in very grave danger."

"You said Mariel helped," Dez said. "Who actually took David? Was Eloise in on it?"

"She didn't say. She told me she wanted to share her truth with me, but didn't want to tell the secrets of others. As far as Eloise, I guess it's possible she was involved, though I understand she gave every impression of a panicked mother in the time prior to her own disappearance. I suspect it was the girls' father who actually took the boy. Elliott Kisbey was a very good man, very loving and protective of his family. What's more, he believed strongly in the world beyond our five senses. He would have believed Mariel's story about Harry, about what he'd said."

Marc leaned forward, putting his papers at risk of toppling under the weight of a shoulder. His eyes carried the intensity of a statement yet to be spoken, one he needed to be heard.

"There's no doubt in my mind," he said. "Had Mariel and Elliott not taken David from that home, his father would have killed him."

18

SULLY DROPPED into the SUV's passenger seat, removing his hood once it was clear no one was around to see him. He waited until Dez was settled in behind the wheel before broaching the topic they'd just discussed with Marc.

"As much as I hate Gerhardt, I've never considered the possibility he might have considered killing his own son."

"All this time, we've been operating under the assumption he wanted answers about David because he's a worried parent of a missing kid," Dez said. "Now I'm thinking he only wants confirmation he's dead so he knows his little Circle is safe."

"And if David isn't dead, he wants the opportunity to correct that," Sully said. He met Dez's eye, looking for answers there. "How do we deal with this?"

"Same way we were going to deal with it in the first place. We offer Gerhardt the chance to find the answers he's after."

"But we can't hand David to him if he's still out there somewhere."

"No, we can't. And we won't. All we need to do is gather enough info to do what you talked about doing in the first place: enough to use as a carrot to dangle. If we can convince him we've got his answers, I'm hoping we can get him to give us Lowell.

Honestly, I couldn't care less about the rest of the Circle. It's just the one member I want."

"But you told me what Paul said. They're all in each other's back pockets. If one goes down, especially one as important as Lowell, the rest go with him. You really think Gerhardt's going to bite on that, especially since he and Lowell are so closely connected in this whole drug experiment?"

Dez's lips flattened into a hard line. "When you put it like that…. Hell, I don't know, Sully. All we can do is try, okay? Just take this one step at a time and see where it gets us."

"Okay, but we've got one massive step to take tomorrow, and that's the reunion. We haven't got room to blow it." He'd been thinking something since they'd left Marc's office, something he knew Dez wouldn't want to hear. "Dez, I think I need to find Eloise again."

"Excuse me?"

"It's possible, given what Marc said, she was involved in her own son's disappearance. I mean, if it were my son and someone told me something like that, I'd do anything possible to protect him."

"Yeah, but that's *if* she believed in prophesies and psychics. Lots of people would have laughed Harry out of the room."

"That's another reason I need to find her again," Sully said. "I want to know for sure, and I want to know before we go to Lockwood tomorrow. The more answers we have going in, the stronger we'll be."

"That's if we get there," Dez said. "Face it, man, we almost didn't walk out of there the last time. Hell, I carried you out the last time."

"So we'll be better prepared this time. Terrence is nearby. He'd be great backup. And maybe we can go armed this time. We can ask about borrowing Emily's gun."

"You're really serious about this." Dez turned to Sully, staring out the windshield at the university parking lot. "I don't like it."

Sully knew Dez wasn't talking about his surroundings.

"Neither do I," Sully said. "But it doesn't make it any less necessary."

DEZ PUT his foot down about visiting The Forks that night, insisting they go in the morning. He put his other foot down against Sully's suggestion he stay at the apartment that night.

"You're staying where I can see you," Dez said. "No way I'm leaving the door open for you to make some middle-of-the-night visit to The Forks without me."

With that, Dez drove the two of them back to his house.

After the obligatory call to fill Lachlan in, Sully spent the night on the downstairs couch. He woke in the morning to find Kayleigh next to him on the floor, stuffing balled-up newspaper into a tied-off jeans leg. Judging by the sheer size of the leg, it had come out of Dez's closet.

"Hey, Kay-bee," he said.

She turned to meet his eye and beamed. "You're awake! Good. You can help me. I'm making a scarecrow for the front step. It's almost Halloween, and Mom said I could make some decorations." She looked back at the jeans. "Dad's pants are too big. I'm running out of newspaper."

Sully laughed, then gave Kayleigh a hand until Dez emerged and told them breakfast was ready.

"Can we make some more decorations today?" Kayleigh asked while Sully cleared the table afterward.

"Uh, Uncle Sully and I have somewhere we need to go this morning," Dez said. "We'll try to be back by lunch. Maybe we could make something before we head out again this afternoon."

"You're leaving again?" Kayleigh's lips formed a pout. "You're always leaving."

Dez turned his frown into a smile, grabbing Kayleigh and tickling her until she broke down in laughter. "But then we're always coming back."

Dez waited until he and Sully were in the SUV before commenting further.

"We damn well better be coming back," he grumbled.

SULLY REMINDED Dez they needed to change. First they made a quick stop at Emily's, who took one look at Dez's bruised face and happily handed over her revolver and a supply of extra bullets. After promising to be careful, they then changed into their grungier clothes at Dez's apartment and set out for the warehouse area where Sully had left the boat from Ravenwood.

The mansion was silent as they emerged from the tunnel and made their way through the house. Ned, it seemed, had grown used to Dez, which came as a relief.

Sully was about to lead the way outside when he was halted by a hand on his arm. He waited while Dez loaded the revolver and relocated it from his back waistband to the front pocket of his jacket. The extra rounds he placed immediately next to the gun, ensuring they were within easy reach.

Dez kept his hand inside the pocket after, and Sully could imagine his brother's fingers wrapped around the gun, prepared to draw and fire or even shoot through his clothing should the need arise. He wasn't about to be bested in a fight a second time— a fact that suited Sully just fine.

They set the same course for the Gerhardt house, concealing themselves in as many bushes and overgrown backyards as they were able until, at last, they reached the right block. Once there, they ducked into the same thick grove of trees they'd regrouped in immediately after their previous disastrous visit to the Gerhardt home.

Dez's eyes were on the street, gaze sweeping each of the

houses in turn. "Any idea which house Terrence and Snowy are using?"

Sully was also scanning the area, looking for an answer to that question. The block largely consisted of larger Victorians, but a couple of smaller, more nondescript houses nestled between the larger properties. "It'll be one of the smaller ones," he said. "The bigger houses would attract the looters and the gangsters first, plus there's more opportunity for an enemy to sneak in and take the occupants by surprise. Terrence will probably be somewhere he feels like he'll attract the least attention and where he has the most control."

"Ordinarily, the bigger places would give him and Snowy more places to hide."

"You've seen the state of the houses here," Sully said. "Raven-wood's mostly stone and brick, so it held up pretty well under the weight of the flood. But most homes in The Forks are wood. A lot of them are rotted out, and upper floors are mainly unusable or unstable. Terrence would know that. Multi-storey places aren't much use around here."

Dez didn't debate the point any further. "So which one?"

Sully nodded with his chin. "I'd say the one with the rifle aimed out the window."

"Jesus, what?"

Sully waited the couple of seconds until Dez had seen what he had: the barrel of a long gun, barely visible where it protruded from the corner of a largely boarded-up window. An overgrown caragana bush covered part of the window, making the gun even harder to see, were you not looking for it.

"If that's a sniper rifle, I'm going to have a few questions for him regarding the death of a certain judge," Dez said. "Speaking of, am I safe bringing him up? Do you think he'll come at you again if I open up that can of worms?"

"I don't know," Sully said. "It's possible. But, honestly, I don't see a way to avoid it. You're right. We need to ask, even if I seriously doubt it was Terrence behind it. He wouldn't have shot at me too."

"Your face was concealed," Dez said. "He wouldn't have known it was you, right?"

Good point. And Dez had another one. "The gun's aimed in our direction. How much you want to bet he saw us moving around in here, and he's got a scope on that thing?"

"Only one way to find out." Without giving Dez a chance to stop him, Sully pushed through the bush, exposing his form to the gun wielder.

"Damn it, Sully!" came Dez's protest from the bushes just before he, too, burst through and took up a spot next to his brother.

Sully waited. The gun, for a moment, remained where it was, so long he began to wonder whether it was simply propped there as a warning to passersby. But then, as he stared, it slowly withdrew. A moment later, the front door cracked open. Terrence's face, and then a beckoning hand, appeared.

Sully and Dez ran over, their pace in keeping with the frantic waving of the man's hand. Once they'd been granted admittance to the house, Terrence tore into them.

"What the hell's the matter with the two of you? Last time wasn't enough? Don't you know the kind of assholes hang out around here?"

Sully didn't have a chance to answer or to offer a friendly greeting before Dez jumped in with his own question. "That looked like a sniper rifle you had levelled at us. Was it?"

"Damn straight. I've got myself a small arsenal here. It's called survival in The Forks. Anyway, I didn't know it was you until Sullivan showed himself. All I saw was movement in the trees. Damn lucky I didn't just cap you. Round here, you shoot first, ask questions later." Terrence turned next to Sully. "The other day, the way you tore into those assholes. How'd you do that?"

"Long story," Sully said. "I'd rather hear yours. Your mom told us Lowell tried to kill you. What happened?"

"I got no proof it was him."

"But you suspect."

Terrence looked from Sully to Dez and back again. He said nothing, and Sully didn't need Snowy's mind-reading skill to know where Terrence's thoughts had gone.

Neither, apparently, did Dez. "We've got no loyalty to Lowell," he said. "We want to take that bastard down more than you do."

Terrence held Dez's eye for a long moment. He didn't share his mother's psychic ability—at least not as far as Sully had ever been made aware—but he was ex-army, a man who'd been forced to live hard, to see the kind of things no human being should ever have to see. He'd learned how to read people as a matter of survival, and he was putting that skill to the test now. For Dez's part, he didn't flinch, and Sully watched as the muscles in Terrence's face gradually relaxed, forming a visible dropping of his guard.

"Mom told me what Lowell did to your kid brother," he told Dez. "The little guy, I mean. I just wanted to be sure you were for real, that it was true and you weren't trying to expose me to your uncle."

"The only thing I'm interested in doing for Lowell is fitting him with a nice, cozy prison cell," Dez said. "Or a casket. I'm fine either way."

Terrence's lips parted in a dangerous smile. "Then you and I have something in common, brother."

Dez crossed his arms. "Before we go any further down that road, there's something I need to ask you."

Snowy's voice sounded as she emerged from the hallway. "Terrence didn't kill the judge. He wasn't even on the mainland when it happened."

Terrence met Sully's eye. "Who the hell you talking about?"

Sully took a chance at speaking the name. "Former Justice Prescott Montague. He lost his job after he was implicated in the death of a teenage boy."

Dez finished the explanation. "Then he lost his life after he threatened to blab something about Lowell and the Circle."

Sully scanned the room. No judge. This was a first, one he believed he could safely put down to the reverse possession. Sully had never considered himself an intimidating person, but he'd begun to realize there were parts of himself that were truly terrifying. Apparently, Montague had grasped that too.

Sully hadn't received an answer to his previous question, so asked it again. "What did Lowell do to make you run?"

"Like I said, I've got nothing to say for sure it *was* him. All I know is I was leaving the store one night, locking up in the back alley, and someone took a shot at me. Then a second. I ducked for cover behind my truck and called it in, but police found no sign of anyone by the time they got there."

"What makes you think it was him?"

"No one else I know has cause to go after me. Lowell paid me to break into the Black Fox the night before Betty Schuster was killed and then her house afterward. I figured later it was a way to try to set me up for a fall if someone started to put two and two together. But I guess that wasn't enough. I might decide to rat him out, after all. I was a loose end he couldn't afford to have hanging around."

Sully's heart sank. "So you didn't actually see him take those shots. You don't have any actual evidence against him?"

"Only what my gut's telling me. That's enough for me."

Unfortunately, it wouldn't be nearly enough for an investigating officer, nor for a court of law. And the additional reality wasn't lost on Sully either, that Terrence's word wouldn't stand on its own against Lowell. Terrence was a medically discharged soldier with a significant psychological chip on his shoulder, and a man who'd agreed to commit break-ins in exchange for a payout. He wasn't what a court would readily deem a reliable witness. It might be his word would be helpful down the road, but it wouldn't be nearly enough on its own.

It was looking more and more like they'd need Gerhardt.

Sully's gaze shifted to the window overlooking the street. The sniper rifle rested there, its business end propped up against the windowsill. "Any chance you can use that to cover us, Terrence?"

"For what?"

"Dez and I need to go back into the old Gerhardt place. His wife's ghost is there and I need to ask her about something. I'd rather we not get taken by surprise."

Terrence shook his head. "I can't leave my mother here for that long, unguarded. There are too many bad people around here."

"I was thinking more along the lines of you covering us from here, maybe firing a warning shot if you see anyone approaching."

Terrence nodded slowly. "I can do that. Least I can do for you after everything you helped me with back then."

Dez harrumphed, and Sully could read the turn of his mind. It really was the least Terrence could do. Sully ignored him. Snowy scowled.

Regardless, Terrence did as asked, exiting the house with them and taking up a spot in the caragana bush beneath the living room window.

"Think we can trust him?" Dez asked as he and Sully made their way a few houses down the street to where the Gerhardt house waited.

"Even if he won't go all-in for us, I think we can count on him for at least this much," Sully said.

"He'd risk exposing himself and his mother, and the fact they've got guns there? I don't know, man. He's got a lot to lose. I wouldn't count on him doing what he promised he'd do."

"So I guess we just need to be more careful this time," Sully said. "Keep your gun ready, just in case."

They reached the house without a problem, and Sully, with Dez at his immediate side, searched the main floor for Eloise. She didn't appear, and Sully led his brother quickly through the living room—the site of the recent attack—and into the kitchen overlooking the backyard. The door was off its hinges, its former frame bent with the heaving foundation, and Sully stepped carefully onto the rear veranda lest it not support his weight. He managed it safely, but Dez had to leap off as the boards cracked beneath him.

Photographs in the police file had shown the backyard to be the sort of place found in a house-and-garden magazine, the pristine wild of an English country garden. It had been all tall flowers, sheltering trees, benches and bird baths. A retreat to get lost in.

Getting lost would be a lot easier now. The couple of large elm trees had died, drowned in the flood, but new ones had sprung up in their shadows. Rose bushes—all thorns and no flowers now that summer was long gone—had overtaken large sections of the yard while caragana had sprouted and spread in places once occupied by flower beds.

If David's spirit was back here, he'd be damn near impossible to find.

But Eloise wasn't.

Sully sensed her before he saw anything, his skin prickling and hair standing to attention on the back of his neck as the feeling of her anxiety reached him. Standing at the base of the veranda steps, Sully turned his head to look back at the house.

She stood framed in the doorway, a spectre of blood and dread as her eyes fixed on the garden where, years earlier, her panic had been born.

"We talked to Marc Echoles," Sully said. "He said Mariel told him what she'd been a part of. Did you know?"

Eloise didn't meet his eye, still fixated on the jungle of her yard. Yet Sully sensed her attention was on him, on his words to her.

Sully pressed on. "Did you find out Mariel helped someone take David that day? Eloise?"

Nothing.

"Someone else was involved. Was it your father?"

She didn't move, didn't adjust her gaze.

"Eloise. I know this is hard, but I need some answers if we're going to move forward. Did you know about the second son prophesy, that your son was in danger?" A logical next question came to him—one that suddenly made all the sense in the world given the intensity of feeling Eloise still carried for David.

"Eloise," he said. "Were you involved? Did you turn your back on purpose that day?"

Her eyes snapped to his, wide and full of pain—and maybe, somewhere in their depths, regret.

"That's it, isn't it? Why you've stayed. You knew your son was in danger and that your husband wouldn't protect him, so you had to do it. You helped make David disappear, and you've regretted it since."

He took a step forward, one foot on a rickety step. It creaked beneath him but held.

"Please," he said. "I want to help, but I need you to communicate with me. Do you know where he ended up? Do you know what happened to him? How did you die? Eloise?"

She stared, saucer-shaped eyes boring into his for a long, tense moment. Answers were in her expression, signs of a knowledge she carried but had chosen to keep secret.

Then, just as suddenly as she'd appeared, she vanished.

"Eloise!" he called out, but she didn't reappear.

"What's going on?" Dez asked, voice near a whisper as if reluctant for her to overhear him.

"I know she heard me but she's shutting me out. She just disappeared on me."

"Why? She seemed pretty eager to talk the last time."

"I think it's because I suggested she was involved. That's got to be it, Dez. She's ashamed. She did it out of love, the same way my birth mother was prepared to give me up to protect me. But I think she doesn't know what happened to him after, and she's scared. What if we find out something bad happened to him after? She'd blame herself."

Dez scanned the backyard with eyes that wouldn't see

anything beyond trees, bushes and ruin. "So you don't see him anywhere back here, then?"

Sully shook his head. "No. Could mean his ghost is somewhere else, maybe wherever he died. But it might be something else too."

He met Dez's eye before providing his other theory, one that might, if true, be enough to help Eloise find the peace she so desperately needed.

"I think it means David is still alive."

19

No warning shots sounded, which suited Dez fine.

He'd kept his fingers wrapped around the butt of the gun the entire time they'd been in the house, mind repeatedly drifting back to the incident the day before. The sight of those men entering the living room, shouting the gang name as they swung their weapons, was unlikely to leave his memory anytime soon.

He and Sully made their way back to Ravenwood, waving at the occupied shrub outside the Waterses' squat on the way. Dez didn't see Terrence wave back, but he did notice the barrel of a gun withdraw from between the branches.

Dez didn't allow himself to relax until he and Sully reached the safety of the opposite shore. It was typical, the gun in his pocket the equivalent of an umbrella; as long as you were prepared enough to have it with you, you never seemed to have to use it.

Sully was quiet, which was nothing unusual for him. Even so, Dez had questions coming out of the visit to the Gerhardt house, ones he didn't think Sully had received answers to either.

"We're not much further ahead, are we?" Dez asked as he helped Sully tug the rowboat into the bushes.

"Not really. I'd hoped Eloise would give us the answers we needed. Now I don't know what to do."

"Maybe this isn't the way to get Gerhardt onside. I mean, if David's still alive, we couldn't tell Gerhardt anyway. It wouldn't be right."

"No, but I think Eloise has a right to know what happened to her son, especially if she was involved as a way to protect him."

Dez thought about Sully's own birth mother who, at just sixteen, had risked everything, including her own life, to keep her newborn son safe. She'd handed him to Emily, allowing the Lockwood nurse to escape with the baby while she'd stayed behind to fight Gerhardt. The psychiatrist still carried a noticeable limp, a lifelong injury he'd sustained thanks to a solid kick by Lucienne "Lucky" Dule. She had found Sully soon after her death at the hands of her own family, and she'd remained a nearby presence in his life ever since. But the same could not, it seemed, be said about Eloise.

Dez agreed with his brother; Eloise deserved to know.

But it would have to take a back seat for now. With the Lockwood reunion beginning in just a couple of hours, they'd have their hands full enough.

"We'll figure out the David thing," Dez told Sully. "For now, we have to get our heads in the game."

Sully's ringing phone set them off course once again.

"It's Forbes," Sully said after a glance at his screen.

"Shit," Dez said. "Now?"

Sully answered, he and Dez staying close to the bushes to ensure privacy—not that there were many people around to overhear anyway. "Forbes?"

"Where are you? I stopped by the apartment but no one was around. Your neighbour across the hall said you were out."

"I didn't think I needed to check in with you."

"Whether or not your name is on record, you're part of an active investigation," Forbes said. "I need to know where you're at if I've got questions."

"So you have questions?"

"I want to know where you're at on your side of things. Have you figured anything out?"

"No. Only that it's looking more and more like David wasn't taken by a stranger. We think it was someone who knew him and was trying to protect him from Gerhardt."

"Who?"

Dez met Sully's eye. It was clear Sully didn't know what to say —not wanting to betray Marc's trust—so Dez took over. He was plenty okay with lying to Forbes. "We're working on that part."

"You realize how big a deal this is, don't you? Solving a forty-year-old missing persons case like that, it would be huge."

Now Sully's expression was something next door to panic.

Dez chose his words as carefully as he could. "I hear you. But it would probably be a good idea for you to sit on this one for now. Don't tell anyone else what we're working on. If it starts getting out, we're going to lose our sources, and that gets us nowhere." No point telling him one of their sources was a dead woman.

"You'll keep me in the loop?"

"We know it's technically still an open police investigation," Dez said. "So, yeah, if we get to the bottom of it, we'll let you know. Then you can do what you figure you need to do."

"You said you think it was an attempt to protect the kid from his father," Forbes said. "Why? Is there info the guy was abusive?"

"Not that exactly," Sully said. "There's this prophesy, one we think might link into Aiden's murder as well."

Sully provided a brief explanation, and Dez wasn't surprised when Forbes snorted at the end of it.

"That's crazy."

"Maybe so," Sully said. "But whether it was true or not doesn't really matter. All that matters is people believed it—enough to cause them to justify the murder of children."

"Children? Plural?"

"We're thinking that's why David was taken from his father, to keep him safe from anything Gerhardt or others in the Circle might try to do."

"Do we have a list of people who were members of this Circle at the time of the kid's disappearance?" Forbes asked. "Maybe you've got it backward. Maybe Gerhardt refused to follow orders so someone within the Circle took his kid."

"I don't think that's it, but we'll keep an open mind," Sully said.

"Where are you going with that next?"

"Nowhere exactly," Dez replied. "But Mom and I are going to ask some questions if we can get close to Gerhardt at the Lockwood reunion today."

"You're going? You're not supposed to be there."

"Hey, the gates will be open and it's expected to be busy. I can't imagine they'd grill everyone who's coming and going. In a sense, it'll be kind of an open house."

"I don't think that's exactly it," Forbes said. "They sent out invitations."

"How do you know?"

"We got one. Well, Greta did. She used to volunteer there."

Dez had forgotten. Greta had been volunteering with senior residents—her birth grandmother, Lorinda, among them—when everything happened with Sully at Lockwood.

"Is she planning on going?" Sully asked.

"She's still doing an inpatient rehab program," Forbes said. "She's not going anywhere for a while yet. But since we've got the invitation and all, I thought I might take advantage."

Dez turned wide eyes on his brother even as he responded to Forbes. "You're *going*?"

"Why not? If you're going, even more reason for me to be there."

"If there was any sort of plan by Gerhardt to kill his son, he definitely won't say anything if there's a cop around."

"That's the only reason you're going?" Forbes asked. "Seems

pretty weak. I mean, why go all the way out there if all you end up getting out of it is a pissed-off psychiatrist who kicks you off the property?"

Dez hadn't been planning on sharing the other reason for the visit, but it seemed Sully didn't have similar reservations.

"That's not the only reason," Sully said. "It's also a way to get me in."

"You? For what?"

"We were thinking, Gerhardt's got some secrets he's had to bury, and what better place to keep them than inside Lockwood?"

"You can't be planning on breaking into his office," Forbes said, voice low in warning.

"Not his office," Sully said. "There's an old wing they shut down years back, one he was using to conduct the drug experiments. If there's anything in Lockwood we can use against Gerhardt, any evidence of wrongdoing, it'll probably be there. I found a set of keys at his old house in The Forks. I think they belong to Lockwood. While Dez and Mom are talking to him, I'm planning on finding a way into the old wing."

"You sure that's a good idea?"

"None of our other ideas have gotten us remotely close to nailing Lowell. I'm willing to try anything."

Forbes was silent a few moments, and Dez and Sully waited him out. It was possible, of course, he'd tell them to stay the hell out of it, that he wouldn't allow them to commit what was essentially an offence and risk contaminating any evidence they found they might be able to use against either Gerhardt or Lowell.

So Dez was surprised by Forbes's eventual response.

"If you're planning on going in there, there's not much I can do to dissuade you," he said. "But I'll tell you this much. If you're going in there, so am I."

A PART OF DEZ—a part buried so deep he could deny its very existence—was relieved by the idea of Forbes going in there with Sully. Forbes was a lot of things, few of which Dez had much use for. But he was also a cop, one with definite career aspirations. Dez didn't trust Forbes with much, but he knew the man wouldn't let anything truly bad happen to Sully—if not out of some moral code shared by every decent human being, then because he could kiss his career goals goodbye if he gave in to fear or spite and turned his back on a civilian in need.

As it turned out, there was one more reason to rest assured Forbes would toe the line: Lachlan would be there to make sure of it.

Dez called him shortly after returning to his and Eva's Gladstone-area home, intending to make sure Lachlan was still up for going to Lockwood. No sense driving out of their way to pick him up if he wasn't.

"Of course I'm going," he said. "Even got us a minivan."

"A minivan?" Dez said. "What for?"

"How are we going to get your brother in there, otherwise? Smuggle him in a trunk?"

Actually, that was exactly what Dez had been thinking, but he left the thought unspoken, given the derision with which Lachlan had said it.

"We can cover him up on the floor," Lachlan said. "They shouldn't be searching vehicles either way, but it will look pretty damn awkward, us opening someone's trunk or hatch and letting some guy out. With a minivan, all he's got to do is sit up and get out with the rest of us."

Lachlan's suggestion put Dez's barely considered plan to shame. Dez, though, had an idea of his own. "I'm thinking we should head over in two vehicles. Mom's coming along now, too, and if I get the boot, I'll need a way to get Mom and me home." He gave it a little more thought. "Do you think you're okay to drive?"

"Hell, yeah," Lachlan said. "But why is your mother going?"

"She was thinking she could talk to Gerhardt parent-to-parent, maybe get him to say something useful to her."

Lachlan chuckled. "I like your mom. Good idea. Here's another one: If you and Mara are planning on tackling that, you can surreptitiously record it for me. That will free me up to go with your brother into the old wing. Not that I don't trust his judgment, but I'd love a look around there myself. There are things only a seasoned investigator will recognize as evidence, and there might be some stuff I'll have to keep him from putting his mitts all over. I'd like to have a look without letting the whole world know I was there."

"As it happens, he'll already have a cop in there with him."

"Who?"

"Forbes Raynor."

Lachlan's response was as expected. "Bloody hell. Who invited that schmuck?"

"No choice. He called asking for an update. We couldn't put him off. Anyway, he got his own invite. His wife volunteered at Lockwood for a while."

"Great," Lachlan grumbled, but he left it at that.

Dez found his mom getting ready in the upstairs bathroom, putting on her makeup while Kayleigh watched, riveted, from atop the closed toilet. The little girl turned her gaze on her father.

"When can I wear makeup?" she asked.

"When you're older," he said. "Like twenty-five."

Kayleigh sighed impatiently. "You're *so* not funny."

Dez and Mara shared a laugh before Dez invented a reason to speak to his mother alone. "Kay-bee, could you go set the table for lunch, please?"

Kayleigh took one more long look at her grandma before returning her attention to Dez. She rolled her eyes, uttering her response through a heavy sigh "O-kay."

Dez waited until his daughter's footsteps faded away on the stairs before addressing his mom. "Are you sure about this?"

"Why wouldn't I be?"

"I'm not even sure I want to go through with it. Too much can go wrong. If we don't play our cards exactly right, it'll raise his suspicions. Hell, he'll be suspicious enough to begin with. The first place he'll go is where he keeps his secrets buried. And if we're correct about that being the old wing, he could run into Sully."

"So we'll play our cards right and make sure that doesn't happen."

"It's not just Sully I'm worried about. It's you too. As of now, you're not on anyone's radar. You're no threat to Gerhardt or to Lowell. You going in there asking questions could change everything. Not only will Gerhardt know you've been asking about his past, you can bank on it he'll tell Lowell. The more I think about this, the less I want you involved."

"And like I've told you, I am involved. Lowell and Gerhardt, they've hurt my family in unimaginable ways. I won't let that go, and you can't make me sit it out. We're doing this together, Dez, all of us, and that's all there is to it."

The statement wasn't completely true, as Eva reminded Dez before he, Sully and Mara left to pick up Emily and Lachlan. Sully and Mara had already headed out to Mara's car, giving Dez a moment to say goodbye to his wife.

"I wish I were going with you," she said. "I hate not knowing what's happening."

Dez scanned the living room. Kayleigh was busy with Pax, giggling uproariously as the dog reacted with predictable confusion to her pretending to throw a ball for him. Dez folded Eva into his embrace, pulling from it every last ounce of warmth he could.

"We need to keep Kayleigh in our sights until this is over," he said.

"I know. That's why I'm not leaving her next door and coming with you. But it doesn't make me less worried about you. Be careful, all right? Keep your cool. And if you need to get out without Sully, you do it. He's got Lachlan and Forbes at his back. You need to trust they won't let anything happen to him."

As much as Dez's instincts ran to protecting his little brother, his wife and daughter came first. If Gerhardt reacted with suspicion—or worse—to questioning about David, Dez knew his place was at Eva and Kayleigh's side. The moment the Circle was alerted to the danger of exposure, there was every chance they would lash out. They'd done it before; Dez knew they'd do it again.

"If this goes sideways, you can count on me being here," he said.

Giving her one last squeeze, Dez left Eva, Kayleigh and Pax and joined Sully and Mara.

THEY TIMED their arrival at Lockwood so Dez, Mara and Emily arrived first in Mara's car. If someone was checking vehicles at the front gate, Dez reasoned he could call back to Lachlan and tell them not to come.

They passed through easily enough, no one on site so much as positioned to check invitations. There was a camera there, of course, which was no doubt transmitting video to a security office, but Sully, concealed as he was beneath a pile of clothes and bedding, would be fine if he stayed down.

Dez turned to Emily in the back seat. "You were right. They're pretty lax about this whole thing."

"They'll have security watching the crowds, but as I recall from the last reunion, they didn't have much to do," she said.

Mara was behind the wheel, allowing Dez—crammed into the front passenger seat of the mid-size sedan—to send a quick text to Sully: *No security at front gate. Just camera.*

Sully responded within seconds with a thumbs-up.

Lockwood was reachable only after driving up a long, treed lane, which then opened to reveal a parking area and a wide expanse of lawn and gardens. The fact vehicles were parked on the edges of the lane told Dez the place was already packed with visitors—a good sign for a group of people aiming to blend into a crowd.

"Maybe we can drop Emily off up on the grounds and come back here to park," Dez suggested.

Emily leaned forward, ensuring her response was clearly heard. "Don't be silly. I'm perfectly capable of walking. Anyway, I think Sullivan, your boss and I will be best served going through the woods at the edge of the grounds rather than cutting across the gardens."

Dez glanced back at Emily. She looked tinier than usual, swimming as she was inside a too-large jacket. "You're sure about going with the others into the old wing?"

"Of course. Out of all of us, Sullivan and I are the only ones who have ever been inside that part of the institution, and he was drugged at the time. They'll need me as a guide. Anyway" —she tapped her purse—"I've got a surefire way to get us out of there if need be."

Mara peered into the rearview mirror at the older lady. "What way is that?"

Uh-oh, Dez thought. One thing about his mom: She wasn't a fan of guns. He was struggling to come up with a satisfactory answer when Emily provided an honest one.

"My revolver."

Mara's eyebrows lifted. "A gun?"

".357 Magnum," Emily said. "And I'm not particularly fond of guns either, my dear. But when you're a smaller woman, and you've been the subject of an attempted murder, you rethink things in a hurry."

Dez watched his mother, saw her eyes narrow slightly at Emily. "It's loaded, I hope," Mara said. Dez's jaw dropped even before Emily had provided the answer.

"Fully loaded with .38 Special. And I've got a box of extra rounds in my purse."

"And you're prepared to use it?"

"If it comes to protecting Sullivan or anyone else, I certainly am."

Mara nodded, a grim smile painting her expression. "Atta girl."

Dez coughed. "Mom?"

Mara pulled into a spot behind a half-ton truck and parked before turning to Dez. "I'm not ordinarily a fan of guns or violence, but I'll happily condone either if it keeps my family safe."

They climbed out of the car, waiting the few minutes until Lachlan pulled up behind them in his borrowed minivan. Dez approached the open driver's window and stuck his head into Lachlan's space, catching a glimpse of Sully poking his head up from the floor area in front of the rear-most seats.

"Anyone know about cameras around here?" Dez asked.

He expected an answer from Sully, so was surprised when Lachlan replied instead. "Besides the front gate, there are a couple on the grounds. More are over each of the main doors and there are multiple inside the main institution. Nothing inside the old wing, though. Would defeat the purpose, no doubt, if the demented doctor and his cronies were caught on candid camera."

"How do you know all that?"

"Hey, I checked," Lachlan said. "If I'm going to be sneaking around the place with a guy who's supposed to be dead, I'm going to cover my bases first. A coroner's investigation happened here a few years back after a patient suicide. Lockwood had to provide a list of its cameras and their locations to the coroner's office."

Dez didn't bother asking how Lachlan had gotten his hands on the coroner's file. It was enough that he had it, and this was one gift horse Dez was happy not to look in the mouth.

Lachlan checked the sideview mirror, eyes studying the proximity to the front gate some distance behind them. "Camera was pointed down as we drove in, and it doesn't seem to have moved. And we're far enough it won't be able to make out any distinguishing features even if it does spot us. I'm thinking Sullivan and

I will make our way toward the building through the woods. Won't be any cameras that way."

"Emily said the same thing," Dez said. "She's going with you. She'll be able to show you the best way in."

"Good," Lachlan said. Then, angling his head toward the back of the van, "Ready, kid?"

Dez circled the van and opened the side door.

"As I'll ever be," Sully said as he un-burrowed himself and stepped into the small ditch next to the lane.

Dez searched for some last-minute advice as Mara pulled Sully into a hug. "Be careful," she said. "Don't force yourself into situations if you aren't certain you can handle it. And call or text Dez or me if you need us."

Dez smirked as he ruffled Sully's hair. "Yeah. What she said."

Sully smiled, but the expression didn't come close to approaching his eyes. "I will. Thanks."

"You okay?" Dez asked.

Sully nodded before taking a deep breath and exhaling in a heavy whoosh. "Let's just do this, okay? The sooner we get in, the sooner we can leave. Text me if you can't find Gerhardt or if it looks like he might be headed in our direction."

Dez agreed, then reluctantly allowed Sully to head off without him, Lachlan and Emily taking up Dez's usual spot at his brother's side. Sully pulled the hood of his coat over his head, and Dez knew it would stay there, his brother's defence mechanism in this place.

Dez stepped up to Mara, crossing his arms as he continued to watch Sully's back. "I don't like this."

Mara settled a calming hand on his arm. "Me neither. But here we are." She paused, long enough Dez redirected his gaze to meet her eye. She smiled grimly. "What say we get this over with, hmm?"

Dez forced himself to keep his eyes from drifting to the woods to the west, not wanting to give anything away as he and Mara walked up the lane toward the psychiatric hospital's grounds. As it happened, he and his mom had plenty to hold their attention, the front gardens swarming with games, tables, food vendors and more people than he'd expected, even based on the number of cars parked on the lane.

"Keep your eyes peeled for Gerhardt," Dez said.

Mara chuckled. "Honey, you're six-and-a-half feet tall. If one of us is going to spot someone in this crowd, it's you."

Dez was still looking for the chief psychiatrist when he turned at the feel of a tap on his back and found Forbes.

"Where are the others?" he asked.

"Walk back to the lane and head into the woods to the west. Text Sull and let him know you're coming. They'll wait for you. And for God's sake, don't let anyone see you going in there."

Forbes narrowed his eyes. "I think I can avoid being followed, thanks." He met Mara's eye and extended a hand. "Ma'am."

Mara met the handshake, but her expression remained cold. "Sergeant."

Dez waited until Forbes had scuttled off before asking the question. "Not that I fault you for it, but what's your issue with Raynor?"

"He was a real jerk to Sully after your dad died. It was all I could do not to pop him in the mouth."

Dez couldn't resist a laugh. His amusement died an abrupt death as his gaze returned to the crowd and settled on a figure bobbing slowly through on the side closest to the imposing Victorian structure making up the main institution. Dr. Roman Gerhardt walked with a cane due to his old injury.

Dez had never before been grateful for another person's permanent injury.

Gerhardt had turned on the charm, smile settling on visitor after visitor, going so far as to embrace an elderly woman who approached him.

"I see him," Dez said for his mother's benefit. "He's busy glad-handing."

CHAPTER 20 189CHAPTER 20 189189

"Perfect. He'll have a harder time telling us to go to hell if he's trying to charm reunion attendees."

Dez took a breath and released it through pursed lips. "Okay, let's do this. Stay close. I might need you to yell at me if I try to clobber him."

Dez wove a path through the crowd, glancing back every few seconds to ensure his mom was still with him. After the tenth check, Dez returned his view to the front in time to catch Gerhardt's eyes settling, saucer-like, on his.

For a moment, it seemed to Dez that Gerhardt didn't know where to look, or whether he should stay where he stood. The psychiatrist's eyes darted first to one side, then the other before finally settling on the massive building behind him. Dez pressed forward, eyes locked on his target, noticing the moment Gerhardt recognized fleeing was futile.

Gerhardt extricated himself from an impending conversation with another visitor, resignation on his face as Dez closed the remaining distance.

Crossing his wiry arms over his chest, Gerhardt levelled a glare at Dez. "What are you doing here? I ordered you off this property, and I intended the order to be a permanent one."

"You'll want to hear us out," Dez said.

Only then did Gerhardt have the opportunity to see Dez's companion, Mara appearing from behind her son's significant form.

Something between surprise and confusion formed on the psychiatrist's face. A smile plucked at the corners of his mouth, the sort of grin that didn't know what it wanted to be when it grew up. "Mrs. Braddock. This is a pleasant surprise. What can I do for you?"

Mara Braddock had years of experience behind her as a family counsellor. She knew her way around conflict: how to avoid it, how to extricate oneself from it, how to use it to solve problems. The tension in her jaw and forehead and the way her lips mashed together told Dez she was struggling to remember everything she'd spent a lifetime teaching.

"Dr. Gerhardt," she said at last. "How are you?"

Dez could hear the anger in her voice, the clipped way she'd addressed the man. But Gerhardt didn't know her well at all. From the way Gerhardt's smile broadened just a little, it was clear he'd mistaken Mara's phoney niceties for ignorance. Gerhardt would know Dez had been told of Sully's allegations, but the fact they were here two years later—the doctor still very much employed and the recipient of unearned respect—would suggest to Gerhardt that Sully's claims had gone nowhere and never would.

Dez couldn't wait to show the man exactly how wrong he was.

Gerhardt's hand lifted a couple of inches and hovered there a moment before dropping, a handshake he appeared to have thought better of. "I'm well. And you?"

"Well, I'm sure as a mental health professional, you can imagine," Mara said.

Dez held his smile in check over his mother's burn.

Gerhardt offered an apologetic nod to match the sudden, slight flush of his cheeks. "Of course. Forgive me."

Mara returned a tight smile, polite rather than conciliatory. Truly forgiving Gerhardt was not something she, any more than Dez, was prepared to do. "We heard about the reunion today, so we took advantage of the opportunity to come out," she said. "It's been over two years, and I thought it was important to take another step toward healing. This was the place I'd hoped Sully would find his own healing. It didn't turn out that way, so now I'm here to try to find a way to put the past behind me."

Gerhardt took a step forward, all kind eyes and warm smile. Fake though they were, they presented enough of a sense of reality as to fool the unwary. "I'm so sorry, ma'am. I wish things could have turned out differently. I will never stop regretting it, that the situation didn't turn out better. I know you likely won't believe this, but I did my very best to do right by Sullivan."

"You're right," Dez said. "We don't believe it."

"Dez," Mara's voice cut in, characteristically gentle, yet with the edge Dez recognized as her "watch it" tone.

He bit back further response, opting to allow his mother to play this through.

She returned her attention to the doctor. "Dez has never stopped being angry about what happened to Sully. I can't blame him, but at some point, I would like him to let go of the anger. I have my own to deal with. That's why I've come. I thought if I could find a way to forgive you, I might be able to find some sort of peace within myself again. Does that make sense?"

"It makes plenty of sense, and I want to thank you for that." He looked back at the institution. "Shall we go inside to talk more privately?"

Mara nodded slowly. "I think that would be a good idea."

With Gerhardt leading the way, Dez walked at his mother's side up the steps and through Lockwood's main entrance. He'd come through these doors so many times in the past to visit Sully, had left feeling hopeless and helpless. This time, he reminded himself, Sully was okay and was very much in control of his own fate. With any luck, he was on the verge of finding the evidence to seal Gerhardt's and Lowell's.

Gerhardt guided Dez and Mara through the building until he reached the keycard-coded door leading to the main offices. Dez had been through here once, and the only thing that appeared any different to him was the fact the secretary wasn't on duty—no big surprise given this was a Saturday.

Gerhardt's office was right near the secretary's, a large, wood-panelled room, likely unaltered much since the place was built in the eighteen hundreds. He used a key to enter the room and flicked a switch to turn on the wall lamps. While Mara followed, Dez hung back a few seconds, just long enough to turn on the record function on his phone's notes app. Only once it was recording did he follow the others.

The wall lamps, Dez noticed, didn't do much to brighten the

room, a reality that accorded with his last memory of the place. Gerhardt pulled a cord on a large desk lamp, the light cutting into a little more of the darkness in the process. Plenty more shadows remained in the room's corners, and Dez repressed a shudder as he contemplated the ghosts who might be lurking there even now, revenge on their minds as they regarded the doctor who was far more unhinged than virtually anyone who'd ever lived or died in this place.

Gerhardt slid in behind his desk, waving grandly at a pair of leather chairs reserved for guests. Dez lowered himself into one while Mara took the other, leather creaking as they sat.

"I have to admit," Gerhardt began, "I'm surprised to see you here. After everything that happened, I had reason to believe you might never find it within you to forgive me for being unable to help Sullivan."

"I wasn't sure I'd be able to," Mara said. "But then I learned something about you, something Dez said you told him a couple of years ago. You said you'd lost a son yourself. I know the pain of that sort of loss. Twice-over, I've known that pain. I realize nothing I do or say can cause you any greater harm than what you already suffer every day."

"Well, yes, that's—"

But Mara wasn't done. Nowhere near, as it turned out. "Sully told Dez you took him to a place he called the Blue Room, that you drugged him and forced him into communicating with murdered spirits."

Gerhardt blanched. "Now, I wouldn't say—"

"Let me finish. I understand your purpose in doing so was to try to discover something about what happened to your own son. Please don't deny it, Doctor. Sully was my son, and I never saw him as terrified as he was during the short time I spent with him between his release from Lockwood and his death in that cave. What's more, I saw the restraint marks and bruises."

"You don't understand," Gerhardt cut in quickly. "Your son was very unwell. He was suicidal when he came to us. He was—"

"Possessed by someone. My son wasn't suicidal, Doctor. He had come under the control of a spirit. And I think you believed that every bit as strongly as I did. You thought maybe, with his gifts, he could help you find your missing son, and you were prepared to do whatever you had to do to tap into that."

"Ma'am—"

"Here's the thing, Doctor. I hate you for what you did to my son. I can't think of many people I've hated more. But I'm torn, because a part of me—a part I wish I didn't have to admit exists —can't blame you for it. I'd like to be able to say differently, but if I had been in your shoes, I might have done the same thing. I don't know what kind of person that makes me, but I do know being a parent comes first. It comes above every other thing. I would do anything, say anything and become anything if it meant protecting my children. I have to believe you are the same."

Gerhardt cleared his throat. Shifted a little in his chair. Cleared his throat again. Finally, he spoke. "What do you want me to say?"

"You could begin with the truth."

"You want me to tell you what Sullivan said was what actually happened. But he was a very disturbed young man, suffering from repeated episodes of psychosis in the time immediately prior to his death. What you're saying, it's—"

"Don't insult our intelligence," Dez said. "We *know* what happened, and we know why. We didn't come here looking for you to deny or confirm anything. We came for another reason entirely."

Gerhardt's jaw tightened, teeth working invisibly within his mouth until he finally answered. "Which is?"

"I'm involved in an investigation into the disappearance of your son," Dez said. "I wanted to ask you a few questions."

Gerhardt narrowed his eyes at Dez. "Why would you do that?"

"Why wouldn't I? We're talking about a young child."

"A young child who was my son. You hate me. Why would you help me?"

"It's not about helping you," Dez said. "It's bigger than that. A lot bigger. My boss, Lachlan Fields, and I received information from a psychic, someone who said they saw Eloise inside your old house in The Forks."

Gerhardt shot forward in his chair. "Eloise? When?"

"Recently."

"But she... I was certain, after all this time, she had to be dead." The dim lighting did not hide the pallor of his face.

"She is dead," Dez said. "It was her spirit the psychic saw. He said she appeared to have been the victim of a homicide." Dez described the injuries Sully had detailed, signs of both a beating and a stabbing. "The psychic said she wasn't much older than she would have been at the time of David's disappearance. That suggested to him she'd died shortly after. Which tells me this whole thing is larger than just your son. Whatever happened to him, it could very easily be connected to the murder of your wife. That leaves me with some questions, such as what role you might have had to play in all of it."

With the pronouncement of the accusation, the psychiatrist reddened.

"How dare you?" he demanded. "How dare you sit there and suggest I had anything to do with what happened to my family? You might not believe this, Mr. Braddock, but I loved them. Whatever befell them, and whatever you might think of me, I would never have caused them harm."

"I'm a former cop, Doctor," Dez said. "Every investigation begins with those closest to the victim. You and I have a pretty shitty history, but I assure you, there is nothing personal behind my questions."

"No?"

"No. So I'm going to ask you right out, and I expect an honest answer. Did you have any reason to make either your son or your wife disappear?"

Gerhardt levelled a glare at Dez, his lips forming a tight line that broke only when he opened his mouth to answer. "No. I did not."

Gerhardt had held Dez's gaze. He hadn't wavered in his reply and he hadn't said more than was absolutely necessary. None of the usual lying tells were present. And yet, Dez couldn't shake the feeling Gerhardt knew far more than he was letting on.

There was, of course, every chance Dez's suspicion was based on nothing more than his hatred of the psychiatrist. But it might also be his read was accurate, and that his biggest mistake would be to ignore his instincts.

His instincts told him Gerhardt was in this up to his eyeballs.

"Why don't you tell us your version of what happened?" Dez said.

"My version? You mean the truth? I was at work and my wife stayed home with David. I received a frantic call from her that afternoon, telling me the police were there and that someone had taken David. The police investigated the matter thoroughly as far as Eloise and I went. We were questioned as suspects and nothing came of it, for one simple reason: We had nothing to do with it. Some lunatic sat there, outside our yard, and waited for the opportune moment. When Eloise went to answer the phone, the man took my son."

That story matched what Gerhardt had told the police at the time, and the one that had become the version of events that had gone out to the media. That told Dez the police, at least, had believed it.

"What happened between you and Eloise afterward?" Mara asked.

"What happens to many couples who lose a child. We fell apart. We blamed each other, we blamed ourselves. We grew distant and barely spoke. She didn't tell me of her plans to leave, simply left a note stating she couldn't bear to live in that house anymore, couldn't bear life without David in it. I found the note when I arrived back from work one day, and I called the police. I thought perhaps she'd gone off to kill herself. When she didn't return, I became convinced of it. It never occurred to me she'd been murdered. This psychic of yours, how reliable is he?"

"Reliable," Dez said.

"Who is he?"

"I'm not at liberty to share that info. What I can tell you is that I'm willing to help you find the answers you've been looking for."

Gerhardt sat back and crossed his arms. "And what makes you think I want your help? You've questioned me, my methods, my very character. I've ordered you to stay away from Lockwood, and yet here you are. You've made it very clear you blame me for Sullivan. Why should I trust you with this investigation?"

"Because you have no choice," Dez said. "You've spent years torturing psychics for answers you couldn't find any other way. We're giving you an opportunity here, a chance to finally lay this to rest."

"And you'll do this for me out of the goodness of your heart, will you?"

Dez was about to reply, but Mara beat him to it. "Not after what you put Sully through. We have a favour to call in, and we'll expect some quid pro quo before we turn over any significant information."

Gerhardt's smile reminded Dez of a snake. "Ah, so now we come to the crux of the matter. What is it you're looking for, precisely?"

This was the part Dez hadn't been sure about. How much could they comfortably share with Gerhardt before they put themselves and their loved ones into a lethal spot?

Mara provided another answer, one that made Dez even more grateful for her presence here.

"You carry a lot of secrets, Doctor, many your job requires you to keep. We'd never dream of asking you to breach the confidence of other families. What we want—what we will demand—are the secrets you carry about our family. We'll help you solve your family's mysteries if you help us solve ours."

Mara stood, ending the conversation without awaiting an answer, forcing Dez to do the same.

"We'll be in touch," she said, offering Gerhardt a cool smile.

Then she left the office, leaving Dez to trail behind her. He glanced back as he passed into the hall, too curious about Gerhardt's response to play this as cool as Mara had. Gerhardt wasn't looking at him, eyes fixed upon the surface of his desk. Whether the man suspected what Mara had been hinting at was unknown, but it was clear he was deep in thought about something.

Gerhardt looked up just before Dez could turn to follow Mara.

"Be careful, Mr. Braddock," he said. "You have no idea how far I'm willing to go to find the answers I need."

Dez's lips formed a humourless grin. "Finally, something you and I have in common."

21

CARAGANAS HAD GROWN over portions of this part of Lockwood, obscuring windows and concealing sections of wall that had been allowed to crack with time and weathering.

At Lockwood's inception, this stone construct was the entirety of the institution, with the main building erected nearer the turn of the century. Lockwood had taken advantage of its new space, launching itself into a new era of mental health treatment. It became not so much an asylum as a place of treatment, and it quickly filled its rooms. The old institution, the home of so much trauma—the site of everything from electroshock to lobotomies—was eventually closed down. Sully had heard blame placed on the presence of asbestos in its walls and ceilings, but he suspected the full answer went beyond the structural. This building held secrets, dark ones the modern-day board members would as soon be kept buried deep within the past.

Talk of demolition had begun, but it had yet to happen. Sully suspected Gerhardt, and possibly even Lowell, had something to do with it. Destruction of the old wing would mean the loss of their experimental space. Connected as it was to a collection of human lab rats—the kind who would talk without being believed—there could be no better location in all of Kimotan Rapids.

Sully followed closely behind Emily as she emerged from the shadow of the woods encircling the hospital grounds. Lachlan remained a fixture at the woman's side while Forbes, who'd caught up partway through their trek, kept as far from the private investigator as he could. An obvious friction existed between the two men, Lachlan possessing the kind of investigative brilliance and acquired respect every working cop aspired to. Forbes's own gifts as a cop ran more to dogged determination, the kind of persistence needed to see plodding investigations through to an end. While equally necessary, stubbornness just didn't come with the same star quality as Lachlan's brand of near-psychic skill in gauging the truth behind a case.

The two men seemed to have agreed to put their mutual dislike aside, though, cooperation and silence required as the unlikely group made its way toward the old wing.

Emily led them to the farthest end of the building. From here, Sully could just make out a portion of the grounds toward the front of the main institution, and several groups of people were visible as they talked. The tinkle of laughter was a distant sound, far enough Sully knew he and his companions could speak without fear of being overheard. Still they kept any thoughts they carried to themselves, following wordlessly as Emily led them from the shelter of the woods and into the few yards of open space separating trees from the building's edge.

In her gloved hands, Emily held the set of keys Sully had pilfered from the Gerhardt house as she pressed between a pair of caragana bushes. It sounded like she said something to Lachlan, and he responded by pushing away some branches, enough to allow Emily to move forward more easily.

It was also enough to reveal a doorway lying at the base of a short set of steps, one the bushes rendered invisible to all but the most knowing eyes.

Sully, with Forbes at his left flank, pushed forward, branches poking at his clothes as he listened to Emily's progress. The jangle of keys suggested she was looking for the right one, and it took a full minute before another sound reached his ears: that of a rusty lock being turned.

The door was unlocked, but entry, it turned out, wouldn't be quite so easy. Lachlan slipped on a set of gloves and took Emily's place, and thudding sounds reached Sully's ears even as Emily stepped up to him.

"Something's holding the door shut," she told Sully. "If my guess is correct, I'd say Dr. Gerhardt had the entrances sealed off from the inside after Nate and I helped you and your mother escape back then."

"Probably boarded up," Forbes said. "It'll need a more forceful touch than Lachlan will manage."

Sully wasn't convinced. Lachlan had reached retirement age, but he was far from weak. Even so, Sully joined Forbes in ducking past the caraganas to reach the door. Lachlan was putting his shoulder unsuccessfully to it, and he turned narrowed eyes on Forbes as the younger man tapped him on the upper back.

"What?"

"Let me have a go at it," Forbes said. "Some things need a younger man's touch."

Lachlan's face cracked into a derisive smirk. "Then you should step aside and let Sullivan at it."

Forbes's snort was more that of an angry bull than an amused recipient of a joke. Luckily, he possessed other bovine qualities that might come in handy: Forbes wasn't tall, but he was solidly built, a short wall of bulky muscle.

Lachlan returned to the other side of the caraganas, and Sully stepped back as much as he could to allow Forbes the room to move. The cop gave the door two precursory shoulders that did little before deciding a kick might be the better option. Forbes jammed his hands into a pair of leather gloves, then gripped the doorframe and lifted a foot. One kick—a solid one by any measure—resulted in nothing but a pained grunt. A second one, though it came with a slight sound of splintering, ended in a loudly muttered curse.

"Maybe we can go through a window," Lachlan suggested to Emily from the other side of the bush.

"It won't work," she replied. "The windows are barred."

Forbes glanced back at Sully, his expression a combination of annoyance and his usual brand of stubborn determination. "This bitch isn't budging. How about I shoulder while you kick? Aim for the spot just above the knob. That seems to be where the block is most solid."

Sully took up Forbes's position, slipping into his own set of gloves as the cop contorted his body to deliver a shoulder blow while avoiding any impact from Sully's boot. Then the two of them went at the door together.

Whatever barricade had been constructed on the door's inner side was a solid one, enough to rattle Sully's teeth as his first kick connected. Yet he felt a little give, enough that Forbes turned hopeful eyes on him.

"One more," the cop said. "Count of three." Forbes counted down without an acknowledging reply, and Sully gave another hard boot to the door as Forbes finished the count.

A loud splintering noise sounded, and it took a final good kick from Sully to send the door crashing inward, a large piece of two-by-four clattering to the floor.

"Quiet," Lachlan scolded as he brushed between Sully and Forbes, flashlight in hand and clicked on.

"There wasn't exactly a quiet option," Sully said.

Forbes settled on a more direct response before following Lachlan. "Asshole."

Sully held the bush back to allow Emily to pass more easily beneath its branches. Her fingers found Sully's forearm and squeezed gently.

"Are you ready for this?" she asked.

He nodded, the expression an unspoken lie. He wanted to be anywhere else right now. Until this moment, he'd had little recollection of how he'd been brought down to the Blue Room, but Lachlan's flashlight bobbing against dusty tiled walls had jarred something loose inside his brain. He saw the tile in his mind, softly illuminated within dim lighting as he bumped along a cracked floor in a wheelchair, brain barely aware, body unresponsive beneath the weight of drugs.

Another gentle squeeze at his arm drew him out of the hazy past, and he looked down to find Emily's bespectacled eyes gazing up at him. "Sullivan?"

"I'm okay," he said. "Just remembering something."

"Try not to," she said, then took his hand as she led him gently into the basement hall.

Sully paused to close the door, sealing them in darkness. He located the flashlight feature on his phone, his flash cutting only a little into the press of shadows as he guided Emily inside. A short distance ahead, Lachlan's flashlight had stopped, its beam fixed on the ground at Sully and Emily's feet as he waited for them.

"Where to?" Lachlan's voice was a muted echo on tile, one Emily responded to by moving quickly into the beam, drawing Sully along behind her. She took the light from Lachlan in her free hand, casting it down the hall and on various doors.

"The old treatment room is this way," she said.

The old treatment room. Sully didn't need to ask to know it was the place Harry had called the Blue Room, its sky-blue walls a deceptively soothing colour likely intended to calm unwilling patients for old-school, torturous procedures.

During his own experience at Lockwood, Sully had been heavily drugged, enough that he'd seen or felt none of the ghosts he might have expected to otherwise see in a place so full of trauma. He was no longer similarly limited.

Dimly lit forms emerged from the shadows around him. A woman, bald and drooling, in a wheelchair. A man, body rocking as he sat curled on the floor, pulling hard at shaggy hair. Most unnervingly, a wild-eyed woman, face partially concealed beneath a tangle of matted hair, moving along at his left shoulder, so close he would have, in life, felt her breath on his neck.

He did his best to ignore the ghosts, but the challenge

wouldn't be an easy one, even with his hood acting as partial barrier. These were, after all, only the ones he could see, each apparently the victim of an unlawful death. But there were others, many others, ones who had died whether by illness or their own hand. He couldn't see them, but there was no ignoring the weight of them in this place, the creeping sensation of dread and desperation they emitted as he moved around them and through them.

Emily had yet to release his hand, and he tried to derive what comfort he could from the touch as he forced himself onward.

Emily paused briefly partway down the hall. Her lips parted in the castoff glow of the flashlight, a signifier of yet-unspoken words. He waited, wondering what she was deciding to say.

Finally, she made up her mind, shining her light on a partially opened door. "That's the room where you were born," she said.

Shadow lay beyond the door, the promise of further darkness beyond.

"You were born here?" Forbes asked. "Jesus."

"Do you want to go in?" she asked.

Sully shook his head before she'd even finished the question. No, he didn't want to go in. He wanted to get the hell away from this room as fast as was humanly possible.

Emily must have read the need in his eyes because she immediately turned and kept going, distancing them from the room and the terrible secrets it held. Lucky Dule had been kept against her will there, had been subjected to God knows what while carrying the unborn baby of the man who'd put her there. This place, all of it, was the stuff of nightmares, and Sully wanted nothing more than to burn all of it to the ground.

He hadn't said it out loud, but with Emily, he didn't need to.

"We'll find justice for her, Sullivan," she said. "I won't rest until we do."

"Thank you," was all he could think of to say. The expression of his gratitude was nowhere near enough, not for this little eighty-something-year-old lady who had nearly sacrificed her own life to ensure Sully had a chance at one.

They continued on, putting a few more doors between themselves and the room. Here, they were closer to the old elevator and the stairs that would lead them to the current institution. Somewhere near here, he knew—somewhere near enough to set his skin crawling—was the Blue Room.

Lachlan found it first. Light burst from the room as a switch inside was flicked, revealing electricity had not been cut off to the old wing despite its supposed disuse.

"I've got a treatment room here," he said, head popping out from the doorway to announce the find. Forbes, too, disappeared inside, leaving just Sully and Emily in the hallway.

"You don't have to go in," she said. "We can wait right here."

It was a good thought. As much as Sully hated the darkened hallway and its ghosts, he liked far less the idea of entering that space ahead, the light bright enough inside to reveal in detail the room that held so much trauma for him.

Yet, deep inside himself, he knew he had to face this. It would be easier with Dez, their mom or Eva at his side, but Emily was fine replacement, one he knew he could trust to watch out for him.

"It's okay," he said. "I need to do this."

She gave his hand a squeeze but didn't make a move toward the room, letting him take it at his own pace. Unfortunately, there wasn't a place in existence that would make this any easier.

Sully stepped forward, closing the distance, keeping his eyes on the dusty floor as he moved. In the light, he could see the trail there, a worn path through the dust made by feet and wheels coming and going from the old elevator. He waited until the moment he'd crossed fully into the Blue Room, when the darker tile of the hallway turned to dusty, clinical white. Only then did he look up.

His eyes bypassed Lachlan and Forbes, went immediately to the bed. He knew he was still standing here, at the entrance to the room, but his mind took him elsewhere. He was no longer on his feet, but restrained on the gurney, Gerhardt coming at him with a syringe while Hackman stood over him with a smirk. He was feeling the prick of the needle in his arm, the sensation of the chemical as it flowed into his vein. He was sinking, further and further, fog separating him from the here and now as the drug took him under. Then, with the press of an object into his hand, a memory not his own exploded in his consciousness until, inevitably, he experienced a ghost's horrific, terrifying death.

Panic seized him, robbing him of breath. He heard a voice, then two, tugging on his consciousness, the way he would hear Dez or their mom or Eva or Ara as they sat with him in Lockwood's visiting area.

A woman's voice—Emily's—reached him first, but it was a deeper, firmer one that broke fully through the haze.

"Sullivan, breathe. Come on. You're okay. Look at me. Hey! Look at me!"

He felt a firm grip on his chin and his head being tweaked to the side. A series of none-too-gentle slaps to his cheek. Then, at least, the fog parted, revealing not Emily or Lachlan in front of him, but Forbes.

Sully blinked once, twice, forcing the remains of the flashback from his brain. Somehow, he'd ended up on the floor, seated and curled against the wall. Forbes was kneeling in front of him, Emily standing just to the side. Lachlan stood back near the bed, but headed for the door and left the room the moment it was clear Sully was okay. He had a set of keys in his hand—Gerhardt's keys —and Sully guessed Dez's boss must have grabbed them while Sully was trapped in the flashback.

Forbes, for now, stayed where he was. "You good?"

Sully nodded, not yet trusting his voice. There was something in Forbes's expression, not an unasked question so much as something needing said. As far as Sully could think, there wasn't much he needed to say. He'd already told Forbes about the Blue Room, about what had happened to him in this place.

A few moments passed before Forbes spoke. "My mother. She was a patient here. I've always wondered...."

The admission, trailing off to silence, jarred Sully, shoved his own trauma temporarily into the background. "What?"

Forbes stood, eyes casting over the room. "Do you think she would have been brought in here?"

Sully pressed back against the wall, using it as support as he drew himself to standing. His legs felt a little unsteady beneath him, but they held. "As far as I'm aware, Gerhardt only used this room to experiment on patients with some sort of psychic ability. Did your mother have anything like that?"

Forbes shook his head slowly, but continued to sweep his gaze over the room. "Not that I was ever aware. I was under the understanding she was treated all right here, but being here, knowing what happened to you, it makes me wonder." He met Sully's eye briefly, before his eyes darted away. This time, his gaze didn't appear to focus. "She suffered a severe breakdown when I was a kid. Dad didn't have any choice but to commit her. She had days where things seemed all right, where I'd visit and she'd seem just like she always had been. But I found out later those days were few and far between. She tried to run more than once, but never made it far before they caught her again. Eventually, she found a way to escape so they'd never be able to bring her back in."

Sully didn't ask. What Forbes meant was clear.

"I'm sorry," he said.

Forbes didn't respond directly. His eyes snapped back onto Sully's. "Can you see her?"

Sully shook his head. He couldn't see her, which probably boded well for both Forbes and his mom. But, as he focused, he believed he could sense her, a protective, loving energy near the police detective. "I can only see the ones who were murdered. But I think she's here, with you. I don't feel like she's upset or anything. She's protecting you. Maybe she always does."

A sheen formed over Forbes's eyes, and he turned away to hide his emotion. "Sometimes I think I feel her around me. I always figured I was just being stupid."

"There's nothing stupid about that."

Forbes nodded. "Maybe it's why I married Greta. I knew she had problems, that she struggled with drugs and her mental health. I couldn't fix my mom, so maybe I set out to fix Greta." He chuckled bitterly. "Didn't work out so good, did it?"

"You did your best."

"My best wasn't good enough."

It was the most real conversation Sully had ever had with the man. It ended almost as soon as it began when Lachlan's head popped back into the room. He met Sully's eye before drifting past Emily to settle on Forbes.

"There's something you need to see. Come on."

Sully was happy enough to leave the Blue Room behind, shutting off the light as he tailed the others to a room across the hall and a couple of doors down.

"Don't turn on the lights," Lachlan advised. "There's a window in here."

The windows were dusty, but enough daylight filtered through that they didn't need additional light to see by. Filing cabinets lined one wall and Lachlan drew their attention there. "There are loads of historic patient files in here, most from before the new institution was built. But I found others, those of patients like Sullivan who were taken to the Blue Room. Gerhardt kept notes—enough to get the authorities asking some big questions."

Sully stepped forward. "Is *my* file in there?"

Forbes caught his arm. "Don't. Don't touch anything, either of you. This is evidence. If we start tampering with it, any search warrant I manage to obtain will be pointless if this ever ends up in court."

"You're already in here when you shouldn't be," Sully said. "That's enough to screw up your case."

"Worse comes to worse, I can say I came in here because I saw evidence you people had broken in. But I need a search warrant for anything not in plain sight."

Lachlan crossed the room, walking past a desk until he

reached a large, windowed medicine cabinet. "Is this plain sight enough for you?"

Forbes, Sully and Emily joined Lachlan, each peering through the cabinet panes at the drugs on the other side. Many appeared old, like they'd been there forever. But a handful, vials containing a liquid injectable, were clearly new. What was more, they were familiar.

"That's the drug," Sully said. "The one they gave me in the Blue Room."

"You're sure?" Lachlan asked. "You wouldn't have been in a position to see the markings on the labels, would you?"

That was true. "Well, they look identical, anyway."

"Easy enough to figure it out, I guess," Forbes said. "We can get this stuff tested at a non-LOBRA lab, see if it would cause the sort of experience you described. Leave it alone. I'll ensure the warrant covers this."

Lachlan rolled his eyes and returned to the filing cabinets. He pulled out a drawer, removed and opened a file and started snapping photos with his phone's camera.

"Hey," Forbes snapped, rushing over to Lachlan. "Cut it out!"

There was no lock on the medicine cabinet door. Sully cracked open one of the doors and snatched a vial from inside, dropping it into a jacket pocket before Forbes would notice. He met Emily's eye and the two shared a small, conspiratorial smile as Sully resealed the cabinet.

Forbes was still arguing quietly with Lachlan as Sully's phone pinged an incoming message from within his pocket. He pulled it out and read the text from Dez: *Mom and I finished talking to G. Fill you in when I see you. Cut it short and get out. Will wait.*

Sully sent a quick text back—*K*—before looking up to address the others.

"Hey, guys, Dez just—"

He halted abruptly as a sound reached his ears, something mechanical from just down the hallway.

"Lachlan, goddammit, stop—"

Sully shushed Forbes, drawing everyone into silence until they, too, had a chance to listen.

Lachlan identified the noise first.

"Bloody hell," he said. "That's the elevator." His eyes snapped from the office door to Sully.

"Someone's coming."

22

LACHLAN SLID the drawer to the filing cabinet shut while Sully ran to the office door. The elevator gears stopped grinding as the car paused a floor above.

Forbes appeared, anxiety rolling off him, at Sully's left shoulder. "We need to get the hell out of here. Now."

There was no arguing the point, but exiting the way they'd come was an impossibility. That became obvious the moment they were back in the hall.

"We can't go back the way we came," Lachlan said, pulling shut and locking the office door. "Whoever that is, they'll see us, or at least hear us before we can get back to the exit. In any case, as soon as we crack that door open, the hallway will be flooded with light."

"The stairs," Emily said. "The ones past the elevator. It's the only way."

Forbes gripped Sully's arm and tugged at him to get him moving. "Let's go."

"Sullivan can't go that way," Lachlan said. "It leads to a hall connecting to the main institution. Security cameras are all over the place. If he's seen—"

"Go," Sully said. "I'll find somewhere to hide. As soon as

Gerhardt, or whoever that is, goes into the office or the Blue Room, I'll head for the outside door."

Forbes didn't need to be told twice. The elevator had started up again, grinding slowly toward the basement floor.

Lachlan paused briefly at Sully's side. "You're sure?"

"Yeah." Sully remembered the vial, and pulled it from his pocket, thrusting it into Lachlan's hand. "Take this and have it tested."

Lachlan appeared uncertain but nodded anyway. Then he jogged after Forbes. Emily, though, wasn't moving.

"Emily—" Sully began, but she cut him off before he could protest further.

"I'm not leaving you here alone." She grabbed his hand and pulled at it. "Follow me. Quickly."

The elevator dinged as it reached the floor and prepared to open. The sound was nearly enough to launch another panic attack, but Sully managed to keep his focus and follow Emily as she moved down the hallway in the direction of the outside door. There was nowhere near time enough to reach the exit, and Sully gave it no thought as Emily led him inside one of the darkened rooms along the hallway. It wasn't until they were inside, concealed in shadow with the door slightly ajar that Sully realized where they were: the room where, twenty-four-and-a-half years ago, he was born.

There was no time to protest Emily's choice of hiding place. The elevator had opened and the sound of movement—a shuffling gait interspersed by the sound of a cane against the floor— reached his ears.

Sully's heart pounded in his chest, breath catching in his throat as he recognized Gerhardt's footsteps.

Sully had lost the most intrusive of the ghosts when he'd entered the Blue Room, but she'd found him again, standing immediately next to him as he sought to control his fear. He thought about Dez, wishing he could call him; since childhood, the sound of his brother's voice was often enough to settle his nerves. That wasn't a possibility, but the thought of Dez brought something else to mind. If Dez saw Forbes and Lachlan emerge from the building without Sully and Emily, he'd flip out.

Sully pulled out his phone, retreating to the nearest corner of the room and facing into it, ensuring the light from his screen wouldn't be visible from the hall. It was, however, enough to further light the ghastly face of the patient who insisted on pressing well into his personal space.

Sully turned his face farther into the shelter of his hood and did his best to ignore the woman while firing off a text to Dez: *Emily and I still inside. We're fine. Take Mom home. Will c u ltr.*

He wasn't surprised by the text that followed seconds later: *Like hell*

Sully sent a reply. *Emily has her piece. Will be fine. Make sure Eva and K ok*

The reply didn't come immediately, suggesting Dez was either distracted or thinking. Sully would have put money on the latter. When at last he responded—*K. Keep me posted*—Sully realized he'd won the brief debate. Problem was, he wasn't sure whether he should feel relieved or despondent.

He sought comfort in Emily, double-checking his phone was on silent and tucked away before rejoining her just behind the door. As if sensing his anxiety, she reached for his hand and gave it a squeeze. It seemed fitting, that the woman who'd taken care of him all those years back was here, doing the same thing all over again.

Another sound reached his ears: footsteps, quieter than the first set. They came from the end of the hall nearest the stairs leading to the adjoining hallway, and for a moment, Sully wondered whether Lachlan had decided to return to question the doctor.

What he heard instead almost put him on his ass on the cold, dusty floor.

"Doctor?"

He knew the voice, had exchanged conversation with its owner only recently.

Snowy.

"My God," Gerhardt said. "You have some nerve showing up here after that escape. One of my orderlies is still off with a concussion thanks to your son."

There was a brief pause, followed by Snowy saying, "I wouldn't do that if I were you. I have information I think you'll want. All you have to do is turn the other way as it relates to my son and me. I want us to be able to come out of hiding, and you're a part of that. If you would just agree to—"

"I'm not making any bargains with you, Phoebe."

"Even after everything I did for you? I gave you all of those psychics. I told you who might be able to help you."

"You didn't do that for me. You did it for you. You wanted out of the treatments."

"All I'm asking is for you to agree to turn the other way should you see Terrence or me in future. All we want is a chance at a life, a real life. Now I don't have much time. He doesn't know I'm here speaking with you. He wouldn't approve of what I'm doing."

"Which is?"

"Betraying a man he and I both respect."

Sully's heart pounded against his ribs as Gerhardt paused in apparent thought. Sully knew without possessing Snowy's gift of clairvoyance she was about to sell him out to Gerhardt.

Escape was now more necessary than ever, but it sounded like Gerhardt and Snowy were speaking not inside an office or other room, but in the hall, just a few doors down. Sully could run, and no one immediately present in the basement could catch him. But Emily might not be as fast, and he wouldn't abandon her here. Anyway, there was the problem of all the staff on the premises. Even if Sully and Emily escaped the building, a simple phone call from Gerhardt would have the gates shut and staff on alert before full escape could be made.

They had no option but to stay put and keep silent.

"All right," Gerhardt said at last. "I'll bite. Who do you mean?"

"I need your assurance."

"As I understand it, your son's problems are rather deeper than just his doings at Lockwood during your escape."

"One problem at a time," Snowy said.

"Fine," Gerhardt said. "I won't make efforts to find either of you in future."

Sully wouldn't have put much faith in anything Gerhardt promised, but Snowy forged on anyway. Whether that was suggestive of her claim she couldn't read Gerhardt like she did others, or whether it was simply a sign of desperate times calling for desperate measures, he didn't know. All he knew was what she said next.

"Sullivan Gray. He's alive."

Another pause, one into which Emily interjected with a squeeze hard enough to crush Sully's fingers.

"He died in a cave collapse shortly after his own escape," Gerhardt said. But the tone was slow and thoughtful rather than immediately dismissive.

"I can assure you, Doctor, he is very much alive. I've seen him. I've spoken to him."

She paused, and Sully was left to wish he shared her ability to read minds.

"Phoebe?" Gerhardt prodded.

"He's here," she said.

"Here, as in Kimotan Rapids?" he asked.

"Here, as in right down the hall."

23

SULLY'S STOMACH DROPPED.

Just a few words, and Snowy had as good as destroyed him.

In the dim light from the hall, he could make out Emily's head as she turned toward him. She'd never be able to see him in the dark, but she didn't have to. She'd know the expression he was wearing without having to look him in the eye.

Sully was sunk. But Emily didn't have to go down with him. That was more than he'd allow.

"Stay here," he whispered.

"No."

"Emily, you have to. I need to face Gerhardt. I don't have a choice. Please, just stay here. Keep your gun at the ready, just in case, okay?"

"I'll call your brother." The tone was hopeful, not threatening. But whichever way Sully looked at it, having Dez here was not an option. He had far too much to lose, and Sully had cost his brother too much already.

"No," he said. "This is about me and Gerhardt. Please, don't involve Dez any more than he already is. Don't worry. I've got this."

Emily sucked in a breath but said nothing more, and Sully

slipped past her before she could think up another argument. Nothing she said could change his mind.

He could hear Gerhardt questioning Snowy further, disbelieving. Sully would have to make this quick, confront Gerhardt before he had time to call in backup. If a search became necessary, Emily would be discovered too. Emily whom Gerhardt had already tried to kill once.

Never again.

Two doors separated Sully from the office he'd just left a few minutes ago. Judging by the light coming from the room, Gerhardt had taken the conversation with Snowy there, no doubt to allow him to use the phone.

He could hear Snowy's voice. "I'm telling you the truth."

"I'm sure you believe that," Gerhardt said. "Don't worry. I'll call in some help to ensure a thorough search of the place."

Sully checked his phone, relieved it still had charge. He opened the recorder app and hit the red button to get it running.

Then he stepped through the door.

"You know, you could just search the floor yourself. Or are you afraid of what would happen if it was just you and me, Doc?"

Sully had kept his hood up until now. Now it no longer mattered. He reached up, drawing it down around his shoulders, revealing his face.

Gerhardt's hand had been on a phone sitting atop the desk; he dropped it like a hot potato when he made eye contact.

"My God… My God."

"Not quite," Sully said. He risked turning his glare to Snowy, who stood this side of the psychiatrist's desk, hands over her mouth as if startled by the sight of the fellow psychic. Sure, she'd known he was there, but seeing him face to face, that was a whole other matter.

"I trusted you," he said.

Her eyes filled with tears, and a sob erupted from her throat. "I'm sorry. I'm so sorry. I just wanted it to end. Terrence, he doesn't deserve this."

"Terrence's biggest problem isn't Gerhardt. That's *your* problem. Terrence's concern is Lowell Braddock. Don't try to tell me you coming here like this was all about you being a concerned mother. You were looking out for *you*."

"You don't understand."

"I don't *understand*?"

"You were here less than three months. I spent years in this place. I couldn't bear it another day. I would have done anything to be free of it, but even when I was out, it was still there, inside me. It hangs over me everywhere I go, the idea I might one day walk into someone I knew from Lockwood, that they might drag me back. I thought if I gave them what they wanted—"

"And now? You're fine living with yourself? What about Terrence? What would he think?"

"He won't know." She took a breath, let it out before shaking her head slowly. "I told you to stay away from this place, didn't I? I warned you. You didn't listen."

Sully understood she was trying to lessen the blame, to alleviate her guilt. Sure, she'd said that. But all it would have meant, had he obeyed, was that Sully would have been fighting even harder to conceal himself. It would have meant Dez, Mara and Eva being questioned and threatened in an attempt to pull from them the truth. The fact Sully was here, that he could face this without dragging his loved ones into it, was actually preferable to the reality Snowy would otherwise have left him with.

He had a second thought, about Terrence. If Snowy had come here in an attempt to settle accounts with Gerhardt so she could come out of hiding, what might it mean about Terrence and his problem with Lowell? Terrence and Snowy needed to stay concealed until Lowell was out of the picture. Maybe Terrence was working on a plan even now to deal with his biggest problem.

Now, though, wasn't the time to ask. He'd probably already revealed too much to Gerhardt about the Lowell situation. The psychiatrist no doubt had some knowledge about his business partner's dirty deeds—he obviously was front and centre regarding what was being done at Lockwood with LOBRA drugs —but Sully wanted to hold onto as much as he could for now.

He shook his head. His thoughts were likely as loud to Snowy as if he'd spoken them, and he sought to pull back, to draw the blinds between his conscious mind and the outside world.

"I know it doesn't mean much to you, and I do understand why you must hate me," she said. "But I truly am very, very sorry."

She turned to Gerhardt. "May I leave?"

His answer was a slow nod, and Snowy beetled from the room as if expecting the psychiatrist might yet withdraw his consent and have her dragged back.

Sully fixed his eyes on Gerhardt as the sound of Snowy's footsteps on the stairs drifted away.

Then he and Gerhardt were alone.

"I thought you were dead," the psychiatrist said. "Where have you been all this time?"

"I didn't come here to answer questions. I'm here to ask them. Are you still experimenting on patients?"

"What are you talking about?"

"Don't," Sully said. "I'm not stupid, and I was never insane. I have an ability you and Lowell exploited for your own ends. The experiments you've been conducting on psychic patients, are you still doing them?"

Gerhardt sat forward at the desk, fixing Sully with a paternal smile so patronizing it was all Sully could do to resist smacking it off. "Sullivan, I know your time here was difficult. But the drugs you were on were very heavy. They had to be. It's likely they made you believe things that—"

"Stop," Sully growled. "You waited until the drugs had worn off before you injected me with the stuff from LOBRA. I was aware. Fully aware. I *know* what happened. I only want to know why. Was it all for Lowell, to help him, or was it for yourself?"

"Now Sullivan—"

"You always wanted to find your son. You never did. The experiments won't end until you do, will they?"

"I don't know what you—"

Sully took a step forward, cutting off yet another denial through movement alone. By now, he knew he'd been naive to hope he might draw a confession from Gerhardt this easily. The man had spent years concealing all manner of sins. No doubt he'd planned, again and again, what he'd do if confronted. There were ways to break him, just like he'd broken Sully two years ago. Talking wasn't it.

Sully felt a tug inside him, a nudge from a part of him. A dark part. If he could feed the hangman by drawing in the disturbed spirits haunting the corridor outside, he could harness the kind of power needed to force Gerhardt's confession. His gaze flicked to the doorway. She was there, the ghost who'd all but stuck to him since he'd come in here. It would be so easy....

Sully shook the thought away. The last time he'd done it, he'd lost himself. He'd nearly killed a man. While he could live with beating Gerhardt senseless, he didn't want a death on his hands. And there was the chance he wouldn't stop there. Emily was just down the hall. If he turned on her, he'd never be able to forgive himself.

Instead, he turned to something else he imagined might significantly weaken the psychiatrist. "Do you still want to find your son?"

"As I understand it, your brother is already working on it. Does he know about you?"

Sully opted not to answer. "I can help you find him."

The smile was back. Sully balled his fists at his sides and held them there. "Why would help me, after everything you believe I've done?"

"Because there's something you can do for me in return. I can give you your son if you give me Lowell."

"Your uncle? Why?"

"Don't bullshit me. You know exactly why."

"I don't know what you expect me to do. Of course I want to find my son. But how on earth do you think I can help you settle your problems with your uncle?"

"You can provide me with information that will take him down. If the authorities and the public are made aware of the drug experiments, of the fact patients are being used as guinea pigs, he'd be finished."

"If all of that truly happened, I'd be finished too," Gerhardt said. "And it didn't happen, Sullivan, whatever you think you remember."

"It happened. I know it happened. You have files in here to prove it. I've seen them."

Shock flitted across Gerhardt's face, but he quickly hid it behind narrowed eyes and tight lips. "You had no right to go through private patient files."

"But I had a right to look at mine. You documented the patients you experimented on. Why leave a paper trail?"

"Any procedure we do here is documented." Gerhardt paused, took a breath he ejected in a sigh before turning tired eyes on Sully. "Look, I know what you think, but anything I've done has been in the best interests of my patients. LOBRA developed a drug that was believed to open up parts of the brain that ordinarily can't easily be accessed. I'm no chemist, so I can't explain how it works, but my hope was that it would allow patients with so-called psychic abilities to not only access their gifts at will, but to control them. I used to believe those with such abilities wanted only to be rid of them; I've since realized differently, that some only want a way to better control the things they can see and do. You're one of them. You don't enjoy seeing spirits, but you embrace it as a part of who you are. Ridding you of the ability, or suppressing it, took from you the essence of your being. Don't you want a way to control it?"

"I have a way to control it," Sully said. "My abilities aren't my problem and neither are the ghosts. It's people like you and Lowell who are the problem." He took another step, leaning on the desktop to put his face closer to Gerhardt's. He was pleased to see the older man flinch. "You haven't done a single thing in the name of helping patients. You've taken advantage of them. You've used them. It ends now, Gerhardt. I'm ending it. You can mitigate the damage to yourself by giving me Lowell. In return, I'll give you the one thing that's more important to you than this job or your own life. If you want to find your son, you'll do what I tell you."

Gerhardt's right hand came up from beneath the desk, more quickly than Sully would have thought possible for the man. In it was a handgun.

"Or maybe," Gerhardt said. "You'll do what I tell *you*."

Sully stared at the gun, a revolver similar to the one Emily owned. He was no expert on guns, but he knew it would be fully loaded. What was more, Gerhart would be prepared to use it.

Sully debated making a comment to alert Emily to the presence of the weapon. It might bring her here, which Sully didn't want, but it would also serve as a needed warning to her. It didn't take him long to decide it was better she knew, for her own safety.

"You going to shoot me?" he asked.

"I don't want to," Gerhardt said. "But you seem to be leaning toward giving me little choice. And consider: The world already believes you're dead. No one knows you're down here. The place is very well soundproofed. And you're an escaped patient who's just broken in and confronted me. It might be I can conceal the whole thing easily enough, but if I'm found out, I have a fairly solid defence."

A sound in the hall drew Gerhardt's attention, and he shifted his aim. Sully wheeled to see Emily standing there, gun in hand and fire in her glare like an elderly, female Dirty Harry.

She opened her mouth, as if to issue an order to Gerhardt, but she didn't get the chance. A shot sounded, a deafening pop that muffled all subsequent sound.

Emily's little body flew back under an impact to her midsection. Sully could do nothing but watch, horrified, as she struck the opposite wall in the hall. There, she slid down until she lay, slumped, on the floor.

Shock gave way to panic.

"No!" Sully cried as he rushed for the hall.

She wasn't moving, yet he didn't see her ghost. With Betty Schuster, he'd noticed her moments after. The fact he couldn't see Emily gave him hope. And yet....

For a moment, Emily was all he knew. He knelt at her side, intending to check on her, but spun at the sound of movement behind him. Gerhardt stood at the door to the office, gun still in hand.

Sully spotted Emily's gun within easy reach. He'd only managed to stretch out a hand for it when another shot sounded. Pain streaked across Sully's middle, the force of the blast flipping him onto his back on the floor next to the fallen Emily.

Gerhardt stood over him as he trained Sully in his sights.

Sully poured every ounce of hate he had for this man into his words. "You son of a bitch. You killed her."

"That's right," Gerhardt said. "And I'm going to kill you too."

24

THE WOUND in his side was like a fire burning, and it would have been enough to buckle him were he anywhere else, in any other situation.

But here and now, his survival depended on seeing past the pain. Seeing past it and ensuring he didn't suffer any further.

The ghosts were here, all three of them, gathered around as observers at a sideshow.

Emily was dead. She had to be. No way she'd taken that slug in the chest and survived.

He'd reached the point of grasping reality, that he might have to kill Gerhardt if he was to get out of here alive and take Emily with him. No way he was leaving her here, in a place and situation that would see her painted as anything less than honourable.

His heart broke for her, and he knew he'd feel even worse later. She'd come here, after all, for him. Gerhardt had pulled the trigger, but her death was on Sully's hands nonetheless.

But the guilt and grief would have to come later. Right now, there was only him, Gerhardt and a gun.

And only one way he could think of to win this battle.

He focused on the ghosts, beginning the process of drawing

them in. Unfortunately the pain and the distraction left him unprepared for the unexpected.

Gerhardt jabbed a syringe into his leg.

Sully gave up on the ghosts, his attention snapping to the sensation of a liquid drug flowing into his vein. He kicked Gerhardt away before he could administer the full dose, then yanked the needle from his leg, tossing the half-full syringe away. He didn't see where it clattered off to, but it was enough that he'd put himself between Gerhardt and the remaining drug.

The doctor backed away a couple of steps, gun still out and fixed on Sully. Sully did his best to keep the weapon in his sights as he struggled to sitting, gritting his teeth as his side pulled painfully.

"Stay down," Gerhardt ordered. "Don't move."

The tone contained no trace of panic; rather, it was that of a man in complete control. Sully tried to refocus on the ghosts, but found he couldn't get there. Dread had set in, the feel of the LOBRA drug winding its way up into his brain, poking into his consciousness, taking him over.

He'd learned over time how to separate spirit emotions from his own, and so more or less block them. But the drug changed that, lowered those defences. As if it were his own, he felt their fear now, these three trapped Lockwood spirits. They circled him, watching pitilessly as he fell before the power of Lowell's drug and their torment. Like many who'd endured the sort of trauma they had, it had become impossible for them to see beyond their own suffering, to sympathize with that of another.

He was on his own.

Sully backed away from Gerhardt, pulling himself along on his backside while scanning the ground for Emily's gun. He couldn't control the spirits in his current condition, but surely he could still fire a gun.

As if sensing the turn of his thoughts, Gerhardt stepped forward, kicking at something on the ground. Emily's revolver slid away, disappearing into the shadows of the hall.

Sully turned back to his enemy. Gerhardt was watching him thoughtfully.

"Mara and Desmond were here at Lockwood just a short time ago," Gerhardt said. "Desmond told me something, that a psychic had seen Eloise's spirit at our old home. I don't think I'd be far off the mark to assume you are that psychic. What did you see? What did she tell you?"

"She didn't tell me anything. Even if she did, I wouldn't share it with you."

"Wouldn't you? You know, it's just occurred to me I've been going about this all wrong. All these years, I've been trying to communicate with my son. Maybe what I've needed all along is to communicate with my wife."

Sully's vision swam, but he was certain he saw Gerhardt tuck his gun under one arm to allow him to remove his wedding band. "Eloise picked this out for our wedding. She was always much better at those sorts of things than I was. It's mine, but in a way, it's really hers."

Perception had changed with the drug. The hallway spun, lights dancing around Sully as his world shifted. Smells were sharper, dust, decay and Gerhardt's aftershave combining pungently enough to make him want to vomit. Sounds were louder; each statement from Gerhardt seemed shouted. The image of the psychiatrist grew larger, and Sully didn't know whether it was real or simply a trick of his eyes until he felt an object—the ring, no doubt—being pressed into his hand.

He'd intended to throw it, as far as he was able. The drug didn't give him the chance.

The vision came instantly. He was back inside the house in The Forks, only it looked different. And he felt different, not like himself. He'd connected to Eloise's ghost, had entered her consciousness, her memory. He was Eloise, and now there was nothing to do but be dragged along for the ride.

She was in the sunlit kitchen, bagging up a sandwich and

placing it, along with a yogurt cup, carrot sticks and an apple juice, inside a Charlie Brown lunch kit.

As usual, Sully's limitation meant the vision was restricted to sights, smell and touch. She was calling out to David; he could sense it based on the turn of her thoughts. And he was aware as she was of David's too-rapid approach from the stairs.

She scolded over her shoulder as she sealed the lunch box. David continued to run anyway, didn't stop until he'd encased his mother's waist in a tight hug.

Bright blue eyes peered up into hers as she turned into his embrace. He was thanking her once again for the train she'd bought him, one she'd seen in a shop window. She'd intended it for his birthday, but Roman had been so harsh with the little boy yesterday evening she'd decided to give David the gift early.

She hugged him back, then laughed inside—only inside—as he begged her to be allowed to stay home from school to play with his new toy.

Her firm "no" led to a pout, but one that turned quickly to a smile. He was a good-natured kid that way, thankfully far more like his mother than his father in personality. And her love for him was boundless.

The memory changed. This time, David was nowhere to be seen, just Eloise and a young woman Sully recognized from photos as Marc's wife, Mariel. She was still very young, likely only eighteen or nineteen. Her face was plaintive and desperate as she revealed a secret to her older sister. Sully couldn't hear the words, but he felt the creeping dread moving through Eloise as she listened. He didn't need to hear to know Mariel was telling her sister of the second son prophesy, the one she'd heard from her friend, Harry.

The two women argued, Eloise locked in disbelief. Roman had proven himself a hard man, but he'd never harm their son. Mariel's friend was obviously out of his mind.

Another memory. David hadn't spoken to Eloise all that weekend morning, had withdrawn to his room with his trains and books and politely refused to come out. When he turned down lunch, Eloise knew something was very wrong.

She sat down on the bedroom floor with him, drew from him at long last an admission. The words went unheard by Sully, but he could see the thoughts as they formed in Eloise's mind, as she pictured what the child described. His father had come into his room last night, saying he wanted to play a game. They took turns holding their breath behind the boy's pillow.

Then the game changed. They'd hold the pillow over each other's faces.

David went first, giggling as he pressed the pillow down. He didn't know why his father looked so serious as he took the pillow for his turn. His dad had told him to lie down. Then he'd held the pillow over David's face, pressing down hard. It hurt. The little boy couldn't breathe at all, even though he tried, and he couldn't tell his father to stop. And he hadn't stopped. Not until they heard Eloise calling.

Eloise wasn't supposed to be back that early, but her art class was cancelled when the teacher called in sick.

She'd arrived home, she realized, in time to prevent her little boy's murder.

Her first thought was to confront Roman, even to kill him. But Roman hit her sometimes, and she knew she'd never win a fight against the man. If she was injured so badly she was rendered helpless, she'd be no use in protecting her son.

She next thought of escape, of taking David with her and running. Running so far Roman would never find them. But there were faults in that plan too. Roman knew people. Wealthy, powerful people. He belonged to a group he called the Circle, and she knew they had eyes everywhere. The kind of resources and skills they possessed collectively, she'd never run far enough fast enough.

She tried anyway. She packed their bags, just one each for her and David. She took the boy's favourite train, of course, and his copy of *Oh, the Places You'll Go!* If she could turn this into a fun outing for them, he would ask fewer questions she didn't know how to answer. She packed several changes of clothes and enough cash to see them through a week or two without having to revert to credit cards. She'd envisioned herself getting a job in a small town somewhere, preferably in a place where she was near enough to see the school. That way, she could watch all the time, make sure Roman didn't return.

She didn't make it. She'd booked them into a motel in a nearby small town and they'd been there less than a day when Roman turned up, furious, at the door. How he'd discovered their location, she didn't know, but she was aware of at least one policeman in the Circle's ranks.

She managed to convince Roman they'd simply gone on a little holiday, arguing honestly that they never went anywhere as a family, and she'd tired of asking him.

He let it go. She didn't.

She knew then there was no other way. If she wanted David alive, she'd need to give him up.

She nearly didn't survive the conversation with Mariel and their father, a kind man who would have done anything for his family. And he did do anything. He helped his girls plot a kidnapping.

He knew a couple, he said, who were unable to have a child of their own. They were desperate, but the adoption process was slow and they'd so far been unsuccessful in speeding it up. Eloise insisted on meeting them, but the best she could manage, given Roman was checking her car's mileage now, was to speak by phone. They were lovely, said all the things she'd told herself she needed to hear to go through with this. They'd let her visit, certainly. They'd find ways to keep her updated on David. She would be a part of his life.

She agreed. They would arrange it well, all of them. Eloise would be "distracted" by a call from Mariel, and their dad would take David from the backyard. He'd drive the little boy to the couple's acreage out of town, and he'd stay there. Eloise would find a way to get there, to explain to him what was happening. She'd take him his favourite things, his trains, his books, the shirts he liked the best. She'd tell him his father was going through a bad time and it was best, for now, that David not be around there. That much, at least, was true.

She stuck to the plan, and when the police came to speak with her, her grief had been genuine. Walking away from David in the backyard had almost killed her, knowing her little boy would never again call this house his home. That he was about to meet someone else he would begin to call "Mommy." She reminded herself again and again as she went to answer the ringing phone that this was for the best, that David's life depended on this. But it didn't hurt less. The police didn't doubt her.

Roman had been furious. He'd started to beat her that night, accusing her of losing their son, but she'd stopped him with a threat, that the police would be back with further questions and she wouldn't lie to them about the origin of the bruises. The police were around a lot with questions. They worked hard to find her son so that she never felt comfortable sorting out a way to visit him. What if they followed her? David's adoptive parents would be arrested. They all would be. All but Roman, who had played no part in this. David would be placed back with him, alone. All alone with the man who had tried to kill him.

So she kept her distance. She didn't try to quell her pain; it continued to serve her well with the police. Some days she went into David's room and never left it. Others, she shut it up and avoided the upper floor at all costs. The house became a prison, just her and the man she'd come to hate with every fibre of her being. She'd stopped him killing her boy, but he'd taken him from her all the same. Sometimes she thought about nothing but how she might kill him and get away with it.

She bided her time, waited until the police investigation and media coverage dwindled, once there weren't eyes on her every move. A little over a year had gone by at that point, a long, painful year. She'd waited until the police and media had reignited interest in the disappearance at its one-year mark. Only then, once the stories were read and additional tips came to nothing, did she act.

She once again packed up her bag, but this time, she took more with her. She'd leave a lot behind but she didn't care. She needed enough to get by, but not so much as to slow her down. And she left a note: *"Goodbye, Roman. I can't bear to live anymore in a place where my boy isn't. Please, don't try to find me. It's better this way for both of us. -Eloise."* He could take it as a Dear John letter or a suicide note. She didn't care either way.

She called a cab this time, ensuring no one could trace her through her car. The cab took her out of the neighbourhood, and she found a friendly woman at a coffee shop willing to give her a lift. She'd considered calling her family, but she didn't want them involved. They'd already taken on far too much. If Eloise was going to take her son back, she needed to keep them out of it.

The lady took Eloise to a car rental place, and she picked out the cheapest model she could find. Then she drove out to the acreage, using the land location she'd been provided, back when she still expected to go out and visit.

The couple had intended to homeschool their adopted son; they'd really have no choice. Word was they had talked about obtaining some forged documents for him under a new name— their name—but Eloise didn't know if they'd gotten to it yet. Whatever the case, it wasn't likely David left the acreage much, and she expected he'd be there when she arrived.

Only he wasn't. A woman answered the door, a lady with pretty features and the sort of build people described as "sturdy." It took a moment, but the woman clued in upon greeting the stranger standing on her doorstep.

David wasn't there. He'd gone fishing for a few days with his father. His father. The strangeness of it struck Eloise, the idea of calling anyone other than Roman David's father. It was odd, but not disagreeable. Roman had never been much of a father to him anyway.

What wasn't so welcome was the realization that if this new man was David's father, the woman Eloise was speaking with was, by extension, his mother. Eloise knew it, of course, had helped to plan for it. It didn't make it any easier, this idea of having been replaced.

The woman—her name was Val, she reminded Eloise—invited her in. She showed Eloise David's room. He'd been playing with his favourite train, the gift from Eloise, on the day he'd been taken from the backyard, and it sat on a shelf in a place of pride, easy access for him to reach it whenever he wanted. It was a comfortable room, warm, cozy and tidy. Plenty of toys, lots of clothes in the closet, books sitting in a shelf just like in his old room in The Forks. It was the photos atop the bookshelf that gave Eloise another moment of pause. There were, of course, none of her. Only these two new parents.

She didn't look more closely at the photos, only a quick glance. It was enough. David wore the largest grin in one of them, the sort of grin Eloise had struggled to pull from him in those later days when Roman had become increasingly dark and unpredictable.

That David was grinning like that for someone other than her was unbearable.

He was happy. Happy, even without her in his life.

It was enough to break her, to steel the resolve to do what she'd come here for.

Standing in the kitchen, she told Val she wanted her son back, that she'd left Roman and intended to start a new life somewhere with David. Val paled. Eloise read the other woman's silence as room to continue her argument.

Something changed. Val's face, moments ago placid and pretty, twisted in anger. No, Eloise was not taking David. The arrangement had been made, and so it would stay. David would not live like that, on the run, for the rest of his childhood and youth.

But Eloise was not backing down. He was *her* son, not Val's. Arrangements could be altered, broken.

The argument continued, became more heated. Val paced,

waved her arms wildly, raged at Eloise. And her voice changed, became deeper, raspy, as if Eloise was dealing with a different person entirely. It occurred to her Val might have multiple personalities, and it became just another reason for Eloise to fight for her child.

And a fight was exactly what it became. The first blow from Val was unexpected, a punch to the face as quick and as sharp as a rattlesnake strike. Eloise buckled under the force of it and fell to the floor. She'd never fought back against Roman; it had always served her better, she believed, to simply take it, as it would end more quickly and with less violence. She didn't know how to fight back, and she didn't now, merely curling into herself as Val continued to deliver kicks and blows to every part of Eloise's body she could reach.

Finally, it ended, just as assaults by Roman ended. Val stalked away, leaving Eloise gasping and sobbing on the floor.

Only it wasn't over. Not this time.

Eloise looked up to the approach of footsteps, saw Val reappear over her.

This time, she held a butcher knife.

Eloise screamed as the knife streaked toward her. They felt like sharp punches at first, the knife blows that struck her chest. She gasped beneath the weight of them, the screams caught in her throat.

Then the blade, coming down again and again at breathtaking speed, arced toward her throat. Eloise tried to move away, to put a hand up to block, but Val wouldn't be stopped. Eloise watched her own blood as it left her body until, at last, darkness stole over her.

25

THE IMAGE CHANGED, darkness giving way to bright light, Eloise slipping away so that Sully reemerged.

It wasn't the light of heaven he was seeing, despite having just experienced the horror of having been murdered. It was a light hanging over his body.

A fiery pain from his middle seized him, reminding him of the bullet wound there. But he forced himself past it, the continued danger he was in leaving him no room for anything else.

He cast his gaze around, noted the familiar sky-blue, windowless walls, the grimy white tile.

The Blue Room.

Sully knew from experience what he'd discover upon trying to move his arms and legs, but he attempted it anyway. He was indeed strapped down, ankles and wrists secured in padded restraint cuffs locking him to the treatment bed. Somehow, Gerhardt has managed to drag him in here, despite any restrictions his disability and age might create. Needs must and all that.

Gerhardt stood nearby, regarding Sully thoughtfully. "You're back."

He was, and he knew what came next. Gerhardt would question him, quite likely with brutal force, even torture. The only escape Sully could imagine came with the three ghosts nearby. He could sense them rather than see them.

It was enough.

He closed his eyes, shutting out Gerhardt's additional questions and demands for answers. Sully locked onto the entities, all three at once. He'd never managed more than one at a time, but then, he'd never tried. He'd do it now. He needed to.

It was palpable the moment he drew their flailing energy into himself, allowed the hangman to consume it. The most startling thing was a gradual lessening of his pain, the burning in his abdomen fading to a dull throb. He felt the hangman's answering laugh, felt it bubble up within his own throat until Sully gave it physical voice.

"What are you laughing about?" Gerhardt's tone was still its usual brand of bitter, but a tremor sounded within the words. Sully didn't blame him. The sound of that laugh had shaken him too.

The hangman pressed forward, urging Sully to allow him to control this moment. Past events dictated the executioner was stronger, more capable of doing what had to be done. Yet, for some reason, this time the hangman hadn't been able to simply take over.

Gerhardt stepped forward. "Answer my questions! What did she tell you? Where's my son?"

Sully snapped his head toward Gerhardt, took pleasure in the way the sudden movement caused the older man to flinch. Sully allowed a sneer to form, the sort of dangerous smile he didn't know he could truly pull off.

"I'm not telling you a damn thing, you son of a bitch. Go to hell."

The psychiatrist took one more step. "You're in no position to refuse me. Now we can do this the easy way or the hard way. You don't want to know what 'the hard way' entails. Now I want to find my son. I *need* to find my son."

A voice, spoken in a solid Cockney accent, sounded in Sully's brain, coming from somewhere deep within. *Now's the time. Let me at him, boy.*

Sully ignored it. For now.

He fixed his eyes on Gerhardt's. "All this time, I thought you were looking for him because you loved him. Because you wanted to give him a proper burial or find some peace for yourself. But all you really want is to kill him."

"What?"

"The second son prophesy. I know about it. I also know you tried to kill David shortly before he disappeared."

Gerhardt opened his mouth to deny it, but closed it again. When he reopened it, a dark smile formed. "I suppose there's no sense denying anything more to you. You're not leaving here alive anyway."

Now, boy!

"Harry Schuster—you remember Harry—he came to our Circle when he was still quite young," Gerhardt said. "Well, we were all young then, I suppose. He convinced us of his abilities, in part because of a tragic car crash he'd predicted that came to pass. He went into these trance-like states and said things. None of us understood it, including him, and it eventually drove him mad. But as strange as these visions were, they always came true. When he came to us with the second son prediction, we were understandably concerned. We'd begun to really get somewhere as a group. We were achieving the things we'd come together to achieve. I, for instance, was able to finish paying off large debts from school and secure myself a job as Lockwood's chief psychiatrist thanks to my contacts in the Circle. I owed them everything."

"So you agreed to kill your own son?"

"It wasn't an easy decision to make. But, by then, Harry was starting to zero in on some people. He told me I was the father of the second son. We decided, as a group, that I had a chance to stop things before the Circle was destroyed. 'When the second son rises, the Circle will fall.' That's what the prophesy says. We were what we were because of each other. The Circle was greater as a whole than any of its individual parts. I owed everything I'd achieved to it. I couldn't allow it to crumble, so I did what I had to do."

Sully thought back to the little boy in the vision, pale-haired, bright-eyed and innocent. Not so different from another child who'd fallen victim two decades later to the same prophesy. Aiden and David. They'd been killed for nothing better than greed and a desperation for power.

Sully's hands balled into fists as he snarled his response at Gerhardt. "He was just six years old."

"Exactly. He wasn't yet a threat. I couldn't wait until he was older, when he'd be able to defend himself. If I waited until I saw the evidence myself, he'd have been too strong for me to fight. If I waited even another year or two, he'd be strong enough to put up a struggle. Struggles leave bruises, marks. If I simply owned up to my responsibility when he was still very young, there would be little to no evidence of wrongdoing. Police would likely ask questions, but there would be no way to prove a murder."

Heat bubbled inside Sully. The hangman was begging to be let loose. Not yet. Sully pinned Gerhardt in a glare. "You fucking bastard."

"I know what you must think of me, but I truly had no choice. The child had to die. Problem was, he disappeared before I could finish it. After the failed attempt I'd made, I had to bide my time, wait until he stopped being so suspicious of me. In the meantime, I became more and more convinced David had gone against my orders and told his mother. When he disappeared, I thought it very possible Eloise had something to do with it. I wasn't certain, given her grief was certainly very real, but it sat there in my brain, wouldn't let go. Finally, she disappeared, taking all possible answers with her."

"Dez told me about a young woman who said she saw David, that he was with you."

"Fifteen years or so after the disappearance, yes. She said she saw him, and I believed what she meant was that he was dead. I thought if I could find the body and prove it was my son, I'd have something to take to the Circle to settle them. Harry, you see, had never stopped going on about the second son prophesy and everyone was anxious. Some of them looked at me like I'd failed them and, you have to understand, failing the Circle is not an option. I would have done anything to find David, to prove to them he was no longer a threat."

Sully thought of Lucky, his teenage birth mother who'd lied to her own family about his existence to protect him. If she'd known about or sensed Gerhardt's true intentions with David, the last thing she would have done was hand him over. And there was the other possibility, that she'd been trying to find a way out of Lockwood. If she could convince the psychiatrist to let her leave, to search for David or his final resting place, she could find a way to escape.

It broke Sully's heart.

You going to cry, boy? Let me out, and I'll make him *cry.*

Sully shook the hangman off. No, he was not going to cry. He was too pissed for that. "I know what you did to her, to Lucky. I know you tortured her. I know you raped her."

That got the response Sully had been after. Gerhardt blanched, his mouth popping open. He snapped it shut before speaking. "How do you know that name?"

Sully had shied away from revealing this last truth, but the reasons not to had dwindled to zero. He found now he wanted this man to know who he was, to reveal himself to him completely, to see what response it would elicit. One of the two of them wasn't leaving here. The truth, if need be, would stay buried within this room.

Sully spoke in a growl. "You got her pregnant, Gerhardt. You got a child pregnant. She gave birth to a son. I'm that son."

Gerhardt gripped the railing of the treatment bed. For a moment, it looked as if it might not be enough to keep him on his feet. Disbelief clung to his features, so Sully kept on, pummelling him with truth.

"She was a good mother, in the short time she was allowed to be. She protected me by slowing you down long enough someone could get me away from here, and she didn't tell her crazy family about me. She gave up everything, including me, to protect me. I was left on a doorstep, and after a few shitty years in the system, I ended up with the Braddocks. It was because of her wanting to give me the best chance possible that I found the family I was meant to be with. But I shouldn't exist. I never should have been born, because what you did never should have happened. You're an evil piece of shit, Gerhardt, and so help me, when I get out of these restraints, you're going to wish I was never born."

Gerhardt had regained some colour, some composure, enough that he was able to speak. "Well then, it's all right, because you're never getting out of those restraints. And you're never leaving this place."

Gerhardt moved across the room to a counter upon which sat a few vials. Into one, he inserted a syringe. "You know what I've just realized, Sullivan? I was wrong about David. I'm glad I didn't succeed in killing him. Because he's not my second son. *You* are. My first boy never truly saw life. He died during a miscarriage. And Lowell. When Harry went to him and told him he believed his brother would harbour the second son, we all believed he meant Aiden Braddock. But it wasn't him. It's you. It's been you all along. You're the one, Sullivan. You're the one I need to destroy."

NOW!

Sully at last relented, giving in to the hangman's demands. He closed his eyes, allowing himself to slide.

The hangman leapt. He snatched onto the spirits locked inside Sully and drew out their energy.

Sully opened his eyes.

Gerhardt stepped back so suddenly onto his bad leg, he fell.

As with Harry's spirit during the battle with Lowell and Hackman, Sully discovered he was still very much present as the hangman came forward. Although he wasn't truly in control of his own body, he felt it nonetheless. Strangely, he found he didn't mind the experience. This wasn't another being inside him, controlling him. This was a part of him. A dark, twisted part, but a part nonetheless.

He feared the hangman: his power, his darkness, what he could turn Sully into. But he couldn't deny that, right now, the nameless executioner was saving his life.

The hangman tested the bonds a moment before pulling at them, using the strength of several energies against the restraints.

Gerhardt had managed to stand, was back at the counter, filling the syringe with shaking hands.

The hangman pulled harder. At last, a crack and a ping sounded as a metal ring shattered and shot off across the room.

One hand free.

One was enough.

Gerhardt didn't look back, focused on his desperate task, as the hangman moved to free Sully's other hand.

Gerhardt turned, rushed to the bed before the hangman had opened the restraint fully. He stabbed the syringe into Sully's yet-trapped forearm but, before he could inject the liquid into his captive, the hangman grabbed the psychiatrist's hand.

A crack sounded within Gerhardt's encased fingers, and he howled. He released the syringe and dropped to his knees, but the hangman held on, two more cracks sounding before he finally let go.

While Gerhardt moaned and writhed on the floor, hugging his broken fingers to his chest, the hangman succeeded in freeing Sully's other hand, then his feet. He yanked out the needle and placed it next to him on the bed. It would come in handy, this substance. It appeared to be the same one Gerhardt had repeat-edly administered to Sully, and no doubt to all the other psychic patients brought down here by force. Only it was at least double the usual dose.

Enough to kill a person.

The hangman stood, testing out Sully's limbs as if revelling in the sensation of being in charge of a body for the first time in ages. In a way, Sully imagined it was true. He circled the bed until he reached Gerhardt's side.

"My, my, how the tables have turned." The voice emerging from Sully's throat was his, and yet not, the deep Cockney accent belonging to another person, another time.

He reached down and, amid the psychiatrist's startled protests, lifted and threw the older man onto the treatment bed. Gerhardt could do nothing as the hangman secured the restraint cuffs, his attempts to defend himself ineffectual against the strength of four separate entities currently taking up residence inside Sully's body. Gerhardt was weak, helpless.

As weak and helpless as a six-year-old boy.

The hangman picked up the syringe. "This liquid. Meant to kill, ain't it?" He met Gerhardt's eyes, saucer-wide in terror. "Works like a charm on people with a third eye. What's it do to people like you? What do you say, doctor? Should we find out?"

"No! Don't you dare. Release me immediately, or you'll regret it!"

The hangman made a tsking sound. "Now, now. Not such a wise move, trying to intimidate the man who holds your life in his hands." He grasped the broken hand and twisted, drawing a wild yell from Gerhardt. "Try again."

"Please! Please, don't do this! Stop!"

The hangman released the hand and stared into the doctor's face, tilting his head as if it would give him a new perspective on the man lying there. "Not so nice being on the receiving end, is it? Go on, beg me. Maybe I'll relent."

"Please. Please! I promise I won't reveal you were here. I won't tell anyone."

"No, you're right there, doctor." The hangman leaned in, locking eyes with the psychiatrist. "You won't."

He jabbed the needle into Gerhardt's arm.

"Stop!" came a voice from the door.

The hangman turned to find Emily standing there, hunched

over and in obvious pain. Sully wanted to go to her, to see if she was all right, to figure out how it was she was still alive—hell, to make sure she *was* actually alive—but the executioner was committed to his task. Sully felt a rush of relief as her eyes met his, eyes containing their usual strength despite the discomfort she was clearly in.

The hangman had other ideas about her place here. "You the one to stop me?"

Emily's lips curled into a smile that shocked both Sully and the hangman. "Stop you? I want to help."

Sully was no less stunned, this time by Emily's stated intentions, but the hangman felt only amusement.

"You're my kind of lady," he said.

Gerhardt's eyes narrowed as he took in the newcomer, making her way to the side of the bed. "Emily Crichton. I should have finished you when I had the chance."

Emily smiled. "Today or twenty-five years ago, dear?"

The hangman laughed. Gerhardt didn't.

"How are you alive?" the psychiatrist asked. "I shot you in the chest."

Emily tugged her blouse open, revealing a layer of black beneath. "Kevlar," she said. "I'm afraid one or two ribs are cracked but, thanks to the hit and run you once plotted against me, I know how to handle pain."

Emily turned to the hangman, flinching slightly as she peered up fully into his eyes but holding the gaze nonetheless. "I know you want to kill him, and I don't blame you. I feel very much the same. But you need to consider something. If he dies by your hand—by anyone's—he'll never leave you. There's a very good chance he'll haunt you until the end of your days. You don't want that, surely."

This gave Sully pause. Unfortunately, the hangman wasn't as convinced. "It matters not to me, pet. I'll consume him like every other evil man I've killed."

"Death is too easy for a man like him."

"So what do you suggest? He needs to know justice."

"I can think of a far better justice for him than death, can't you?" Emily returned her gaze to Gerhardt. "You've spent your career torturing and traumatizing patients who weren't like others, those you felt could be of benefit to you. Perhaps the most fitting punishment would be for you to become one of them. How would you like that, Doctor? To be locked away inside your own damaged mind, a patient within your own facility?" She took the syringe from the hangman's willing hand. "I think if we're careful with the dosage, we can ensure just such an outcome, don't you?"

Gerhardt's face froze.

The hangman laughed, wild and deep, as he held the psychiatrist's arm against the bed, squeezing to make a vein pop. Emily waited a few seconds, until a thick bluish line showed through the flesh of Gerhardt's arm. Then she inserted the needle.

"No!" Gerhardt screamed. "Stop! You can't do this to me! It will kill me!"

"Like you've killed," the hangman said. "Seems fitting." He turned back to Emily. "What do you say, milady? Shall we?"

Emily ignored the hangman, focusing entirely on Gerhardt. "I don't get any pleasure from this, and I assure you I have no intention of killing you. But I do need to stop you. I've lived with the guilt of turning a blind eye to your evil, of what that meant for Lucky Dule. I won't let you hurt anyone else."

She injected the drug into Gerhardt's arm.

A furious yell broke off midway as shock overtook his features. Sully had no way of seeing inside the man's head, but he knew what he was feeling. Sully had been here too many times before. He could see it in Gerhardt's face as the drug he'd injected into numerous patients seeped into his own vein, set its course through blood, its final destination his brain.

Fear played out across Gerhardt's face. Part of Sully felt guilty, but only a small part. The psychiatrist had shown no mercy to the patients he'd forced into his current position. He hadn't batted an eye at the pleas, the tears or the screams. He'd destroyed lives, and likely taken a few.

Emily had given him only a partial dose of what Gerhardt had intended for Sully.

It was more than enough.

Psychics had been guinea pigs for Lowell because their brains, he'd reasoned, were more open. Gerhardt had happily allowed it to meet his own ends.

The problem for Gerhardt was he was no psychic.

Sully didn't know what he'd been expecting, but he'd been mentally preparing himself to view a seizure or even death.

Instead, after a few moments of useless struggling, everything went quiet.

Gerhardt was alive. He was breathing and his pulse, when the hangman lifted a hand to check, was a solid, healthy—if not a little too rapid—thrum against fingertips. Gerhardt blinked once, twice. But the eyes didn't focus, fixed on a spot in the water-stained ceiling.

What caught Sully was the way the eyes looked. Wide open between blinks, they held an expression of the deepest terror. What he saw was anyone's guess. All Sully knew for sure was the man had come to resemble the haunted and tortured spectre of Harry Schuster.

Sully could think of nothing more fitting.

Pounding footfalls sounded in the hall, had the hangman spinning in place, prepared to do battle with whatever new threat this might be. Instead, a few seconds later, the image of Dez came into view, sliding to a screeching halt in the doorway and breathing hard.

"Sully? Mom and I ran into Terrence just as we got to the car. He told us his mother sold you out. We ran all the way back and had to figure out how to get in. Mom's standing watch outside. Are you—What's wrong with you?"

At first, Sully thought Dez must be referring to the blood on his clothes from the gunshot wound. Then he noticed Dez was focused entirely on his eyes.

"It isn't him right now, Desmond," Emily said. "It's a man speaking in an English accent."

Sully felt the hangman's anxiety as he regarded Dez. Why, he didn't know.

Dez at last looked away from Sully's face, gaze settling where it ordinarily would have to start with. "God, is all of that blood yours? Sully—"

"We need to get out of here," Emily said. "But we can't leave Gerhardt like this. Help me get him out of this room."

The hangman didn't need additional help, easily lifting and carrying the psychiatrist into his office and settling him in his chair. Emily, meanwhile, busied herself gathering up the used syringes, both of which she wiped clean of any prints before wrapping Gerhardt's limp fingers around them. One—the remainder of the dose he'd been injected with—she placed at his side, next to his good hand.

"Don't he look all nice and cozy?" the executioner said.

Dez appeared at his side. "Stop talking like that."

"Like what, Red? This is how I talk."

Dez's eyes widened, his expression an approximation of Gerhardt's. "Christ, Sully, what happened to you?"

Emily moved forward and took Sully's still-gloved hand. "You can let go now, Sullivan. We're safe now. You can come back."

Sully knew it. But this wasn't like a separate personality. It was him, or a part of his soul anyway. The longer the hangman stayed up front, the stronger he felt, as if he was continually devouring more of the spirits he'd taken in.

As if he was trying to find a way to stay in control.

Sully wasn't about to let him. He couldn't. Anyway, it wasn't fair to the patients whose spirits he'd sucked in. They deserved peace, not the eternal torment of possession.

The hangman's protest was audible, a snarled, "No!" But

Emily was right. This part of his life, the Lockwood part, it was over. He didn't need the hangman's strength here anymore.

He pulled the darkness back, stepped back fully into himself.

The pain hit him the second he released the three souls, but it was not what it was, and nowhere near what it should have been.

He'd been shot. He knew he had. He had plenty of blood on the front of his shirt to prove it.

He lifted his T-shirt, exposing a belly covered in blood—enough to draw an anxious Dez even closer.

One of Dez's hands joined Sully's in a search for the wound. "What happened?"

Emily had temporarily disappeared into the hall, and she returned in time to answer the question. "Gerhardt shot him."

Dez's head snapped toward her. "Jesus Christ, what? Sull—"

"I'm okay," Sully said, just as his fingers finally settled over a small pucker in his skin, to the right of his belly button and a couple of inches down.

Dez knelt for a closer look. "This is it?" He examined it a moment before turning startled eyes up to his brother's face. "Sully, this wound looks like it's a month old. It's mostly healed."

Sully shook his head. No, he didn't have an explanation.

While the brothers had been distracted by the injury, Emily had been bustling around the room as quickly as her own injuries would allow. Now, she appeared at their side, Gerhardt's lab coat over one arm and an urgent tone in her demand. "We need to leave here. Now!"

"Are you okay to walk?" Dez asked her as they followed her from the room and back down the hall. "I can carry you."

She managed a light chuckle. "As much as I'd enjoy being carried by a handsome young man, I'll be fine. But I do think I'll need a hospital. Sullivan should get looked at too."

Sully shook his head. "I can't, Em. But it's okay. I can't explain it, but it doesn't feel that bad."

Dez wasn't sold. "Sully, I don't think we have a choice. You've been shot, dude."

"If it's not bad enough I'm not supposed to exist, how the hell am I going to explain a rapidly healing bullet wound?"

Dez shrugged before stopping suddenly in the dark of the hall. "Damn. Blood. Sully's DNA's in the databank. If someone finds it here—"

"There's no blood that I saw," Emily said. "The bullet must still be inside Sullivan, so there's no exit wound. That would have lessened the external bleeding, and I'm thinking his front must not have come into contact with much. The only blood I could see was on Gerhardt's lab coat, and I've taken that with me. Sullivan was wearing his gloves most of the time he was in here, as was I, so no fingerprints. I did wipe down the syringes, just in case, and I placed them next to him so someone might think he injected himself. And I picked up my gun and replaced his in the drawer and picked up the spent casings. No doubt he'll have gunfire residue on him. I wiped some from his face, but there's not much I can do about the rest of it. I couldn't think of anything else to clean up offhand."

Dez raised his eyebrows. "Damn. You're good."

Sully grinned. "Yeah," he said. "She is."

26

THEY SPENT two days lying low, waiting to hear about Gerhardt.

Dez had filled Lachlan in on what happened as soon as he dropped Emily off at the hospital. The private investigator had hightailed it back to Lockwood so he could be on hand once the search for the missing psychiatrist began, as it inevitably would. Just as well, too, because very few staff members, it seemed, had knowledge of the continued use of the old wing or Gerhardt's illicit use of it.

They'd found him, Lachlan later told Dez, where he'd been left, a partially loaded syringe next to the fingers of one hand. The other hand had been inexplicably broken in several places. Some were surmising he'd fallen on it. Given his longtime leg injury, falls for him weren't unheard of.

Dez had managed to convince Sully to stay at his house, and he'd make Emily come, too, once she was discharged. They didn't exactly have the space, but it felt better to Dez to have everyone under one roof where he could keep an eye out.

On the second day, Dez received a call from Lachlan, telling him Forbes wanted them to go over to discuss what had happened. Not the police station—Forbes had insisted on that— but at his house.

Dez and Sully left in the SUV to pick up Lachlan. It would take them out of their way, picking up his boss before going to Forbes's, but it was just as well. Dez wanted to talk to Sully first. With everyone around, he hadn't had much opportunity. They'd managed to hide Sully's bullet wound from Mara, concealing the worst of the blood on his shirt and hoodie by doing up his overcoat. Her discovering Sully had been shot—and that her boys had effectively lied to her about it—was unlikely to go down well.

"How are you feeling?" Dez asked a few minutes into the drive.

"The bullet wound? It's fine. Like, weirdly fine."

"It doesn't make sense, man."

"I know. I've been thinking about it, and the only thing I can come up with is that having all that extra energy inside me helped my body to heal more quickly. I mean, I've always healed fairly quickly, but not like this. It's the only explanation that makes any sense."

Dez shrugged. The idea of it, of his brother being able to consume and use spirits to heal himself was so out there, it made his head spin. Yet he wasn't about to complain about something that had, quite likely, kept Sully alive.

"I guess that makes as much sense as anything," he said. "What about the rest of it? Going back there and everything? You okay with that?"

He gazed over at Sully and was met by a smile. "Yeah, D, I am. I never thought I'd say it, but I really am. Facing it—facing *him*—it was like an exorcism or something. Just as well, because I need to go back there to try to get those ghosts to cross over. They shouldn't have to be stuck in a place like that."

"After, you know… what happened, do you think they'll appear to you again?"

"I don't know, but I have to try. Especially given the way I had to use them."

That touched on the other topic, the one Dez hated having to bring up. Really hated having to bring up.

"Hey, Sull. About that. What *was* that?"

"You're not talking about the reverse possession."

Dez kept his eyes on the road as he shook his head.

"It was the hangman," Sully said.

"I figured that much out. And I've seen what happens when he ends up in control. I mean, it was obviously him at the Gerhardt house that day. But he was, like, fully present this time, having conversations and everything. Even your eyes changed, went all pale—like on someone who's been dead a while, only shinier. Is that, I don't know, normal?"

"Not exactly," Sully said. "I felt like I had to let him take control so I could stay alive in there, so I could escape. Gerhardt had me strapped down to the bed, and he was going to inject me with enough of the drug to kill me. I mean, he actually said he was going to do it. I've got the whole thing recorded."

This was new. "You recorded it?"

"I thought I could get a confession from him. And I did. He admitted he tried to kill his son, and he admitted he was going to kill me."

"What about Lowell? He say something about him?"

"Yeah. He mentioned him. I'd asked him about the second son prophesy, and he talked about Aiden's death, and how Lowell had done it."

Dez's heart gave a solid thud. "Jesus, Sull! That means we've got him!"

"Maybe. I don't know. I'm kind of thinking Gerhardt just comes off sounding like a lunatic. It's enough to raise questions, definitely, but Gerhardt's not in any condition anymore to provide a statement or testify at trial."

"I've seen cases where recorded statements have been played for juries where the person who initially said it was dead or otherwise incapable of testifying. It happens."

"Statements given to police, maybe. This, I don't know...."

Dez didn't bother arguing the point. Come right down to it, he didn't know whether it would be usable in court against Lowell.

Forbes was the Major Crimes investigator. He'd be able to provide some advice on the matter.

They arrived at his house forty minutes later, and Forbes waved them in.

"I called in sick," he said. "I figured we needed to discuss this privately."

The police sergeant waited until they were all seated around his living room before launching into it. "Thanks to Lachlan, they found Gerhardt in his office in the old wing. We've been questioning staff left, right and centre, and barely anyone claims to have been aware the old wing was still in use. They'd been told it was unsafe due to asbestos, so were ordered to stay out of there. For my part, I believe them."

"Gerhardt only had a handful of people present during the experiments," Sully said. "Hackman's dead. Lowell was there a few times. And the other one we now believe to be Reynold Dunsmore. I don't doubt some of the other orderlies were in on something and maybe a nurse or two; it's pretty hard to cart patients around in the dead of night without at least a couple of night staff noticing. But I wouldn't be surprised if most people around there had no clue."

"All of that's definitely being checked into," Forbes said.

"How is Gerhardt?" Lachlan asked. "Any updates?"

"He's still in hospital," Forbes said. "Medical staff is trying to figure out what to do, but given the experimental nature of the drug, they're at a loss. Unsurprisingly, they've brought LOBRA in to offer advice. Lowell is distancing himself from it, of course, saying he doesn't know anything about this drug. While the vials are labelled with some identifying information—enough for Gerhardt to know what he was using—it doesn't have the necessary identifiers as to where the drug came from. You can bet your ass Lowell's working as we speak to obliterate any evidence of the stuff in his labs. Not much we can do about that, I'm afraid. We don't have nearly enough for a search warrant. Good news, I guess, is this should mean the drug experiments are over."

"As for Gerhardt, he appears to be in a semi-vegetative state, but his brain is showing unusual signs of activity. Neurologists aren't sure what to do with him, other than send him back to Lockwood. I mean, he sits up fine, he can be spoon-fed and everything, but he can't communicate. It's like he's stuck inside his head. The worst part is the expression on his face. Twenty-four-seven, he looks like he's seeing his own death coming for him."

For anyone else, it seemed a cruel outcome. For Gerhardt, Dez decided, it was justice.

"What about Lockwood?" Sully asked. "What's going to happen to it?"

"They've got someone filling in as psychiatrist over there, a young woman who'd apparently tried for a spot there in the past. The board loved her but Gerhardt put his foot down against her. With the only opposition gone, I'm thinking she's a shoo-in for the chief job now. By all accounts, she's got a great reputation. Won a humanitarian award for the work she did in some Third World countries and all that."

"Cass Jacobson," Lachlan supplied. "I heard about her." He met Sully's eye. "She's good. Really good. She'll do a fine job around there, and she's a sweetheart to boot. Gerhardt's polar opposite. I understand she's in the process of re-evaluating every patient there to ensure she agrees with the diagnoses."

Sully smiled, and Dez mirrored the expression. In many cases, Lockwood served a purpose, and a useful one. It was helpful and even necessary to many of its patients. But to others, those like Sully, it had been a living nightmare. It sounded like that was about to end.

"What about the files?" Lachlan asked. "They still there?"

"Yep, all accounted for," Forbes said. "We seized them all as evidence, and we're trying to make sense of them now. Most of them don't identify the patients other than by numbers, and they're only a record of the secret treatments, not the legitimate patient records. The proper records are upstairs, in the main office. Based on what we know about Sullivan's experience, I think I've managed to pick out his file. But there are others—a lot of others—we haven't been able to put a name to.

"I'll tell you this, the info contained in those files is pretty damning. It confirms what you've told us. Gerhardt made notes of what patients reported having seen, he noted the quantity of the drug used in each case and whether sedative was required to calm the patients afterward. But we found something else, something even better. He video-recorded some of the sessions. It's pretty damn obvious how terrified the patients were, how unwilling to undergo these supposed treatments. It makes him look a damn sight more unstable than his patients."

"Anyone else there?" Sully asked.

"You're wondering about Lowell," Forbes said. "Sorry, no. There was a video of you, but Lowell wasn't in it."

"He wasn't there every time," Sully said. His tone sounded the way Dez felt. After everything they'd been through to get to this point, it would have been too easy, finding Lowell in one of those torture videos.

"Is there *anything* connecting Lowell to this stuff?" Dez asked.

"Not by name. Gerhardt covered up others' involvement, I suspect. But given the nature of the drug involved, I can't imagine any lab besides LOBRA being able to come up with it. Our own lab has been looking at it, and they've never seen anything like it."

Dez thought of something. "Sully, the drug Lowell was giving you a couple of years ago, the one you were taking around the time you started seeing Harry. Maybe it's similar."

Forbes raised an eyebrow. "You have any left?"

"Not personally," Sully said. "But you guys seized some back then, remember? I think your lab tested it. I think Lowell told you it must have been some kind of street drug."

"Shit, I forgot about that," Forbes said. "I'll check with the lab, see if we have the samples on hand. If we can compare the two, it could be we'll be closer to pinning something on Lowell."

Dez met Sully's eye. There was one other thing, although he wasn't sure Sully was prepared to hand it over.

Ultimately, Sully pulled his cellphone from his pocket. "There is one thing, Forbes. I recorded part of my conversation with Gerhardt."

"What? Why the hell didn't you say that earlier?"

"Sorry. I wasn't sure what to do with it. It's got my voice on it, and I'm not supposed to exist, remember?"

"Let me hear it."

Dez hadn't heard it yet either, and his blood ran cold as the recording played through. He listened as Gerhardt admitted to what he'd tried to do to his own son in the name of this stupid prophesy, what he planned on doing to Sully. But the turning point came as the psychiatrist dug further into Harry's vision, and what it had ultimately meant for Aiden Braddock. Dez fumed as he listened to the cold, clinical way the doctor spoke of the two small boys, both targeted by an organization fuelled by greed, power and wealth.

The recording ended abruptly after that. Dez was livid, damn near shaking with it, but he calmed slightly as his brother's hand settled on his shoulder and squeezed. Dez exchanged a quick look with Sully. He knew there had to have been more to that recording; it cut out just after Gerhardt announced his intention to kill Sully. Dez suspected his brother had done some editing, had gotten rid of the parts that might incriminate him or Emily or would raise questions given the later appearance of the Cockney-accented hangman.

"What happened after that?" Forbes asked.

"I guess my phone died, but Emily suddenly appeared. She had her gun and she threatened Gerhardt into letting me go. There was a struggle. I grabbed his hand at one point and he fell. I think he broke it, but I couldn't tell if that happened when I grabbed him or when he hit the floor. Anyway, we knew he had a gun—he'd already shot Emily—so we got out of there."

It was the story they'd rehearsed, a way to explain away

evidence that might be uncovered. No one had known whether it would be enough to convince investigators—Lachlan's tight-lipped expression suggested he, at least, smelled a lie—but if Forbes thought the same, he wasn't making a point of it.

"I'm going to need your phone," he said.

"For what?"

"I need to take it to our tech guys so they can extract the audio clip you've just played."

Dez was about to protest—the tech guys would be able to remove far more than that if they wanted to—but Sully beat him to it. "Sorry, man. I'm not turning it in. Like I said, I'm not supposed to exist. There's stuff on here that could burn me. I'll email you a copy of the recording."

"Copies aren't good enough. Not for evidence. There's no way to ensure tampering didn't occur."

Sully took another long look at his phone. "Can you guarantee me this is enough to nail Lowell?"

Forbes waited until Sully looked back up at him. "Nope. But it's enough to start asking some questions."

Sully held onto the phone for another moment, then dropped it back into his pocket. "I'm sorry. That's not good enough. Once Lowell clues in I'm alive—and he will once this recording starts getting out there—none of us are safe. I could deal with it if it was just me, but it's not. It's my family too. I need to find more, some-thing we can concretely pin on him. Something that will take him out of play for good."

Forbes leaned forward. "Are you sure that exists?"

Sully seemed to be doing his best to form a smile. "It has to. I don't want to think about the alternative."

FORBES'S PHONE ringing a few minutes later signalled a pause in the conversation. He took the call out of the room and Lachlan excused himself to use the bathroom, leaving Dez and Sully alone in the living room.

Dez studied a row of family photos on the upper shelf of a bookcase while Sully knelt beside him to scan the titles. Charles Raynor's face grinned from one of the photos, his arm draped around his son's shoulders.

"Bad Luck Chuck in happier days," Dez grumbled, his tone reflecting his disdain for the man.

While Charles was well-enough liked by the community, he'd run up against his share of problems as Kimotan Rapids' longtime mayor —leading to the nickname coined by one of the unsuccessful mayoral candidates in the last civic election. The massive flood four years ago was a veritable disaster for obvious reasons. Another was a corruption scandal that had nearly unseated him. Flynn Braddock had been given the unhappy task of liaising with the feds on the corruption allegations, an extra-uncomfortable task since the mayor doubled as head of the police commission. Nothing had come of it except Flynn's belief Charles harboured hopes of seeing him out of a job one day.

It turned out Lowell solved the problem for Chuck.

Sully hadn't acknowledged the comment and, when Dez looked down on the top of his brother's head to see why, he noticed Sully's gaze fixed upon something in the bookshelf.

"What is it?" Dez asked.

Sully's hand shook slightly as he drew a book from the shelf, a battered copy of Dr. Seuss's *Oh, the Places You'll Go!*. He stood, taking the book with him as he flipped the cover open.

An intake of breath caught in Sully's throat, and he exhaled a half-whispered, "Oh, my God."

Startled by his brother's inexplicable reaction to a children's book, Dez peered over his shoulder. Inside the front cover was inscribed, "To my boy. Wherever you go, carry me with you. Love forever and ever, your mom."

"Sully, what?"

"This book. She showed me this book."

"Who?"

"Eloise."

Sully next scanned the photos on the shelf. His face paled as he settled on one, taken when Forbes was just a little boy, both his parents next to him.

"Oh, God. Dez...."

"What? You're freaking me out, man."

Sully replaced the book on the shelf and caught Dez's sleeve, tugging him out of the living room, through the kitchen and into the backyard. Only then did Sully reveal what disturbed him, his tone hushed to keep the conversation private.

"You remember what I told you when we were at Lachlan's, and he had the photo of Eloise and David? I recognized something about David. He looked familiar, but I couldn't place it. And then, when Gerhardt gave me his wedding band? Dez, the book, the photo. Forbes is *David*."

Dez stared at Sully, trying to comprehend what he'd just said. "But Sully, that.... How is—"

Sully cut into Dez's failing attempt at speech. "It all makes sense. When the four of us went into Lockwood the other day, I had a panic attack and Forbes talked me through it. He said something to me about his mother having been a patient there before her suicide. He wasn't talking about his birth mother. He was talking about his adoptive one—the one I saw flipping out and killing Eloise."

"Hang on. I thought Chuck and his wife, whatever her name was, were his birth parents."

"Her name was Val," Sully said. "And, no, they weren't. A couple of years ago, when Forbes was questioning me about Betty's murder, he asked me something about whether I'd ever wanted to find my birth parents. I told him I figured he was asking because he was adopted himself. He didn't deny it, just shut the conversation down. Now I get it."

Dez whistled low before speaking. "Jesus. How much do you think he remembers?"

"He hasn't said anything about Gerhardt, about having any recollection of him as his father."

"You think he would have just forgotten him like that?"

"What I do know is that he didn't have much of a relationship with him. Most of David's time was spent with his mother. I got the distinct impression Gerhardt's always been a workaholic, and when he was around, he was the kind of father a kid would rather forget."

"The whole suffocation thing. I wonder if he remembers that?"

"It could be he blocked the memory. It happens sometimes with trauma."

"Maybe," Dez said. "We need to talk to him about it."

Sully caught Dez's arm before he could return to the house. "Wait, Dez."

Dez turned, met his brother's eye. Sully's expression—furrowed brow and slightly parted lips—suggested some sort of internal conflict was raging. He gave Sully a moment to get his thoughts together before voicing his question. "What?"

"I don't know, I just…. Are you sure we should tell him?"

"He has a right to know. Hell, maybe he already does."

"I don't think he does. I think he might have some vague memory, but I think he's found a way to put a lot of it behind him. He made a new life with the Raynors, and I know he's really close to his dad. I get that. I found you guys, and you weren't just my adoptive family. You were my *family*, and you were all I needed. I don't know, sometimes maybe it's better not to know the truth."

Dez scanned his boot tops, hearing more in Sully's statement than he'd perhaps intended. "You wish I hadn't told you about Gerhardt, don't you? I'm sorry. I really wish I hadn't said anything."

"No, I'm glad you told me the truth, Dez. It gave me the chance to confront him with it. But Forbes won't have that same chance now."

Dez met Sully's eye. "Except he's involved with the investigation. If it comes out he is who you're saying he is, he'd be in a major conflict situation."

This time, it was Sully gazing down at his boots. "Yeah, I guess."

"Listen," Dez said. "Why don't Lachlan and I go talk to Chuck, see what he has to say? I mean, we do need to sort out what happened to Eloise, don't we? You'll need to help her move on."

"Yeah, you're right. She needs answers too."

Dez settled a hand on Sully's shoulder, then moved closer and draped his arm fully around his brother, pulling him into a half-hug as they turned back toward the house. "Come on. One problem at a time, all right? We'll get this sorted out."

"Thanks, D."

Only then did Dez shake his head at the absurdity of the situation.

"You know what's weird?" he said, his hand on the door handle. "Never in my wildest dreams would I ever have pictured myself giving a damn about Forbes's feelings."

27

CHARLES RAYNOR WAS A BUSY MAN, so busy it seemed at first he would have no time to talk to Dez and Lachlan.

"He's swamped today," the receptionist in the mayor's office said. "He's preparing for a meeting with the city planner this afternoon. If you'd like to leave me your names, I can—"

Lachlan, though, had an ace up his sleeve. "Eloise Gerhardt. If you could just pass along the name to him, I'm sure he'll see us."

The receptionist's face was the picture of confusion, but she followed through, picking up her phone and dialling. "I'm sorry, sir, but Mr. Fields has asked me to provide you with a name. Eloise Gerhardt."

A pause followed, and a lengthy one in Dez's approximation. He cast Lachlan a quick side-eye, checking for a reaction. Lachlan's face held a smile, the sort of cat-got-the-canary grin he'd likely worn into his share of suspect interviews during his storied policing days. Dez would have hated to be on the receiving end of one of those smirks had he ever landed on the wrong side of an interview room.

At last, the receptionist provided the answer Lachlan, at least, seemed to be anticipating. "End of the hall, corner office on the left."

Charles occupied a massive space, floor-to-ceiling windows on two sides, making the office appear even larger. Given the mayor's office was on the twenty-second floor of City Hall, it boasted some of the best views in the city, looking out over the urban sprawl of Kimotan Rapids, the river close enough to watch the boaters in the warmer months.

Charles stood at one of the windows, casting his gaze somewhere beyond this office, possibly even beyond the city.

"What can I help you with?" he asked. No polite greeting he was so known for. He simply sounded exhausted.

"Mr. Mayor, I'm Lachlan Fields and this is—"

"I know who you are." Charles at last turned to face them. Dez wasn't surprised the politician's characteristic grin was down for the count. "I don't have much time to talk. Please, make this quick."

Lachlan took a seat in one of a set of plush chairs this side of the mayor's massive desk. Dez remained standing.

Lachlan had just taken a breath to speak when he was interrupted by Charles, his eyes having settled on Dez's large form. "You're Deputy Chief Braddock's son. I hadn't clued in right away for some reason."

"I am, sir."

The mayor took a few steps and, to Dez's surprise, extended a hand to him. "I know it's two years too late, but allow me to extend my condolences. I know Flynn and I didn't always see eye to eye, but I've come to respect the job he had to do. It can't have been easy."

"It wasn't," Dez said. He still wasn't sold on the guy, but decided to be big about it. He thought his dad would want that. "Thank you," he said before breaking the handshake.

Charles motioned to the other guest chair. "Please, have a seat."

Lachlan waited until Dez and Charles had sat—the latter not on his own chair as Dez had expected, but on the edge of his desk, facing his two visitors. It could be it was an attempt at appearing open—more open than he intended to be. Or it could be the way he normally was. It was anybody's guess until the questioning started.

"Let me begin by saying we've managed to piece a few things together," Lachlan said. "We've been working on solving the disappearance of David Gerhardt, and the trail's led us to your doorstep."

Charles paled. Dez guessed the mayor now regretted his choice of seat.

"Are you all right, sir?" Dez asked.

It took a few seconds to get an answer, but Charles at last replied, "Fine." The hushed sound of the word made him sound anything but.

Dez opted to take over. The situation required tact Lachlan didn't often use. "We've learned a fair bit about the kind of life David lived in the Gerhardt home. He was close to his mother, and she was good to him, but his father was a sociopath who we believe tried to kill him. As a result, Eloise set out to find a way to protect her child. When she found out she couldn't do it alone, she was forced to look for another solution. We have information that you and your wife were that solution."

Charles stood shakily, keeping one hand on the desktop to balance him as he circled it. Once in front of his chair, he collapsed into it. His eyes, usually full of smiles whenever a TV crew was nearby, appeared nearly dead by comparison. "Where did you come by this information?"

"We have a source," Dez said. "Someone who made some connections and brought them to us."

Charles sat forward, imploring eyes settling on Dez and Lachlan in turn. "How much do you want? I have no doubt you're being paid by someone for your services. I'll pay more. Just please, whatever you think you've learned, I need you to keep it to yourselves." His eyes widened. "God, Forbes doesn't know, does he?"

"He doesn't remember?"

"He remembers his birth mother, but he doesn't remember much about her besides her first name. He's blocked a lot out, I think. Val and I took him to a child psychologist after he came into our lives, given we were informed about the attempt on his life. The psychologist said Forbes remembered something about not being able to breathe, but little else. He didn't seem to remember why, and said nothing about an incident with a pillow. That never changed throughout his youth, nor did he ever mention anything about Roman Gerhardt.

"He asked me once, when he was a teenager, who his birth parents were. He'd never discussed it before that, although he'd sometimes talk about his memories of Eloise. I talked to him about her, the good person she was, how she'd allowed us to raise him because she was unable to do it herself. He said he had no memory of his father. I told him a partial truth, that he wasn't a good man. Forbes didn't question me further. I think part of him wanted to know more; that's natural. But I think he was afraid too —afraid of what he might find if he went looking. As far as I know, his search for answers began and ended that day."

"How did the boy end up in your care?" Lachlan asked.

"I knew Eloise's father. He was a good man, a kind man who loved his family dearly. His wife died young and he brought the girls up himself. There was nothing he wouldn't have done for them and for his grandson. When Eloise and Mariel went to him with what Gerhardt had done, and how Eloise's attempt at escape with the child had failed, he helped them arrange a new family for Forbes. Eloise knew Gerhardt might let her go if she was alone, but he'd never let her take the child. She needed a permanent solution, so they faked his kidnapping. Her father brought Forbes to Val and me, and we raised him as our own."

"How did you avoid being found out?" Dez asked. "I mean, it was all over the news."

"We kept his presence a secret for a long time. We homeschooled him, and we didn't take him out anywhere for a while. But we quickly realized it was no life for a child, so we moved. We left the province entirely, settled down on an acreage. We continued to homeschool him, though. Too many eyes in the public school system. If I have one regret, it's that we didn't do more to ensure he had some friends growing up. He didn't. We couldn't afford a situation where someone recognized him. It got easier when he got older. He looked different: His hair darkened, he grew taller and broader, his facial features matured. I had been working for a small-town police service, but I really wanted badly to work in Kimotan Rapids. Anyway, Val's health had deteriorated by then, and she was back in KR. It was a long way to go to visit, but there wasn't any help for her where we were living."

"Help?" Dez asked. "You mean Lockwood?"

Charles's gaze snapped down to his lap. "I know what you must think of me, putting her into that place with that monster." He returned his eyes to Dez's. "But you need to understand, Lockwood was all there was. It still is the only dedicated mental health facility within a three-province radius. I'd tried taking her to a regular hospital, one with a psychiatric unit. They looked after her there for a time. But it soon became apparent her breakdown was not to be of short duration. The episodes were coming more and more frequently, and she was rarely herself. Sometimes, the people she became scared me. I worried about leaving Forbes alone with her when she was like that. At any rate, it quickly became clear Lockwood was the only option.

"I met with Gerhardt first. I wanted to see whether he showed any indication of suspicion of me or my wife, something to show he knew about us. But he didn't. He actually seemed kind in his dealings with Val. I've heard that about him, that he could be remarkably good with his patients, despite the way he treated others. I felt I had no choice. God help me, I had her committed. Then one day, I got a call from Gerhardt saying she'd managed to take her own life."

Lachlan edged forward slightly in his chair. "Did you suspect that, perhaps, he'd had a hand?"

"I did, naturally, question it. I insisted on an autopsy, and I asked the pathologist to check for any signs of foul play. Given I was working with the KRPD by then, I had an existing relationship with the pathologist, and I'm certain he told me the truth. He assured me there were no signs of anything untoward. She'd hanged herself, no signs of a struggle, nothing in the toxicology to suggest she'd been drugged. I think she knew she was ill and wouldn't get better. She just couldn't deal with it anymore."

"I'm sorry," Dez said.

Charles offered a small smile and nodded his thanks.

"Can I ask you something else?" Dez asked. "Are you familiar with a group called the Circle?"

"I'm aware of them, yes."

"Are you a member?"

"No. I was approached around the time I started working in civic politics, but I turned them down. I knew enough about the Circle to know I didn't trust their tactics. And I knew Gerhardt was a member. I would never join anything that would put me in proximity with that man." He met Dez's eye. "To be honest, I've always wondered whether that was where the corruption claims originated. I made some enemies in the Circle's ranks when I refused to join, and I think the false claims might have been a way for them to get back at me. And I also wonder whether they weren't eager to have one of their own members in the mayor's office." He sat forward, his gaze intensifying as he regarded Dez. "I'm afraid I was very embittered by the whole thing at the time, and I took it out on your father. I know he was only doing his job; I'd been a police officer myself, of course, and I knew how it worked. I sure wish I could take back some of the things I said to him."

"It's okay," Dez said. "I'm sure he knows, wherever he is." That could have been right here, for all Dez knew. Only Sully would know for sure.

Something else needed to be discussed, the most difficult topic. Charles seemed like a good guy, and Dez wasn't thrilled about having to broach the topic of Eloise's murder, but there was no way around it. She'd never been found, and she deserved to be.

Thankfully, Lachlan fielded that one. "Did you ever find out what happened to Eloise?"

"No," Charles said. Dez saw no tells he was readying for a lie. "Val and I suggested she could come around for occasional visitations with Forbes, but she never came to see him. I think at first, it was hard for her to get away, what with Gerhardt being how he was and all of the police and media attention on the case. Val and I, too, felt very hemmed in at that point, like we couldn't move a finger for fear of someone seeing and reading into it." He paused, thinking. "You know, come to think of it, Val did tell me once that Eloise came to see Forbes. He and I had gone for a fishing break that time, I think. I remember asking because Forbes found a bag stashed by the stairs containing a few of his things from his old life: books and toys and things like that. Val said Eloise had dropped the things off and left."

"And you're sure that's what happened?"

"Of course." Charles sank slightly in his chair. "Why? Are you suggesting something more?"

"I'm afraid so, sir," Lachlan said. "We have reason to believe Eloise was murdered by your wife."

"That's absurd!"

"Is it? You know how deep emotional strain can sometimes trigger people with dissociative personality disorder. Our information is that Eloise went there that day to take her son back. Understandably, Val was badly shaken and upset by this, and we believe she lashed out violently. I don't think she fully knew what she was doing, if that helps. It's quite possible she would have been found not criminally responsible for the offence. But I think if you were to search the property, you might find that Eloise is still there somewhere."

Charles stared at Lachlan a long moment. Then he crumpled. His face dropped into the shelter of his hands, and he sobbed, shoulders quaking with the rush of emotion.

Dez pitied the man.

Close to a minute passed before Charles uttered anything more. What he said came out as a muffled moan behind his hands. "Oh, Val. Val, what did you do?"

Another half-minute ticked by before Charles withdrew his hands. His face was a mess, eyes red and tear-filled, skin mottled, nose running. He grabbed a tissue from a drawer and blew his nose, then needed a second.

"Are you all right, sir?" Dez asked.

Charles nodded, but the movement didn't match what Dez was seeing. "I'm sorry. God, I—" He wiped tears from his cheeks before returning his gaze to Dez. "I didn't know. You have to believe me. I didn't. But, heaven help me, I suspected something might have happened. That bag didn't just contain toys and books. There were clothes and a few toiletries. I understood why she'd want him to have some of his favourite things, but the rest didn't make sense. Not unless the explanation was what you've just suggested. I wondered. I did. But I didn't ask. Val gave me her explanation, and I didn't question it, because the alternative was unthinkable. I was a police officer, and I knew something was off. I did search for evidence to show something had transpired, but I never found anything—no blood, no hair, nothing broken, no notable injuries on Val. I did notice our butcher knife was gone, but she said she'd broken the blade so had thrown it out. Oh, God, you don't think—"

"We think so, yes," Lachlan said. "I know it isn't easy to hear. You knew Val best. Do you have any idea what she might have done with the body?"

Charles shook his head. "I never even accepted she'd done anything wrong. I didn't ever get as far as trying to think where a body might have been concealed. One thing, though, she wouldn't have kept Eloise at the acreage. She wouldn't have risked either myself or Forbes finding her. This happened before we moved away, and we lived very near the Black Woods. It's quite likely, I suppose, she might have taken the body there. Oh,

God. I know what you need to do, and I understand it, but this will ruin Forbes and me."

"You had nothing to do with it," Lachlan said. "I believe you on that. I'll go to bat for you publicly. It could be with the right public relations, the impact on your career can be minimized."

"I appreciate that, but it isn't my career I'm talking about. It's my relationship with my son. He was close to Eloise. He talked about her all the time as a child, and he always asked why she didn't come to see him. I'm worried he'll think I had something to do with either the death or with covering it up, or that he'll blame me for not doing enough to prevent it. Regardless, this will bring the truth out, and that will break us. He'll never see me again."

"I think you're overthinking things," Dez said. "If he's as close to you as I think he is, he won't give up on you just like that. He'll be upset, no question, but you didn't do anything wrong. Hell, you didn't even lie to him. You didn't know either."

"But I suspected, and did nothing. That's bad enough." Charles sighed. "My God. What am I going to do?"

Dez exchanged a look with Lachlan. He knew how miserable he must look when Lachlan took up the baton once again. "Leave it with us for now, all right? It might be there's a way to do this so no one ever needs to know. I mean, there's little use now, is there? Val's gone, and Gerhardt is as good as. The people left behind don't deserve to be burned over this."

Charles met his eye, gently raised brows and a slight lift at the corners of his mouth suggesting hope had dawned at Lachlan's words. "Thank you. Thank you both. I'll do what I can to help."

Dez and Lachlan took their leave, standing and heading for the exit. Lachlan turned back before opening the office door.

"Forbes is investigating the Lockwood case. We might have to tell him something so as to avoid a conflict. Should it come out about his relationship to Gerhardt, it could affect the admissibility of any evidence he's gathering."

Charles nodded tightly. "I understand. I'll try to figure out how to break it to him."

Dez smiled. "One thing I've learned about Forbes. He's a tough bastard, and he stands by his family even when things aren't so good. Maybe you're not giving him enough credit."

Charles returned the smile. "Maybe you're right. Thank you, both of you."

Lachlan gave the mayor a lazy parting salute and led the way from the room.

28

THE SOUND of a car pulling up outside had Sully peering out the window of Dez's Riverview-area apartment.

He'd called Forbes and asked to meet with him. He hadn't said about what. It wasn't the sort of thing you could say over the phone.

Having buzzed the man in, Sully took the few moments he had to steel his nerves for the upcoming conversation. He'd been in this same room when he'd learned Gerhardt was his father. It was about to play host to a repeat.

Sully had insisted on coming alone. Although Dez and Forbes didn't hate each other as much as they once had, the old tensions hadn't completely eased. The last thing Sully wanted was Forbes on edge before he'd even broken the news.

A knock on the door signalled it was time to get this rolling. Sully answered, and the Major Crimes detective swept into the room.

"I haven't got a lot of time. We've got a lot on the go with the Lockwood investigation. As you can imagine, we've got piles of people to talk to, so—"

"I won't take up much of your time, but I'm thinking you

might have to shelve your role in the investigation once I'm done."

"Why would I do that? It's the case of a lifetime."

"I thought Lowell Braddock was the case of a lifetime."

"This could lead us to him. That's what I'm hoping anyway."

No sense delaying the inevitable. "Sit down, okay?"

Now Forbes appeared suspicious, head angled away, narrowed eyes fixed on Sully. "Why?"

"Humour me."

Forbes sat on the pullout. Sully had made it back up into a couch for the meeting, and he lowered himself into a spot on the other end, giving himself one last moment for thought.

"You asked me once if I ever wondered about my birth family, remember?"

Forbes pondered the question, as if trying to recollect when he'd asked the question. "I think so. Why?"

"I said I thought you were curious because you were adopted yourself."

"What's your point?"

"You are, aren't you?"

"Adopted? Yeah. So? My dad is my dad."

"I know. I get that. The Braddocks are my family. I never questioned that. Thing is, when I found out about my birth family, it made me wish even more the Braddocks were my blood."

Forbes gave a slight shrug. "Blood doesn't always matter. Not about the important things."

"I know. I guess what I'm trying to ask is whether you're interested in knowing more about your birth family. I mean, do you remember them?"

Forbes shifted in his seat. "Why are you asking me this? It's none of your business."

"You're going to have to trust me when I tell you it kind of is. Please. I promise I have a point."

Forbes heaved a suffering sigh. "I remember my birth mother a little. I don't think I could even describe her in any great detail anymore, though. It's been a lot of years and I don't even have a photo of her."

"Do you know her name?"

"I remember people calling her Ella. I don't know more than that. My parents never gave me a last name, and I never asked for one. I was happy where I was. I didn't need more."

"But you still wondered. You wondered enough to ask me about my experience."

"Of course I wondered. Who wouldn't? Doesn't mean finding out is a good idea. I mean, if you had the chance, wouldn't you want to unlearn the shit you know now about your own birth family?"

"Maybe. Maybe not. I don't know. Sometimes knowing is hard, but it gives you the chance to make choices you wouldn't have been able to otherwise. Knowing about them, it's helped me know myself better—not the good side, but the other part. I think we have to understand the darker parts of ourselves too. Meeting the Dules let me do that. I could see where that part of me came from, so maybe I can figure out how to control it."

Forbes crossed his arms. "You're working around to telling me you know who my birth parents are, aren't you?"

"I guess I am, yeah. But I won't say anything more about it if you really don't want to know."

Forbes uncrossed his arms, started to cross them again, then used them to lean forward, into his lap. He remained silent a while. A long while.

Sully waited.

At last Forbes spoke. "I have good memories of Ella, nothing but good. But there's this other thing. It's always felt like a dream kind of, a nightmare, this feeling of suffocating, of knowing I'm about to die. Her voice, it saved me. I kind of remember her voice, I guess. That's all I've got. Blonde hair and a voice." He sat up, meeting Sully's eye. "I have no memory of my father. I know I had one, but I have the impression he wasn't around much. She was a good person, though, right?"

"Yeah," Sully said. "She was."

"Do you know why?"

"Why what?"

"Why she gave me up. My parents always told me she wasn't in a good place in her life, that she was in a situation that made raising a child impossible. They never said what that meant, and I never asked. I always assumed she was a drug addict or something."

"She wasn't," Sully said. "She was with a horrible man who made life impossible. She tried to escape the situation with you, but he found the two of you and made you go back. Then something happened that made her realize she couldn't protect you anymore. The only thing she *could* do was find someone else to raise you, someone who could give you a better life, a safe and happy life."

Forbes hadn't moved, body still angled forward, toward Sully. He'd lost some colour, and Sully questioned whether Forbes could handle what he was no doubt about to ask. "This something that happened. What was it?"

Sully took a breath, let it out slowly before answering, holding Forbes's eye as he did so. "Your birth father, he tried to suffocate you with a pillow. Ella returned home unexpectedly and interrupted without knowing it. She only found out about it later because you told her."

Forbes blanched, gaze redirecting to the wall. "It wasn't a nightmare."

"I'm sorry."

"I thought maybe I'd almost drowned or something, but it was —Jesus Christ." Forbes returned his eyes to Sully's. "How do you know all this?"

"She showed me."

"Ella."

Sully nodded.

"That means she was murdered."

Sully nodded again.

"How? Was it my biological father?"

Sully had considered this moment, this question. The truth, he knew, would shatter Forbes, might destroy every positive feeling he still carried for Val Raynor. She was a killer, yes. But she'd also been a severely mentally ill woman who'd snapped only because she believed the child she'd come to love as her own was about to be taken from her forever. It was unlikely Mara or Flynn would have reacted violently to Sully's birth family showing up and trying to take him, but maybe they would have. Either way, they wouldn't have let him go peacefully.

Val's reaction had been her brain's way of dealing with it. Horrible and as wrong as you could go wrong, yes, but the result of mental illness, a part of herself she couldn't control. Sully didn't have DID, but he knew what it was to lose control to a dark part of himself, to nearly kill while in that state. How could he blame Val when he wasn't so different?

Had it not been for Gerhardt, Eloise wouldn't have been in the position to have to give up her child in the first place. And Val wouldn't have been placed in the position of needing to defend the chance at motherhood that had been so unexpectedly granted to her.

Maybe it was Sully's loathing for the man doing his thinking for him, but right now, he had no problem making Gerhardt out as the architect of Eloise's brutal fate.

"I'm not really sure," Sully said in answer to Forbes's question. "I think it was."

Forbes's head lowered, brows settling over his eyes. "Who is he? I want to see to it he's dealt with."

"He has been dealt with," Sully said. "There's no easy way to say this. Forbes, your mother's full name was Eloise. You were born David Gerhardt, and you've been the subject of a missing person file since you were six years old. Your father is—"

Forbes fired off the couch, backed away a couple of steps. "No."

"I'm sorry, but it's true. The book you have in your shelf, the

Dr. Seuss one from your birth mother. She showed me that. And she showed me her memories of you as a child. It all came together at your house, when I saw the book and the photo of you as a kid."

Forbes shook his head. "I'm not that man's kid. I can't be. Not him."

"I've been saying the same thing since I found out about my own past. I debated telling you because I know what it makes me feel about myself, coming from someone like that. But I also know you're in a conflict situation with this case, and you have the right to know, to make some choices about what you do going forward."

Sully stood, facing Forbes fully. "I know it probably doesn't help much, especially coming from me, but I really do know what you're going through. And I know you're not big on talking, but if you ever want to, you can talk to me." He smirked. "I'm dead anyway, right? I'm as silent as the grave."

The heat and the panic hadn't left Forbes's expression, and Sully had to struggle to hold his ground as Forbes took a quick step forward, closing the distance between them. Forbes stared into Sully's face as if looking for something there.

"You're telling me…. You're telling me we're brothers?"

It was Sully's turn to pale. It felt stupid now, but in all this time, he hadn't even considered this other very real truth. "Yeah. Yeah, I guess we are." His lips quirked.

Forbes reached out slowly, fingers touching and then bunching up the front of Sully's hoodie. Sully waited, uncertain whether he was about to get shoved to the ground or hit.

Instead, Forbes only shook him gently, letting his breath out in a little "huh" sound. His lips turned up at the corners.

"I don't fucking believe it. I've got a brother."

THE FORKS WAS QUIET, a chill in the air promising winter on the horizon. Sully pulled his jacket tighter around him.

A cold breeze had proven enough to keep most people off the streets today, allowing Dez and Sully to move unhindered as they made the trek between Ravenwood and the Gerhardts' old house.

Just as well, because they had some anxious company this time: Forbes Raynor.

They paused in the bushes outside a house within view of the Gerhardt place. Sully had led them in a different direction this time, ensuring they wouldn't easily be within sight of the house where Snowy and Terrence were staying. Not that it would do much good. Snowy would know he was here, regardless.

He paused to rub at his middle. A dull ache had formed with the exertion of the hike. It was annoying, but he didn't dwell. He knew it could have been—should have been—far worse.

Dez hadn't missed the movement. "You okay?"

"Yeah. All good."

Dez wasn't likely sold, but he dropped it anyway. "Any chance of us avoiding Snowy? I'd rather not see that little traitor again if I can help it."

"If she's around here, she'll know where I am. I don't know if her gift has any sort of radius or whatever, but we'll be too close no matter which way we go."

"So we'd better make this quick."

"Gerhardt's basically gone, Dez. Whatever risk she posed is gone too." Sully scanned the street one last time, relieved to find it still quiet. "Ready?"

"Yeah, let's get this done."

Sully started to push through the trees but was drawn up short by the realization Forbes had yet to say a word. He'd been quiet on the boat ride over, and he'd muttered a few curse words as he was briefly assailed by Noisy Ned inside Ravenwood. But he'd kept to himself after that.

It hadn't initially struck Sully as unusual; Forbes wasn't much for conversation at the best of times. But this silence possessed a different quality, one built more of tension than introversion.

Sully halted Dez with a hand on his arm before returning his attention to Forbes. "You okay, man?"

"I never believed in ghosts," he said. "I think even after everything I saw you do, I never really bought into it somehow. But, God, man, you're telling me she's really still there? In that house?"

Sully nodded. "Yeah. And I think seeing you will help her."

"I know that's what you told me, and that's why I came. But holy hell."

Sully gave Forbes a minute, watching as the thoughts played out across the man's face. Dez's tree trunk arms folded over his chest, the picture of impatience. Sully didn't blame him, the realization things could go way wrong in The Forks all too obvious after their past visits. But Forbes was who this was about today. Forbes and Eloise. They'd do this on their terms or not at all.

But when Forbes showed no immediate sign of emerging from his thoughts, Sully decided some gentle pressure was in order. "I know this isn't easy, but staying in one place for too long around here isn't a good idea. The sooner we can get in and out, the better."

Forbes acknowledged Sully with a stiff nod. "Right. Right, let's do this, then."

This time, Dez led the way, pushing through the trees before Forbes could again delay things. Sully followed, keeping Forbes next to him as they approached the street. Sully tugged Forbes into a jog as they crossed the road.

They stepped onto the Gerhardt property, keeping quiet, waiting on conversation until they were inside. Sully led them into the sitting room where he'd first set eyes on Eloise, wondering if she'd sense her son's return. When he didn't see her within the first minute or so, he tried calling out.

"Eloise? Are you here?"

He was met by silence.

"Nothing?" Dez asked.

Sully shook his head, then turned to see Forbes heading for the staircase leading to the upper floor. "Hey, Forbes, watch it. The stairs aren't in great shape, and neither is the upper floor."

Forbes didn't answer but stalled at the base of the stairway. Sully joined him, peering into the older man's face to try to get a read of what was playing out within his mind. He'd gone pale, eyes wide as he stared into the shadows above.

"You okay?"

"I used to dream about this house. As I got older, I thought I must have made it up."

"You remember it?"

"Kind of. Not really. I don't know." He looked away from the stairs, focusing on Sully. "I think my bedroom was up there."

Sully gazed from Forbes to the stairs and back again. "You want to go have a look?"

"I don't know." Forbes paused another long moment, then, without further conversation, started gingerly up the steps.

Sully glanced back at Dez. "You're okay staying here?"

Dez patted his coat pocket. "I've got Emily's gun this time. I'm plenty okay. I'll keep an eye out and call if something comes up."

Sully nodded and followed Forbes.

Having reached the second floor, Sully had intended to tell Forbes where the room was. He discovered there was no need; Forbes drifted straight there as if in a daze, no instructions necessary.

By the time Sully reached David's bedroom, Forbes was in the midst of it, arms hugged across his chest, back to Sully.

"Forbes?"

A sound somewhere between a gasp and a sob came from the older man, and Sully took a couple of steps forward, gaining Forbes's side while hoping the floor would accommodate them both. It creaked, but held. Just as well, because the broken-down state of the building was the least of Sully's concerns at the moment.

Forbes's eyes had covered over in a sheen of unshed tears. He brushed at them and trained his gaze from the bookshelf to the opened closet to the toys on the shelf.

"Forbes?"

"I remember this," he said. Then his eyes settled on the bed, and awe changed to dread. "I remember all of it."

Sully sensed her before he saw her, a presence at the doorway leading to the hall. He turned to find her there, wide eyes fixated on the greying blond hair of the newcomer.

"Hey, Forbes," Sully said. "She's here."

Forbes turned slowly, as if uncertain whether he wanted to see. Unsurprisingly, there was nothing there for him *to* see. "Where?" he asked.

Sully allowed Forbes to follow his gaze. "Doorway." Then he turned his attention to her. "Eloise? This is Forbes Raynor. I know it's been a lot of years but—" He broke off the introduction as she shot forward, stilling only once she stood directly in front of Forbes. She studied him, as if both recognizing something within the man and looking for something familiar. When a smile broke upon her face, Sully knew she'd found it.

"You don't need me to tell you," Sully said to her.

But it was as if he'd ceased to exist. Everything in this moment came down to just two people: Eloise and David. He was all she saw as she brought up a hand to brush at a stray strand of Forbes's ordinarily neat hair.

"Sullivan? What's going on?"

"She knows you," Sully said, voice coming through a smile. "Who you are, I mean."

"Is she okay?"

Sully nodded. "Yeah. She's okay. More okay than I've ever seen her."

It was true. Even as they stood here, the injuries on her were beginning to fade, the stains and rips on her clothing disappearing.

"Can I talk to her?" Forbes asked. "I mean, she'll hear me?"

"Yeah. I think she'd like that."

Forbes glanced at Sully, flinching slightly as he eyed him. "It feels weird, doing this while you're here."

"I can leave."

"Then I won't know what she's saying back."

"I think it's kind of obvious what she's saying back, don't you?" Sully smiled, then left Forbes to it, heading back down the stairs and to Dez.

Dez was staring out the living room window, eyes hard as he watched for potential threats. "How's it going?"

"He's talking to her now, I think."

"And she's okay?"

"I think she's almost ready to go, so yeah."

Dez nodded, then took a break from his surveillance duty to grace Sully with a smile. "What you do, it's pretty cool, you know."

Sully returned the grin. "It has its moments." He turned his gaze to the world outside the broken window just as Dez did. "Anything going on out there?"

"Just Terrence lurking from what I can tell."

"Terrence is out there?"

Dez nodded with his chin. "By those shrubs across the road. I was contemplating inviting him in. Guess I owe him for clueing me in that you were in trouble back at Lockwood. You good with me getting him?"

"I'm not really thrilled at the idea of seeing Snowy again, but it would be good to talk to Terrence."

"I don't see her, just him."

Sully nodded his agreement, and Dez waved a hand out the window. A moment later, a bald head popped up from the bushes.

Terrence jogged across the road, gun in hand, and entered the house. "How the hell'd you make me out there?" he asked Dez.

"Sorry."

"Guess I'm getting rusty." He turned to Sully, and his face

cracked into a wide grin as he knocked knuckles with the younger man. "How ya doin', kid?"

"Good, thanks. You?"

"Decent. Heard you and the old lady took care of Gerhardt."

Sully raised his eyebrows. "How'd you know that?"

"Hey, my mom?" Terrence said by way of explanation.

It was all Sully required. "Right. Of course."

The mention of Snowy caused Terrence's face to fall. "Listen, man, I want to apologize to you for what she did. I didn't know until it was too late. You need to believe me. She got it in her head she wanted to face her past, and I figured I could get us in there and out without being seen. She's had a lot of nightmares and flashbacks, and I know firsthand how running from your past doesn't help you heal. You saw me through my own demons by helping me face them, and I figured I could do the same for her. Worse came to worse, I knew I could bust my way out of there easily enough. But it turned out she wanted to go for another reason altogether."

Sully nodded. "Me."

Terrence's smile carried shame. "I just thought she was going to use the bathroom. Next thing I know, she's gone. When she came back, she looked like hell, and she admitted to me she'd sold you out to Gerhardt. I was gonna go in there to get you myself when I saw Dez and your ma. Figured you'd have things cased between you, so I bailed and got Mom out of there.

"Listen, I know this won't mean much after everything, but she really does feel like shit about what she did."

Dez faced Terrence, a sour expression marring his features. "No offence to you, Terrence, but good."

Terrence faced Dez. "I don't blame you for being pissed. If it was my brother, I'd be out for blood. All I'm trying to tell you is I'm sorry. I didn't know."

"We know that," Sully said.

Dez shrugged. "Doesn't erase what she did though."

"I get it. But you need to understand, we've been living a half-life out here. She keeps talking like her life is over anyway, but she wants something more for me. We're stuck in hiding because of two men: Gerhardt and Lowell Braddock. She figured she could take care of Gerhardt by making a deal with him, trading info for her freedom. That would leave just the one obstacle."

"We share that obstacle," Dez said. "Now we've got Gerhardt dealt with, we're hoping Lowell will be falling alongside him very soon. We haven't figured out exactly how we're going to get there yet, but it's coming."

"I don't know what I can do to help," Terrence said. "But if you need me, I'm here. Honestly, I'd love to be there when the son of a bitch goes down."

A creak on the stairs had them turning to see Forbes making his way down. His eyes were a little red, but he otherwise appeared okay.

He was most of the way down when he spotted Terrence, and the sight of the stranger pulled him up short.

"It's all right," Sully said. "Forbes, this is Terrence. Terrence, Forbes."

The two men exchanged a nod of greeting before Forbes turned to Sully. "Does he—"

"Know about me? Yeah. Both that I'm alive and can see ghosts."

Forbes nodded and took a breath. "I know I told you I wanted some privacy, but the conversation seems kind of one-sided to me, so...."

Terrence chuckled. "Yeah, I know how that goes. Tell ya what, I'll leave you to it. I'll keep an eye on the place from the road, fire off a shot if I see anything I don't like."

Dez clapped Terrence on the shoulder. "Thanks. I appreciate it. And thanks again for coming to me about Sully the other day."

"Anytime. And, hey, I owe him." He turned and pulled Sully into a bro hug, thumping him a couple of times on the back before releasing him. "You take care of yourself, kid. Call me if you need me. I mean it."

Terrence having taken his leave, Sully returned attention to Forbes. Eloise, now fully healed, appeared beside him, one hand hovering near one of his.

"I told her all about how good my life was after she gave me up, how close I am to my dad—the dad who raised me, I mean. And I told her none of it was her fault, that she's shown how good a mother she was by making that kind of sacrifice. I guess I need to know what she wants to say."

"She's been saying it all along," Sully said. "She loves you, that's obvious. And she's happy now. I think she got trapped here after she died, so she had no way of knowing what happened to you." Sully stopped there. The reality was, Eloise had to have been petrified by the possibility of Val Raynor turning on her adopted child; if she'd snapped once, she could do it again. What Eloise couldn't have known was that Charles Raynor wasn't about to let anything happen to the boy. He'd made sure of it, in a way that ultimately proved tragic.

Sully thought it might be best for Forbes to never know the full truth.

"I want to find her, give her a proper burial," Forbes said. "And I want to find evidence of what happened. If Gerhardt did this, I want the world to know. And if it was someone else, they need to face justice for it."

Sully turned to Eloise. "What about you? Is that what you want?"

She shook her head, the movement quick and decisive. No, she definitely did not want that. Sully didn't have to ask to know her thoughts had travelled the same paths and had drawn the same conclusions.

"She doesn't need anyone to find her body," Sully said. "And she doesn't need any more justice. Gerhardt's paid for his crimes, and she's just found the only thing she ever really needed. You're the reason she was stuck here, Forbes, and you're the reason she can leave."

"Leave?" Forbes turned to the space Sully had been watching, his eyes fixing on the spot where Eloise stood. "I only just found her again."

"Her staying here, it isn't right," Sully said. "And I don't think people we love ever really leave us. They just go somewhere we can't see."

"Even you?"

"Even me."

"So how do you know?"

Sully shrugged. "I don't. I guess sometimes, you just have to have faith."

Forbes smirked. "I never used to know what that meant. I've had to develop it in spades since I got to know you, Gray."

Sully smiled at Forbes before turning it on Eloise. She drifted up to him, settling a hand alongside his face. It was a thank you, no need for words he couldn't hear.

"You're welcome," he said.

She deepened the touch, sending a thought into his brain. This time, unlike the others, the thought was calm, and it held there: a set of wind chimes, jangling gently in a breeze.

"What is it?" Dez asked once Eloise had broken the connection.

"I think she's telling me she'll let Forbes know she's around by playing with wind chimes." Having received a confirmatory nod from Eloise, Sully turned to Forbes. "You have some?"

"No," Forbes said. "But damn sure I'm gonna go out and buy some now."

Sully watched as Eloise approached Forbes. She rested a hand over his heart, and a peace stole over her face as if she'd felt the thrum of his life beneath shirt, flesh and bone.

Then, with one more gaze up into the face of her son, she was gone.

29

SULLY PEERED through the mesh eye holes of his rubber mask, a poor approximation of a ghost if ever he'd seen one.

Dez had bought the stupid costume for him, cackling maniacally as he'd stuck the mask over his little brother's head. Dez had seen something hilarious in the idea of a trick-or-treating Sully dressed as a ghost.

All Sully saw was his first chance at an evening where he was something other than the ghost he'd been forced to become.

Kayleigh tugged on his hand, jack-o-lantern shaped candy bucket already half full as it bounced along next to her, threatening to spill its contents onto the sidewalk.

"Come on!" she said. "You're going to love this next house. They always decorate it really awesome. One year, they even did a haunted house in the garage!"

This year, it turned out, they'd done one, too, and Sully held onto Kayleigh and pretended to be scared as she squealed at the animatronic creatures, ghosts and ghouls the family had set up. It took a lot more than that to spook him. A hell of a lot more.

As it stood, this was the best night he'd had in years.

Given the current state of his life, he knew it couldn't last.

Forbes was waiting for him at Dez and Eva's when Sully returned with Kayleigh an hour later.

The police detective, seated in one of the living room chairs, wasn't bothering to hide a smirk as he regarded Dez's scarecrow costume. If Dez was staying home with Eva to hand out candy instead of coming trick-or-treating, he had to dress up; Kayleigh had insisted, and Sully had done absolutely nothing to back his brother's arguments.

"What's he supposed to be?" Kayleigh asked as she regarded Forbes.

"We're trying to figure that out," Dez grumbled.

Kayleigh's face lit up at the perceived game. "Door-to-door salesman?"

Forbes pulled out his ID wallet and flipped it open to reveal his badge. Kayleigh glanced at it before peering up at her father. "He doesn't look like a policeman."

Dez chuckled as Forbes scowled. "Hey, she said it."

Forbes eyed Dez and Sully. "Is there somewhere we can talk?"

Dez knelt in front of Kayleigh. "Honey, why don't you go put on a movie downstairs? We need to talk to this guy about boring stuff for a bit. We'll come down and join you, after. Don't eat any of your candy until Mom or I check it, okay?"

"How long will you be?"

"Not long. Go pick something out and start watching."

Kayleigh rolled her eyes and headed for the basement stairs. Eva, Mara and Emily—newly released from hospital and a guest in the Braddock house—joined the men in the upstairs sitting room, Mara casting Forbes a dark look as she sat. Sully could guess where her mind had travelled; while he'd forgiven Forbes for his actions two years ago, mothers were not so quick to forget.

"Sergeant," she said.

"Ma'am." Forbes peered up at Dez. "Does everyone—"

"They all know what's going on, yeah. What's up?"

Forbes leaned forward. "We had the Lockwood drug tested, and we ran it against the one we seized a couple of years ago from Sullivan's apartment. The two match up, same substance. Only difference is the one Sullivan had back then was in pill form, and it was less concentrated. The Lockwood stuff is administered intravenously and is significantly more potent. Two years later, the chemists at the lab we use are still stumped. All they can tell us is that the drug is a psychotropic of some type. I'm not heading up the investigation anymore, for obvious reasons, so I had no say in it when the new lead took the drug to LOBRA for additional testing. I understand he spoke to Lowell directly. Lowell's denied any knowledge of the drug, other than to promise to check it out for us."

"If he knows the drug's in the hands of police, he'll tear down any evidence he has of its production," Mara said.

"If I were to guess, I'd say he probably started the process as soon as Gerhardt was located in the old wing."

"Any change with Gerhardt?" Eva asked.

"Still in the same state. He's not really in a coma, but he's not able to respond to much outside stimulus either. They've run a couple more MRIs, and still the same thing: plenty of activity in the brain and corresponding spikes in his heart rate and blood pressure. But whatever's going on in his head is staying there." Forbes's lips formed a tight line. "Wish I was a big enough man to say I feel sorry for him."

Mara glanced around the room at each of its occupants before returning her attention to Forbes. "Lowell will conceal all evidence of his involvement in the Lockwood experiments; we know that. But I think we can safely assume this will nonetheless put him on edge. He'll know he's being watched. Our biggest problem isn't just finding something to pin on him; it's keeping ourselves and each other safe while doing it."

"From my end, I'll do what I can to protect you." Forbes ended the statement with a smile. "I know we got off on the wrong foot, ma'am, but I've come to a few conclusions since then. In short, I believe Sullivan, and I'll do my best to get you some justice for Deputy Chief Braddock and Aiden."

Surprise gave way to a softening of Mara's features, the corners of her mouth turning up as she regarded the detective. "Thank you, Sergeant. That means a lot to me. To all of us."

Forbes nodded and stood. "I'll leave you to it, then. Please keep me posted on anything you hear or see, anything you think might aid me in the investigation."

Mara stood, too, then crossed the room and shook Forbes's hand. "You be careful. Your investigation isn't official. Until you have something substantial enough to take to your commanding officer, you're more or less on your own. That puts you at great risk if Lowell learns about your activities. If you need help with anything in the meantime, call us."

"I will, ma'am, thank you."

Sully and Dez showed Forbes out while Mara, Eva and Emily went to join Kayleigh. Forbes had his hand on the door handle when he turned back toward the brothers.

"There's something else," he said. "I didn't want to bring it up in front of everyone."

Sully expected something about Forbes's feelings about his birth family. What he got was much more unsettling.

"Greta left the treatment centre," Forbes said. "Didn't even bother to check herself out, just went out the window last night. I've been looking, but I can't find her. No one knows what happened. She seemed to be on the straight and narrow, and was kicking the drugs. Last time I saw her, she told me the cravings had dropped right off. She was so much different from the woman you knew. She was like the woman I married." Forbes took a deep breath and let it out in a huff. "I don't know what to do."

"Maybe Lachlan can help find her," Dez said. "He's good at that."

Forbes's gaze had settled on the wall, but now it snapped to Dez's face. "That's not why I told you. I don't want a search for her to become a big thing. She has too many secrets—bad secrets

—and investigations always entail overturning a person's life. If she's found out, I'll lose her forever. I'm telling you because she's targeted Sullivan in the past, and there's every chance she might try again."

"But she did it because of the influence of her family," Sully said. "They're not in the picture anymore, so what's the problem?"

"I don't know," Forbes said. "And that's the problem. I have no idea why she took off, so I can't say what her plans are. One thing's for sure: If she's unstable enough to walk away from treatment like this, anything's possible. Just watch your back, okay? Just until I can find her."

"You know, it's more likely something in treatment triggered her, and she went off somewhere to get a fix," Dez said. "She'll turn up."

"Probably," Forbes said. "But I can't take a chance of it being something else." One side of his mouth quirked up. "I may be new to this whole big brother thing, but I'm pretty sure looking out for him is one of my jobs now."

Thankfully, Dez waited until Forbes was out of earshot, back in his car and driving down the block, before responding. "Big brother. The guy doesn't know the first thing about it."

"He's trying, Dez. That's something, right?"

Dez shrugged. "Guess it beats him looking for ways to arrest you. Let's just keep in mind, where big brothers go, you've already got the best."

Sully met Dez's goofy grin with one of his own. "Yeah, no arguing that."

Dez patted Sully on the shoulder. "Come on. Let's go see what Kayleigh's picked out. If I have to suffer through *Princess Bride* again, so do you."

"I'll be right there. Just need the bathroom first."

He didn't really have to go, but he needed a moment to himself. He'd spent the past few days in this house—save a quick surreptitious trip to Lockwood with Dez to rescue the trio of trapped ghosts—and time to himself was hard to come by.

And he needed it. With everything that had been going on—the David investigation, facing his past at Lockwood, dealing with the fact he had a new blood relation—Sully had put the manner of his own creation onto the back burner. None of it, none of the good things he'd done or the people he'd helped, erased how he came into being. He could change people's lives for the better, but he would be forever helpless to change the one thing he so desperately wished he could.

So here he was, staring at the bathroom sink faucet as he tried to get up the nerve to look in the mirror.

He hadn't studied his own reflection since discovering the truth about his background, and he wasn't keen to now. But he'd have to face it sometime, would have to accept this part of himself if he was going to find a way to exist within his own skin.

He hadn't seen his birth mother's ghost since back at the Dules' old house in The Forks, and he hadn't expected to either. She'd told him she would stay close to her mother and sister and would return to him if they were closing in again. Her image was in his mind as he forced his head up, hoping to find parts of her in his reflection. The more he resembled Lucky, the fewer traces of Roman Gerhardt he'd find.

The initial glimpse of his own face had him averting his eyes. He returned to studying the sink, his hands clenched around the sides of the bowl.

A small, white hand reaching for his made him jump and turn.

She was there. Lucky. The petite, pale, blood-covered teenage girl who'd given him life and then saved it more than once. Large, kohl-rimmed blue-gray eyes stared up into his before going to the mirror. He followed her gaze, saw the two of them side by side in the mirror, mother and son, him eight years older in physical age and six or seven inches taller. She moved a little closer, sealing the remaining distance between them, her energy joining his at the edges. The bite of cold against his left arm and hip was uncomfortable, but he didn't move away. The rest of him, the parts inside himself that really mattered, were enveloped in enough warmth to render the chill meaningless.

He found it there, just as he needed to. His height and body structure, there was no getting away from the fact those were Gerhardt. But from Lucky had come his eye colour and shape, the fine bone structure in his face, even the soft half-smile she was giving him now. Her hair was dyed purple, but he knew from photos in Lachlan's possession that it was naturally a shade very similar to his own. As his gaze moved from his own face to hers and back again, a small shred of hope took root inside him.

"I'm not like him, am I?" he asked.

She shook her head.

He sought out and held her eyes in the mirror. "I'm so sorry this happened to you. There are no words for how wrong it was, how wrong I am for existing the way I do. I'm only here because something awful happened to you, and that's not right."

He watched the mirror as she turned to face him. It was obvious she was demanding he meet her, so he turned to gaze directly down into her eyes. A chill against his hand told him she'd touched him, and then he was flooded with a memory.

Hers, not his. The image of a crying, blood-covered newborn baby held tight in her arms. Her first image of him. And it wasn't revulsion she'd felt, nor horror or pain. It was the most intense joy, her vision clouding through tears so she'd had to blink them away. And love. The kind of love Sully had not yet had the pleasure to feel for another human being. He loved his family, and he loved them intensely. But this, this bond between a young parent and her child, was beyond anything Sully could describe.

She didn't hate him or regret the fact he'd come into existence.

He completed her. He gave her meaning. And he was the first real joy or love she'd ever known.

Her hand came up to touch at his face.

And then the smile slipped from hers.

Another image, this one not of her or of him, but of Greta. She was peering from a window, a street below shadowed by the night. From one of the shadows emerged a blonde woman pushing a wheelchair. In the chair sat a thin woman with a pointed face, which lifted until a set of cold eyes met with Greta's. A smile, as icy as the rest of her expression, formed, and she lifted an arm, index finger extending and retracting in a "come here" gesture.

For a long moment, Greta didn't move. She stood frozen to the spot as she regarded the two women. While the younger one appeared slightly anxious, the woman in the wheelchair showed every sign of confidence, as if nothing stood between her and the power she still held over the young woman inside the treatment centre.

The vision ended, leaving Sully chilled and disquieted.

Because there was no doubt in his mind what Lucky was trying to tell him.

"The Dules," he said. "They're back."

AFTERWORD

Thanks so much for reading! I am continuing to work on the next Sullivan Gray books, and would be pleased to keep you updated on future projects and release dates if you would like to join my mailing list. As an adding bonus, a growing anthology of short stories, entitled *Haunted: The Ghosts of Sullivan Gray*, is available as a gift to subscribers. Visit my website at hpbayne.com to sign up.

The books in *The Sullivan Gray Series* can be read as stand-alones to some extent, each with a plot that wraps itself up by book's end. But there is a deeper plot that threads throughout the series so, for that reason, I always suggest the books are best read in the following order:

Black Candle

Harbinger

The Dule Tree

Crawl

Hollow Road

Second Son

Spirit Caller

As always, I wanted to take a moment to thank my family and friends for their incredible support. I am incredibly appreciative of all the people in my life who have been at my side throughout this journey.

A big, Dez-sized thanks also to my hawk-eyed editor Hannah Sullivan and to my absolutely stellar team of advance readers. All of you help to ensure each of the books is all it can be and more, and I am so very grateful to you.

And, of course, a big thank you to everyone who's picked up this and other Sully books. I thank you from the bottom of my heart for making my dreams come true every day.

ABOUT THE AUTHOR

Fascinated by ghost stories and crime fiction, H.P. has been writing both for well over two decades, drawing on more than fifteen years in a career in a criminal justice setting. Raised on a farm on the Canadian Prairies, H.P. enjoys reading, portrait drawing, travel and spending time with family and friends.

For more information, visit H.P.'s website at hpbayne.com.

Manufactured by Amazon.ca
Bolton, ON

33100044R00164